FLOTSAM

AND

JETSAM

FLOTSAM
AND
JETSAM

TWENTY-ONE
CURIOUS TALES

RORY O'SULLIVAN

Matador
Unit E2 Airfield Business Park,
Harrison Road, Market Harborough,
Leicestershire. LE16 7UL
Tel: 0116 2792299
Email: books@troubador.co.uk
Web: www.troubador.co.uk/matador
Twitter: @matadorbooks

ISBN 978 1803134 833

British Library Cataloguing in Publication Data.
A catalogue record for this book is available from the British Library.

Printed and bound in Great Britain by CMP UK
Typeset in 11pt Minion Pro by Troubador Publishing Ltd, Leicester, UK

Matador is an imprint of Troubador Publishing Ltd

For Jackie

THE TALES

FLOTSAM AND JETSAM

*...this was his first body; a youngish woman, not
unattractive and, on closer inspection, thankfully... not dead*

He had walked along that beach hundreds of times before and discovered numerous interesting and useful items, but this was his first body; a youngish woman, not unattractive and, on closer inspection, thankfully... not dead.

It took him over an hour to get her back to his shack, or The Ritz as he had christened it. It wasn't that she was particularly heavy, but she was just a dead weight, so he had to construct a sort of stretcher from bits and pieces of wood on the beach, tied together with some blue nylon rope that he had picked up a couple of days before, with his anorak stretched across it. He managed to roll her onto it and then drag it the half-mile or so back to his shelter. *This is when you really need your mobile phone*, he thought to himself, and he hadn't had that thought for... however long it was that he had been there... six months maybe...? He wasn't sure. Inside, he checked her pulse, which she still seemed to have, and her breathing was regularish, so once he had heaved her onto his bed, he left her to come round in her own time. Once she was conscious again, he would think about what to do next.

He had been reading for a while, when he looked across at her.

'How long have you been staring at me?' he asked, in a tone that suggested amusement more than anything else.

She blinked, looking around her unexpected landing place. 'What's your name?' she asked in reply.

'I picked you up off the beach... earlier this morning...' No response. 'Did you have some sort of accident?' ...Still nothing. 'Is there someone I should get in touch with? I can walk to the village... it's about an hour away.'

'How long did you say I've been here?' she asked.

'Couple of hours maybe, something like that.'

'Sorry, what did you say your name was?'

'I didn't... I... don't have one anymore.'

'What, someone stole it?'

'No.' There was a pause.

'I suppose I should say thank you,' she offered half-heartedly.

'Depends whether you're grateful or not.'

'That's very astute of you.' They were off to an interesting start. 'If you haven't got a name... what am I supposed to call you?'

'Tell you what,' he said, 'I'll call you Flotsam.'

'So I call you Jetsam, right?' She was quick.

'Right,' he agreed.

In time, the names got shortened to Flos and Jet, but the idea was still the same. That first day consisted mostly of not asking obvious questions... waiting to see if any explanations were offered... they weren't.

Later on, she did ask, 'Is it okay if I stay here for a bit?' when it was clearly already too late to go anywhere that evening.

4

'Sure,' he said, and left it at that, not really knowing exactly what she meant by "a bit".

When it got dark, he asked her, 'Fancy something to eat?'

'Thanks, but I'm not really hungry,' she said, but when she saw him opening tins and boiling up pasta, she changed her mind.

'Everything's either tinned or dried,' he said. 'I've got provisions for probably six months... it was a year... but I've eaten half of it.'

'Is that all you eat?' she said. 'What about fresh stuff, fruit and veg and water?'

'I sometimes go to the village for vegetables and fruit, and there's a stream that runs down to the sea just behind the shack. It's probably why the shack was built here.'

'So it's your shack then?' she asked.

''Tis now,' he said.

They sat in silence and ate tagliatelle with chopped tomatoes and mixed chilli beans, followed by instant coffee, from a huge catering size tin, with powdered milk.

'Michelin Stars?' he enquired.

'That would be nice,' she replied.

There were two rooms to the shack – living room and bedroom nominally.

'You can have the bed tonight,' he offered, feeling thoroughly gallant.

'What about you?'

'I'll be fine here,' he said.

When he woke up, he was back at school, in the sixth form, at a Christmas disco, THE Christmas disco to be more accurate, and Anna was there, in the corner with her friends. He had fancied her forever, but there always seemed to be another bloke in the picture somehow. But there she was tonight, just with girlfriends. It was his chance if he had the bottle. Then they were outside, in the school car park, and she seemed as keen as he was, if he was reading the messages – which he was. Suddenly the letter came into focus, the one she'd written to him when he was at uni. Sorry and all that; it had been great; he was a lovely person... and then the all-time cheesiest phrase... let's remember the good times. Let's not, he thought. And now he had Marianna on his knee, laughing and gurgling, and Anna was out in the kitchen doing something... and then suddenly back at the disco again and he couldn't work out why... and he wanted it to stop... and then it did.

Why suddenly called Flotsam...? That wasn't her name. Her parents called her Marigold, but she always told people it was Marie, Marie Baptiste. Marigold... just too embarrassing. Parents – Kingston and Dimple Baptiste – children: boys – Maceo, Bijoy and Farukh... girls – Carmen and... Marigold. Where did that name come from? Not enough that you got different skin... you got to have a different name too. In the street, it's okay. We're all the same... more or less, you know. In school, you're never the same. College. Never the same... work... never the same. Now I got new skin, white skin... smooth blonde hair... now called Flotsam.

The light woke him up. He felt stiff, really stiff. He was sprawled out on the floor on a pile of clothes and stuff for some reason. Then he remembered why. He tried to focus, but too much was going through his head, not much of it making any sense. So he made a decision... to go for a swim. When she peeped through the makeshift door, the place was empty. Had he gone...? Where to...? When was he coming back? Would he be coming back? She thought about leaving before he did. But to go where? And why? She went outside and sat on the bench, which was made from two oil drums and a bit of rough planking, and she tried not to think; not to think about what had happened; not to think about what might happen next. She sat there for a while but he didn't come back, so she went inside again. When he returned from his swim, maybe an hour or so later, neither of them really knew how to play it, so instead of talking, they didn't. He made some sort of porridge which he ate with enthusiasm and she out of politeness; then she suddenly said she was going for a walk. 'Planning to come back?' he asked.

She looked at him, trying to gauge the meaning behind the question. In the end, she said,

'If that's okay with you... Jetsam.' He laughed, and she smiled.

Not much was any clearer by the time she got back. Plan A had failed, and she didn't really have a Plan B, so... play it by ear, she thought. He was thinking very much the same sort of thing, but maybe for different reasons. The one thing he was excellent at by now, having had plenty of practice, was not talking, and that seemed to suit them both pretty well for the time being. Luckily, it was fairly good weather for March, so they spent most of their time outside, which was good since inside was not exactly salubrious . At one time, it had been a nice enough beach hut, not designed for living in but solid and comfortable. When it had been abandoned, most of the furniture and fittings had just been left, as though someone had definitely intended to return but changed their mind, for whatever reason, and left it, "Marie Celeste-like", with a copy of the *Guardian* still on the table, giving a precise date of departure. Of course, there was no electricity or running water, but there were candles and a stream, a calor gas heater and a little camping gas stove that he had acquired, so that covered most bases. It was survival camp.

And so the days passed, quietly and largely uneventfully. She did a bit of the cooking, if you can call it that, and she was tempted to tidy the place up a bit but thought better of it. At first, they only spoke when necessary, and that was comfortable for them; then they spoke occasionally, about politics and society and philosophy... heady stuff. They never spoke about themselves. And the days seemed to turn into weeks, though neither of them was counting. But the nights... the nights were different.

> *When he woke up, he was in the water and he knew he couldn't swim. He was shouting out for help, but Anna was on the boat and she was waving to him and laughing; and then Anna was holding Marianna over the edge of the boat and the little girl was waving her arms and kicking her little legs and they were both laughing. Then he was on the beach shouting something. Then he was back in the boat, but Anna and Marianna weren't there. Where were they? He could smell the bacon and burnt toast... was it Sunday breakfast? Then slowly the water closed over his head.*

We are all sitting round the table – Ackee and Codfish as usual on Sunday. Red Stripe beer for Dad and the boys, coconut milk for us. Boys arguing with Dad same as ever... always in trouble somehow... get a proper job, he says... you're not boys now... don't expect me to support you forever. Carmen saying she wants to leave school... get a job at a hairdresser's. I got a letter, I say... what letter? says Ma... offer letter, I say... offer to go to university... long silence. Why you want to go there? says Dad... waste of time. I'm in the big dining hall and I'm sat at a table... just me. I'm wearing my new clothes... on my own... all white faces looking at me... whispering, whispering... what's she doing here...? English Literature... what do you want to be here for, girl? I'm saying to myself. I'm in my room... I'm in the library... I'm in the lecture hall on my own... Congratulations, Ms Baptiste... You can keep your degree, I say. What good will it do me? What good, what good, what good? and she wakes up sweating.

It's maybe two months, something like that, who knows. Only the food stores are keeping count. Now they are easy with each other in a different way... close but not intimate, if that makes sense. They start to talk a bit more openly. Little bits at a time... where she's from... where he's from... his job before... her job before... that sort of thing... tit for tat. Never the reason for being there, not even close. But the troubled nights... they continue, her in his bed, him on a newly constructed put-you-up. They walk a lot together, along the beach, but not towards the village. Sometimes they walk separately, and that makes walking together better. He's got quite a lot of books in the shack; it turns out that he did English Literature at university too, so they discuss Salman Rushdie and George Eliot and mostly disagree. They go into the village occasionally; she needs to get some clothes and there's a charity shop; Jet gives her the money, not much, he doesn't have much of the £500 he brought with him. That would run out eventually anyway. They try fishing without much success, well, without any success really, so it's back to tinned tuna and sardines. "Life in the slow lane", he would have called it once; that's when lanes meant something to him.

Now Anna's face appeared to him more and more frequently; sometimes laughing, sometimes questioning, sometimes blank and blue. Sometimes her face turned into Marianna's face, but he couldn't reach her. That was the worst thing... not being able to reach them.

The girls in the office were whispering, whispering again, only it wasn't really whispering. She was meant to hear. She was the researcher; she was meant to be in charge of them. Why does she wear those clothes...? Fuzzy hair... strange smell... how has she got this job...? It's raging inside her now... like a fire that's been lit... and it won't go out... she's grabbed the taller one, Penny, by the collar of her blouse... she's shoving her against the cupboard door... she wants to choke her... to shut her up. Now she's outside the building... she can't go in again... she's sitting on the pavement crying, and people pass by but don't say anything.

He seems to be drifting in and out of consciousness. Anna's face appears, then Flos' face... she's wiping his face with a cool cloth... now he's under the water again, and he's struggling to get to the surface but he never reaches it. He's lying on his own bed in the shack, just for a moment, then everything disappears again.

Penny's dead... she must be... everyone is screaming at her... her dad is screaming at her... her mum is crying... Mr Lloyd, her boss, is handing her an envelope... he's shaking his head. Now her mouth is full of codfish; so full, it's choking her... and her father is pushing more fish in... and he's laughing now... and she's choking. And there's Jet's face over her as she lies on the floor, on the bed, and he isn't laughing or shouting. She drifts away.

He's holding Marianna in his arms, trying to wake her up, but she won't. And Anna is beside him, but she can't help because she's dead... completely dead. So he sinks below the surface, slowly, calmly, and they come with him. But she can't remember how she got onto the beach... how she got onto the stretcher... he thinks she's dead... maybe she is... if she is... that's okay, it's okay.

It's dark when he opens his eyes, so he can't see her, but he knows she's there. There beside him, on the bed. He doesn't know how he got there. It doesn't matter anyway, because she's there, beside him; he can hear her, sense her, knows she's there.

'Are you awake?' she says, out of the darkness, and he's not sure whether the voice is real, but he thinks it is.

'Yes,' he says, and waits for her to say something else.

'You were... in a bad place,' she says. 'I helped you onto the bed... that's all I remember.'

'How long ago was that?' He's confused, because... he doesn't even know why he's confused.

'The shack was shaking and rolling around. I thought it must be a storm or something. So I got you onto the bed... but then I don't remember what happened.' She was silent for a while. 'Then I woke up, a few minutes ago, I think.'

The bed's a wreck... pillows on the floor... sheets draped off the side and end... and an atmosphere in the room... like... like after Armageddon.

They lie side by side, unseen, unseeing and silent.

'My name's Dale,' he says suddenly.

She hesitates at first, then says, 'Mine's Marie... I mean... Marigold.'

They both smile blindly, then he feels across the bed and finds her elbow, then her hand; she links her fingers between his, and they wait quietly for sleep, which slowly, gently, engulfs them.

They have each decided where the next step might take them, a sort of plan at least.

THE VISITOR

...she was sixty-seven, with a good few more years left in her, but at a loss to know what to do with them. When the knock on the door came, she would have to start making decisions

Perhaps the problem was that she didn't really fit into any of the boxes. That's what she told herself anyway. She wasn't old enough to be vulnerable; she wasn't ill; she wasn't poor; she wasn't without friends, or at least close acquaintances; but she was still… lonely, despite everything, and there wasn't a box to tick for that. It was a grey area; she slipped through the net, or whatever euphemism you chose to use.

It certainly hadn't always been like this. Once, her life had been full, busy, hectic even. A husband she could always rely on, always until the diagnosis, until the hospitalisation, until the funeral eighteen months ago. Was it really eighteen months? His funeral had been the last "family occasion". She had been in touch with his side of the family since, of course, with lots of lukewarm invitations and kind words, but nothing that meant anything really. It had always been a fairly disparate clan, flung wide across the country and with little more than a surname in common.

And her own children: a son, a translator, living with his family in Paris; one unmarried daughter in Sidney; and another semi-detached one on some remote Scottish island, the name of which had always escaped her. They had all come to the funeral, which was no mean feat in itself and had been lovely, and stayed in touch via the miracle of FaceTime, almost too often at first, but time marches on. They had their own families now, their own lives to lead, and she had always made it abundantly clear that she would never allow herself to be any sort of burden to them. So, the offer of Christmas in Paris, romantic as it might sound, had little appeal, and the much-discussed trip "down under" was still in the early stages of planning, and might well stay there for a while yet. The Scottish island option was not on offer, which was just as well probably.

She had had a sister once... but that was a long, painful time ago. Ah well. There had also, at some point, been mention of distant cousins on her husband's side, but they were so vague as to be little more than mythical. So she had arrived at this point in her life; sixty-seven, reasonably fit in mind and body, comfortably off and presumably with a good few more years left in her... but at a loss to know what to do with them. It was Christmas Eve and she felt... lonely.

It had been a strange sort of year, and that was an understatement if ever there was one. Last Christmas had been difficult enough; only six months since... The Paris brigade had come over for four days and they had tried to be normal. She cooked Christmas lunch with all the usual banter that attends it. They'd played some family games for the children; they'd even tried to watch the Queen's speech, which they hadn't done for years, but gave up halfway through. By the day after Boxing Day, everyone had had enough and it was with a guilty sense of relief that she saw them off at Heathrow. And since then… well, from March onwards, her life had been almost surreal.

The first "lockdown" actually had the one advantage of novelty, a sort of wartime spirit that most people had never experienced before. Having to stay in your house all day wasn't exactly the Blitz, but it did feel very odd. And then going out for your permitted exercise walk. The girl next door showed her how to do the supermarket shop online, which was quite a challenge, but she ended up quite enjoying her newfound skills. And whilst there wasn't any rationing, you still had to really think about what you were going to eat, plan the week's menus, even try out some new recipes, instead of just popping into the shop every couple of days for the usual. She knew she was fortunate, very fortunate, in fact; others would have been finding it far more difficult, impossible even. The second lockdown was different, and despite being less rigorous, it definitely felt more intrusive. The house felt bigger, emptier, less comforting. She missed things more: her weekly choir; her ladies' monthly lunch club, and just seeing people for a coffee and a chat. It all began to feel as if it would go on forever. And now with the promise of a vaccine at last, there was light at the end of the tunnel, but if you listened to the radio, it was still a pretty long tunnel.

When the doorbell rang, she debated with herself. It was past her six o'clock "watershed" for unexpected visitors. It could be the girl from next door, very sweet, very practical, always concerned that she was on her own, and so on. She knew she should be grateful when people showed concern, but somehow she always ended up feeling slightly patronised, even though she knew it was well meant. Of course, it might just be a parcel; they seemed to come at any hour of the day or night now. Was she expecting anything? She couldn't remember. Then a cold dread came over her; please don't let it be the vicar from St Matthews. Rev... somebody or other. She had only gone back to the church on that Sunday on a whim; she wasn't religious and didn't want to be, but some people are just determined to save you whether you want it or not.

The bell rang again. If she ignored it, they would probably just go away. The sitting-room lamps were on – but so what? She didn't really care if people thought she was rude not answering; they were rude just turning up and ringing her bell uninvited. If she turned the lamps off, that would make it clear that she wasn't receiving visitors, and then she felt annoyed at having to think up evasion strategies. Perhaps she should just open the door and see who it was, and whilst she was pondering this course of action, the bell rang again, which, unexpectedly, made her jump.

She had had a chain put on the front door last year when one of her neighbours had had her door forced open by a former partner who was well over the limit. The same thing wasn't going to happen to her, but it made her nervous all the same, so now she always kept the chain on when she was in the house on her own.

She opened the door as much as the chain would allow and peered out into the gloom. Her heart stopped. There, silhouetted against the streetlight on the opposite side of the road, stood... her husband. She slammed the door shut and leant back against it in utter panic. She tried to gather her wits. *Breathe*, she thought. *That's what they say, isn't it?*

Breathe. She took a deep breath and tried to decide what to do next. Three more breaths. She was overreacting. It was just such a shock. He looked so like him. Poor man, standing out there wondering what on earth was going on. Another deep breath, then she would open the door again. Slowly, she took hold of the catch; slowly, she turned it; slowly, she inched the door open a crack and looked out. 'Ahh!' She slammed it shut again. It was him, it was... but... but... *Don't be ridiculous,* she said to herself... *it's not him... obviously, it's not.*

More breathing, and then a muffled voice from the other side of the door. 'Hello... hello... look, I'm sorry if I frightened you.' She listened, unsure what to do. 'Sorry,' the voice said again. 'Shall I go away?' Another pause.

'Who are you?' she whispered to the door, and then realised that he wouldn't be able to hear her. So she took a breath and shouted, 'Wait,' at the top of her voice. She listened. No response. Then, in a flash of inspiration, she lifted the letter flap and shouted again. 'Who are you?'

Two eyes appeared in the narrow window. 'I'm your cousin,' he said. 'Well, not actually your cousin, a sort of distant cousin of your husband, your late husband, that is.'

She swallowed and tried to think, but her mind was still racing. 'My husband didn't have any cousins... not that I know of,' was all she could think to say.

'No, well, we weren't in touch, not since we were very small children,' came the reply, in a tone of voice that sounded weirdly familiar. She looked at the eyes, so unnaturally framed, and was intrigued and unnerved in equal measure.

'So what do you want?' she found herself saying, then immediately thought how unfriendly that must sound.

'I read about your loss last year and meant to get in touch then, but it wasn't until this week I was in London, so I thought I would look you up. Look, I'm terribly sorry if I frightened you.' He sounded so genuine and warm and strangely familiar. She was alarmed and confused and she felt she should just tell him to go away. But she didn't.

'What's your name?' she asked, but when he told her, it meant nothing to her.

'I'm sorry,' he said, for what seemed like the umpteenth time. 'I shouldn't have come, shouldn't have bothered you. You're probably very busy. Look, I'll leave you to get on with things, sorry again.'

And then, and she really couldn't explain why, she said, 'Wait' again. Another pause. 'You'd better come in.' What on earth was she doing? she thought to herself.

There was an extraordinary family likeness, and not just physical, though that was unnerving. It was in his bearing; slightly stooped, not athletic but still strong somehow, substantial and… familiar.

As soon as she had let him in, and he was safely ensconced in the sitting room, she disappeared upstairs. She knew it was ridiculous, but she felt she had to change out of her jeans and sloppy top, and it also gave her time to think. When she reappeared a few minutes later in skirt and blouse, with a quick smudge of lipstick and having run a brush through her hair, she had formulated a sort of plan. She would offer him a coffee and give him half an hour to say whatever it was he wanted to say, and then she would politely apologise for curtailing their conversation, as she had to go out... to meet a friend. Actually, this sounded highly unlikely with the current restrictions, but come to think of it, his being there was hardly complying with government instructions.

'Coffee?' she asked.

'Thanks.'

'White?'

'Black, no sugar, please.'

Does that mean I have to do the cafetière? she thought, but then grabbed the jar of instant. She didn't have any biscuits in the house.

When she came into the sitting room, he stood up, which somehow didn't seem over formal or phony, just very polite. Before he sat down again, he took out his wallet and produced a small photo, black and white, a family holiday snap, and handed it to her. 'I thought this might amuse you,' he said. They were much younger, of course, but she couldn't fail to recognise her mother– and father-in-law, who had never liked or approved of her, and in front of them in shorts and vests were two small boys, about seven or eight, she guessed. 'That's the two of us in front,' he said, 'on holiday in Torquay. I went with them several times when I was very young, which was kind of them because I wouldn't have had a holiday otherwise.'

She wouldn't have recognised her husband, not at that age, but the similarity between the two boys was uncanny.

'I can leave you the photo if you like,' he said. 'I've got another similar one.' It was a sort of identity document, she decided. Proof he was who he said he was. He placed it on the mantelpiece.

The really extraordinary thing was how easy it was for them to talk, but the truth was, it was she who was doing all the talking. Generalities at first, about the epidemic and how things might pan out. Then Brexit and what that would all mean in the long term. Then family stuff and, gradually, more and more personal things. Had she stopped to think what she was saying, she would almost certainly have been more circumspect, but it was just so easy, so natural to open up.

When she came to think about it later, it was probably the first time she had really talked, talked freely and honestly like that for years, long before she had been on her own. All the things she had wanted to say over the years were suddenly coming out. How she had felt as the kids were growing up, and when they each flew the nest in turn. How she felt when her husband was diagnosed; nobody had ever thought to ask her, as if her feelings weren't really important at that moment. But they were, they really were, and now, somehow, she had permission to express them.

More than an hour had flown by, and now she just wanted to keep on talking; it was as though knots that had restrained her for years and years were gradually being untied, one by one. 'Do you fancy a sandwich?' she asked, in what even she recognised was a desperate attempt to keep the evening going.

'Thanks, that would be great, if it's no bother,' he said, and she breathed a sigh of relief. She had bought a wholemeal loaf that afternoon to do her over Christmas, so that was fresh, and she found a tin of salmon and the nub of a cucumber.

She had also, rather daringly, she thought, bought a couple of bottles of Chardonnay, which were sitting in the fridge. She congratulated herself on being so organised. And so the evening went on, and she felt her pent-up stress and anxiety slowly draining away with the wine.

Two rounds of sandwiches, a bottle and a half of Chardonnay, and more coffee – the cafetière this time – and it was ten o'clock. 'I really ought to be making a move,' he said, and her heart sank. 'But I can't go before I ask what's next for you?'

If talking about the past, and even the present, had somehow been ridiculously easy, facing the future was impossibly hard. 'That's very cheeky of me,' he said, 'none of my business.'

He was about to get up when she said, 'No, wait... I would like to... talk about it,' though she had absolutely no idea what she had to say. There was a pause.

'When I left school, I didn't go to university, though I could have. Lots of us girls didn't. I went straight into the Civil Service, Inland Revenue; and the thing is, I was very good at what I did. I got promotion unusually quickly and I was told that if I stayed in the Service, I could go a long way. Some women had really successful careers. Then, of course, I got married and never went back. Never worked after that, never needed to. My place was at home and, to be honest, I didn't complain. Line of least resistance, I think. But since I've been on my own, these last months, it's got me thinking. I had a brain then. Maybe I've still got one. Surely there's something I could do with it, even at my age. It's probably a silly idea.'

'No, absolutely not. You mustn't think like that,' he said. 'There are opportunities out there, especially in the voluntary sector. Someone like you would be invaluable to a whole host of charities.'

'Do you really think so?' she said.

'Absolutely. Get in touch with a few local ones, see what they say. If you tell them the sort of things you could do, I'd be astonished if they didn't fall over themselves to sign you up.' And with that, he did stand up. 'Thanks for this evening. I've really enjoyed it,' he said.

'I can't quite believe how it started out with me slamming the door on you. I'm so sorry about that,' she said.

He made his way to the front door and turned. They stood facing one another for an awkward moment, then they both laughed into a brief hug. 'Thanks again,' she said.

'What for ?'

'My Christmas present.'

'What Christmas present ?'

'The best possible one,' she said. 'Hope.' He smiled.

At the gate, he turned. 'Good luck with the charities,' and then he set off. She gave a surreptitious look up and down the road to see if anyone had seen them. She rather hoped someone had.

Whether it was the wine or not, she had the best night's sleep she had had for ages. When she woke with her alarm at 7.30, she lay in bed for a while mulling over the events of the previous evening. Then she realised... it was Christmas morning. 'Happy Christmas,' she said to herself. The kids would be FaceTiming her before long and she had so much to tell them; so many new resolutions, even before the New Year.

She showered and dressed, went downstairs, put on the kettle and drifted into the sitting room. 'It's a new beginning,' she said to herself. 'At sixty-seven, it's a new beginning.' Then she noticed the photo where he had left it on the mantelpiece. She picked it up and looked at it. There they were, the dreaded in-laws, and in front of them... was... one... small boy... one. She stared at the image for a few moments, then she smiled to herself, took a deep breath and marched into the kitchen to make herself some toast.

THE FLOAREA PRIZE

...the eldest of the four Floarea sisters was Eleina. She was clever, hard-working, ambitious and, most importantly of all, totally unscrupulous. The young poet Paul Mallary hardly seemed a match for her

Sometimes, a poem just doesn't want to get finished. Poems have a mind of their own, don't they, a life of their own, an independence from their author? Well, this is what Paul Mallary felt anyway, and this was precisely what he was now experiencing.

Mallary had very particular views on poetry, and they failed to chime with current fashions. For example, he loathed the term "Poetry Slam" with a passion, considering it to be little short of oxymoronic. Poetry, in his opinion, could do a multitude of things, but "slamming" was not amongst them. In fact, he was not really in favour of poetry being spoken out loud at all, his argument being that if a poem had any real depth (and he saw no point in poems that had none), then grasping its full meaning and appreciating its beauty took more than hearing it once, especially if that happened in a bar or similar venue. Poems needed to be read, and reread, and then read again, to allow the words to do their magic. Comic poems may be an exception – ditties or limericks, and song lyrics obviously – but not serious poetry. His own writing might be described as traditional in character, rather formal in style, and yet accessible for some reason.

So it may surprise you to know that Paul Mallary, far from being some stuffy old professor of ancient verse at a third-rate university, was, in fact, a part-time landscape gardener in his late twenties, married to the charming, wise and endlessly patient Maria, manager of a small independent health food shop, and father to Michael and Elizabeth, exceedingly naughty, spoilt and quarrelsome two-year-old twins. None of which helped the frustrated writer in his present pursuit: to complete his poem. He had been at it, on and off, for three weeks already.

There were just twelve years covering the four Floarea sisters, in descending age order – Eleina, Sophia, Andreea and, the baby at eighteen, Iolanda. They were striking in appearance, and each gifted, to different degrees, in one way or another.

Iolanda had started to dance as soon as she could walk, and dancing was her entire life. Despite the pulling of numerous strings and the calling-in of countless favours, she had failed to secure a place at the National Academy of Dance, a situation she regarded as "their loss", and in response she had simply created her own dance company, something you can only do if you have sufficient money and gall. She not only engaged twenty fledgling dancers, boys and girls, thrilled to be offered professional work, but also choreographers, designers, technicians, administrators and crew, all prepared to risk involvement in this speculative venture if the money was right. She had booked venues and was in the process of building a performance programme; so, not short on confidence then.

Andreea was the musician of the family, a pianist and singer, though not at the same time, as she would point out caustically. She had studied music at Guildhall in London, at the same time as having private piano lessons with Helena Golda, one of the most revered teachers in the capital, and now at twenty-one, and back in the States, she was already giving concert performances in established venues around the country. She sang for her own pleasure, and that of her friends.

Having tried her hand at numerous and diverse visual arts – painting, pottery, graphic art, even dabbling in filmmaking – Sophia had finally alighted on photography as her chosen career, and whilst black and white portraiture was hardly groundbreaking stuff, she did have a certain flair for subject matter, happy to record the down-and-outs of New York's underclass and juxtaposition them against glossy images of her own society friends. She had had several one-woman shows, self– financed, of course, that had at least divided opinion, which Sophia was more than happy to settle for.

Which leaves Eleina, who had no creative talent whatsoever; what she did have was a talent, if you can call it that, for getting her own way. She was clever, hard-working, ambitious and, most importantly of all, totally unscrupulous.

So, where did this fascinating female quartet spring from, with its colourful cocktail of talents, their dark eyes and dark hair and athletic bodies? Well, Alexi Floarea was a Romanian refugee, who arrived in the United States without a penny to his name, a neurotic wife, Juliani, and two small daughters. He was a shoemaker by trade, but not just any old shoemaker. He was, and would prove himself to be, quite simply the finest maker of ladies' footwear in the entire country. Within a couple of years of his arrival in his new homeland, he had emphatically made his mark on the American footwear industry. Within five years, Floarea Shoes were the most sought-after item in the discerning lady's wardrobe. He had opened three shops and employed only the very best craftsmen, but every single pair of shoes he sold had received his personal attention (or so he said).

By the time Iolanda was born, Alexi was a very rich man. By then, he had diversified into designer clothing, perfume, jewellery and racehorses; he had established an empire. By the time Iolanda was eighteen, Alexi was dead – a heart attack – Juliani had been committed to a long-term mental institution, the businesses had been sold for unimaginable money, and the four sisters had the world at their feet.

Iolanda was still single, and intended to stay so; Andreea was unhappily married; Sophia was married for the second time; and Eleina always had a partner, but not always the same one.

The poem that Paul had been struggling with was about his mother, or to be more precise, his relationship with her. The title, which might well change eventually, was *Only My Mother*, and it was intentionally ironic. The family lived in his mother's house, but only now she had died, since Maria had never felt exactly welcome there whilst her mother-in-law was still alive. "Your little shopgirl" was how the formidable Mrs Mallary used to refer to her son's fiancée, and even after she was diagnosed with leukaemia, and Maria had done everything in her power to support her, Joanne Mallary continued to resent the woman who had replaced her in her son's affections.

The poem was an attempt to reconcile Paul's feelings of guilt with his resentment at his mother's intransigence. The human response to forces that threaten the individual had been the enduring theme in Paul's work, the quality of which had been increasingly recognised both in the relatively rarefied circles of poetry appreciation, but more significantly in the much broader realms of general literary criticism. He had been regularly published in several magazines and periodicals, and his latest volume of poems had sold reasonably well, for poetry, that is. If he could just increase his output enough to sustain a public profile, then he could at least consider giving up the gardening; but yet again his dear mother was providing an irritating stumbling block.

There was so much in this poem that Paul was happy with; its exploration of the meaning of the word "only", for example. He played around with its breath of inference, from the *cruelly dismissive* to the *supremely exclusive*. It seemed to have a strange universality to it, somehow mirroring or perhaps even encompassing the very concept of Motherhood. He even toyed with the idea of coining the word "onlyness", but thought better of it in the end. However, he still felt uncomfortable about something. He substituted words and phrases, but that made matters worse. He tried redrafting the final verse, but that didn't appear to be the problem. He tried starting from scratch again, which he knew was a mistake, and he was right. The really annoying thing was that he felt that the piece was so nearly right, he was so close; so close, in fact, that he did something that he promised himself he would never do. He let someone else read the poem before he was satisfied with it. Maria always read his work before he sent it off to the publishers, and he did have great faith in her judgement; but this was different, showing her a poem that he himself was unhappy with.

'Seems good to me,' she said. 'Reckon you've hit the nail on the head, I think.' And Paul didn't know whether that was fantastically helpful, or of no use to him at all. Her comment verged on the frivolous, and yet it stated very simply that she couldn't see the problem with it. It took a particular sort of bravery for an artist to submit his work for scrutiny on the approval of another person, however intimate, but, in the end, that is just what Paul did.

The idea of establishing an international prize for the arts, equivalent to the Nobel prize in status, had not been Eleina's in the first place. Randolph Vaughan, her then partner, had come up with it, almost accidentally, whilst watching some awards ceremony on television, but Eleina had immediately recognised the potential of such a scheme, and her imagination went into overdrive. She could envisage a Nobel-style structure; various categories – music, visual arts, theatre and dance, literature, and perhaps even a multi-media prize – to give the whole thing a thoroughly modern feel. There would need to be committees, to draw up lists of nominees, and then select winners, or should that be Laureates? There would need to be accreditation, from national and international bodies, to give the prizes authenticity and kudos; there would need to be huge media contracts, to ensure world-wide exposure; and there would need to be serious sponsorship, to guarantee the long-term finances. The Floarea Foundation would provide the seed funding, just to ensure the whole thing was established as a global homage to the family name, but thereafter it would need to be commercially viable. And somehow, quite extraordinarily, it had all come true.

By an irresistible mixture of audacity, charm, persuasion, bribery, blackmail and the offering and accepting of sexual favours, like confetti, Eleina had managed to pull it off. Each of her sisters chaired an appropriate committee, with Eleina herself chairing the literature committee, and Randolph Vaughan covering multi-media; and then various luminaries from each particular discipline were coerced into serving as committee members. She had taken a permanent suite at the Waldorf, to act as her headquarters, and from there she controlled and manipulated the entire enterprise. The great, the good and the hopelessly ambitious beat a path to her lair, to beg, bribe or offer up their souls to gain favour that might lead to fame. The entire suite was wired for surveillance, so nothing went unrecorded, and no opportunity was wasted to exploit the incriminating images or indiscreet conversations that Eleina herself meticulously planned, choreographed and then executed with self-conscious relish.

And thus, the Floarea Prize was established. Enormous monetary prizes, and unparalleled publicity, ensured that no artist, however supposedly reclusive or self-effacing, ever turned down the invitation to be included on one of the category shortlists, and over the years the names bearing the title "Floarea Prizewinner" began to read like a history of twenty-first-century culture. Unbelievably, even this didn't satisfy Eleina for very long, and she dreamed of an even more prestigious award, covering not just the arts but science, the humanities and public service of all kinds; an award to be made once every five years to elect the "greatest living human being". Even for the stratospherically ambitious Eleina, this was surely a step too far, and her sisters, who were the only people capable of doing so, thankfully dissuaded her from pursuing this idea, at least for the time being. She would have to satisfy herself with the title of "Doyen of the Creative Arts".

On his father's rather sudden and unexpected retirement, David Crowther found himself in charge of Thistle Publications, a once proud and significant player in the world of poetry publishing, but no longer the force it had been, especially since the advent of digital publishing. Whilst the company was not actually in debt, which was certainly something to be grateful for, its prospects looked modest at best, and the most sensible course of action would probably be to wind the business up before it died on its feet.

But then a very strange thing happened. Without a secretary, whom they had had to let go, David was sorting through his post one Friday afternoon, when he came across an A4 envelope containing a six-verse poem entitled *Only My Mother,* by Paul Mallary. This wasn't particularly odd in itself, though hard copy submissions were generally discouraged these days; no, what was odd was the effect that the poem had on its reader... it enthralled him; it mesmerised him; in short, it completely captivated him.

David had some vague recollection of the name Mallary... a couple of modestly selling, slim volumes perhaps, that sort of thing, but he had never met the man and knew almost nothing about him. Yet here was this extraordinary poem, which clearly worked on so many different levels at once. It would speak to sons, to daughters, to mothers, to wives, to priests, to social workers, to politicians; it would actually speak to humanity. It was insightful, non-judgemental, lucid, lyrical, unputdownable, to use that awful phrase, and it demanded, simply demanded, an appropriate response.

It was an insane idea, but after two hours of pondering what to do, David decided to publish the poem on its own; not in a collection or anthology, just the poem by itself, beautifully printed on handmade card. His father would call it a ridiculous plan, and of course it was, but it would be a relatively inexpensive mistake if it proved to be so, and what did they have to lose? As it turned out, *Only My Mother* was an absolute sensation, and far and away the most successful poem the company had ever dealt with.

It started slowly, a few thousand copies, at two dollars a throw; then it found its way onto social media somehow, and it was away. Once the national networks had picked it up, within a couple of weeks it had had to be reprinted and had broken through the half-million-copies mark. But the really odd part was that people wanted to hold a hard copy... in their hands; not just hear it, but touch it and read it, and reread it and then read it again. Within the year, it had sold over five million copies and been translated into twelve languages. Like Walt Whitman in the nineteenth century or Sylvia Plath in the twentieth, Paul Mallary came, somehow, to represent the spirit of the age, and the somewhat bewildered poet was established as one of the leading voices of his generation.

An encounter between the two was, of course, inevitable, once Paul's fame could no longer be ignored, and Eleina had managed to overcome the jealousy she always felt towards anyone else's success. She had seen photos of this handsome young poet many times, and although she was almost twenty years his senior, she looked forward to adding him to her long list of amorous conquests. She made meticulous arrangements, involving elaborate diversionary plans, for his wife and children, which would allow her an entire day with Paul to accomplish her aims. She had well– rehearsed strategies to pre-empt any crisis of conscience that her victim might suffer, and she felt confident that by the time she had finished with him, he, as so many before him, would be her loyal creature. Paul was no fool, however, and no innocent either. He knew perfectly well of Eleina's reputation, and of the purpose that lay behind his invitation to the Waldorf suite, but he felt, perhaps rather foolishly, that he would be able to turn this situation to his own advantage. The scene was set for an interesting duel, though neither combatant had allowed for their opponent's unexpected reactions, or for their considerable resolve in the face of adversity.

Ten o'clock in the morning is clearly a bit early for cocktails, but convention meant nothing to Eleina, and a couple of very dry Martinis was always a good opening move. She ensured that hers was well diluted in the mixing, and he managed to surreptitiously pour most of his into a magnificent-looking succulent that sat on the small table beside his chair. It was something of a moot point whether seduction came before business or the other way round, but, on this occasion, Eleina decided to at least set some ground rules about where their relationship might lead, with the bedroom held in reserve, if greater persuasion were needed. The offer of "poetic immortality" was decidedly grandiose for an opening gambit, but it was worth testing the water, she felt, and without knowing the nature of the man, he might just fall for it. He didn't; in fact, he was surprisingly dismissive of the entire "Prize" culture, saying that he would prefer to leave any enduring judgement of his work to history. That certainly took the wind out of the lady's sails, so she quickly moved on to pecuniary advantages, confident that Paul's recent success would have given him the taste for the good life, a situation she felt sure he would wish to continue. She explained that sudden fame could just as soon disappear without some sort of substantial back-up, and nothing was more substantial than the accolade of "Floarea Prizewinner". But surely even she could not guarantee that an individual would actually win any given prize, Paul suggested, rather mischievously, to which Eleina responded with her most beguiling smile. 'How sweetly innocent you are,' she whispered, leaning in towards him.

And so this exchange of offerings and delicate refusals went on for some time, until Eleina eventually began to tire of it, deciding that perhaps the time had come for less resistible temptations. She excused herself, leaving him to "think it over", only to reappear moments later in the bedroom doorway, and the fact that she was exceptionally well preserved, for a woman in her forties, was clearly evident through the flowing chiffon gown she had changed into. The apartment lights seemed to dim of their own accord, and the strains of soft bewitching music seeped into the air. The hairs on the back of Paul's neck stood to attention as an unaccustomed fear and panic flooded over him, and he began desperately to assess his chances of escape. The poor man was in mid-ponder when his temptress turned her back on him and began to walk slowly towards the bed, allowing her flimsy covering to drop to the floor in her wake.

Jeeze! Paul thought to himself, his mind racing and his heart pounding. He knew he was seriously out of his depth, when a line from his own poem came screaming to his rescue: "And there in woman's guise, and in its lies", and suddenly he remembered that the whole thing was just a charade; a cheap, shameless trick; all just a "woman's lies" to feed her ego, her lust; not for sex, surely, but for power. He took a deep breath.

'I think I'll pass on that one, if you don't mind,' he found himself saying, and he went over and quietly shut the bedroom door. He lingered a moment too long, frozen by his own courage, when the door, to which his hand was still attached, burst open again, and Eleina, the vision of a classical furry, swept back into the room and roared at the trembling poet.

'You're finished, you hear…? You little worm. Dead meat… all doors forever closed to you… do you understand…? Finished.' She was very cross indeed. Paul steadied himself; he realised that his opponent's display of outrage and threat of retribution actually belied her real position. He swallowed hard.

'Not necessarily,' he said quietly. Once again, he had taken her by surprise.

'What do you mean? "Not necessarily", she snapped. 'You stupid kid, don't you realise that I can just crush you… like an ant?' There was still plenty of bravado, but perhaps that was all it was.

'You must admit, it would make an interesting scoop… this little encounter we have just enjoyed,' he said, still not quite sure how she would react.

'You wouldn't dare,' she threatened. 'And who do you think would believe you, when I deny every word of it?' Now he knew he had her.

'Everyone. Everyone would believe me. You know that as well as I do,' he said. 'It's what everyone has known for years… they just haven't said it.'

Three months later, Paul Mallary was unanimously voted winner of the Floarea Prize for Literature, and Eleina Floarea graciously presented him with his substantial cheque. She then made an uncharacteristically self-deprecating speech, in which she thanked everybody she could think of for everything that had ever happened, and then announced that she would be stepping down as President of the Floarea Foundation, so that she could devote more time to her beloved charity work. After a moment of stunned silence, she received a standing ovation, though the motivation for the enthusiastic applause was not altogether clear.

QUIET ALICE

…there was nothing physically wrong with her voice; it was not that Alice would not speak, but that she could not

T here are just some families that are golden, aren't there. Intelligent, good-looking, successful couples with just the right number of wonderful children, and everything they touch seems to turn to gold. And then, as if that's not enough, they are exceptionally nice people as well; it doesn't seem fair really. Christian and Claudia met at the LSE, both gaining firsts in Economics, before taking a year off to do voluntary work together in South America. On their return, Christian got a job with Lansdown and Cresswell, one of the top city banking firms, and Claudia worked for a while for a lobby group promoting women in politics.

When Christian Montgomery Berkley married Claudia Louise Augusta a year later, it was one of the social events of the year. Minor royals, society A-listers and numerous showbiz personalities were amongst the 600 or so guests; the tabloid press predictably labelled it a "fairytale" wedding. Five years on and Christian was already a junior partner at L and C on a seven-figure salary with the same again in annual bonuses, and Claudia, having duly produced one son, Toby, and one daughter, Isabel, was running her own business from their stunning Richmond home, headhunting exceptional women to serve as directors on the boards of the top Footsie 100 companies. The dearth of female directors was an embarrassment to many of the companies, but finding suitably qualified and experienced candidates was very tricky, which meant that Claudia's services were very much in demand, which, in turn, meant that she could charge almost whatever she liked, as long as she produced the goods. Her secret was, of course, to find the talent in America, where women had played a leading role in business for decades, and though they weren't two a penny, they were available at the right price. So for Mr and Mrs Berkley, life couldn't really have been much sweeter.

When Claudia found out that she was expecting again, very much to the couple's surprise, there was a moment when they wondered if another baby was really a good idea. Toby and Isabel had both started school, and their family life was pretty well organised. They had kept Imelda on, now more as a housekeeper than a nanny, but she could obviously revert to her former duties easily enough, so they eventually decided to go ahead with the baby, albeit with reservations.

In the end, whilst the pregnancy went very smoothly, the birth itself certainly did not. There were complications from the moment Claudia's waters broke on a family walk round Richmond Park, a protracted and painful labour and finally a preeclampsia scare that ended happily but with an exhausted mother and a perfect, if very small, daughter.

Alice Francesca weighed in at just six pounds, and unlike her brother and sister, who had both taken after their father with blond hair and blue eyes, the latest addition had dark eyes and wisps of raven hair, echoing her mother.

The family had taken their summer holidays on Sardinia for many years, so they knew the island pretty well, and Christian had decided exactly where he wanted to build his villa, overlooking a small private beach on La Maddalena archipelago. He had employed a fantastic Sardinian architect, Ignatziu Murgia, who had an international reputation for designing ultramodern houses but with a traditional Moroccan feel to them – arched windows and vaulted ceilings were two of his signature features – and using local materials wherever possible. Christian, who always did the holiday booking, told Claudia nothing of his plans, saving the project as a surprise tenth wedding anniversary present to spring on her when they arrived on the island for their family holiday.

During the run-up to the holiday, Claudia hadn't been feeling particularly great, which was very unlike her. She was really looking forward to getting away, but on the plane over she felt rotten and just hoped that once they arrived it would pass, and so she said nothing to Christian about it.

As they pulled off the main highway and into the drive of Villa Ephesus, the sight that greeted them was simply stunning. The building was a symphony of glass and stone, with numerous wraparound balconies and gently sweeping pan-tiled roof slopes. And as though set on its own island, the house had an enormous swimming pool that emerged from each side of the building and spread right across the front, with an elegant bridge leading across it to the front door. It was utterly breathtaking, and Christian, who had only seen photos of it during its construction, was delighted; it had exceeded even his expectations. He turned to his wife, who had been uncharacteristically quiet on the run from the airport, ready to announce triumphantly that this was her anniversary present, when he realised that Claudia was slumped in her seat, deathly pale and suddenly struggling to breathe.

It was a small private funeral, immediate family and one or two very close friends only. Toby and Isabel sat on either side of their father, but Alice, who was only just five, stayed at home with Imelda, despite her protestations. Throughout Claudia's final illness, which lasted just four months, Alice had become increasingly agitated and was only allowed to see her mother occasionally, when her mother was feeling up to it, and whenever the little girl asked if Mummy was getting better, she was gently reassured, for fear of distressing the child further.

The house in Richmond was strangely quiet over the weeks following Claudia's funeral; screams and laughter were replaced with hushed tones and whispers, everyone creeping about as though trying not to disturb a patient who was no longer there. Christian submerged himself in his work and hardly spoke to his children; Toby and Isabel only spoke to Imelda and then just at mealtimes, and nobody noticed that Alice didn't speak at all.

As the weeks turned into months and nothing in the household changed, it was Imelda who finally pointed out Alice's silence to her father, but he dismissed it as shock, and assumed it would resolve itself given time. It didn't, and reluctantly Christian had to recognise that his daughter needed help of some sort, though his GP, excellent when it came to sports injuries, was clearly out of his depth with a child's psychological problems. He did, however, recommend a Harley Street consultant who diagnosed selective mutism and offered a course of therapy which involved weekly visits over a six-month period, costing some £12,000 and achieving precisely nothing.

The problem was not that Alice *would not* speak, but that she *could* not. And it wasn't a physical disability; there was nothing wrong with her voice. Indeed, if you listened in at her bedroom door after she had gone to bed, you could hear her having long conversations with her toys, and she was able to read aloud at school, and even at home sometimes to her father, but that was the limit of her speech. She was simply unable to have any conversations with either adults or her peers, and as months and eventually years passed in this state, Alice developed her own strategies to cope with people, and with life.

Whilst all three children were at the same private prep school in Highgate, Toby and Isabel were able to keep a protective eye on their little sister, who, not surprisingly, was often the victim of teasing, not to say bullying. The school was extremely sensitive to the girl's plight and did its best, without specialist expertise, to support and encourage Alice in every way it could. But once Toby and then Isabel moved on to senior schools, Alice became ever more isolated and introspective, and as she edged towards puberty, Christian found himself further and further out of his depth, and increasingly reliant on Imelda to cope with his daughter, but the question of which senior school Alice could attend had to be addressed sooner or later.

The Carl Herring School occupied a pair of splendid Regency terraced houses in Chisholm Road on the edge of Richmond Park. It had two further sites: a large house in Park Street just half a mile away, which served as boarding accommodation for the twenty-three boys and girls who lived too far away to be day pupils at the school, and the second, a retreat near Ringwood in the New Forest, set up to provide a variety of outdoor activities for the pupils. The school catered for just seventy– five children of secondary age, all of whom were experiencing a variety of serious psychological problems. Just to describe the educational regime at Herring as individually child-centred is to hopelessly oversimplify the school's philosophy; the character of the school certainly owed a debt, which it freely acknowledged, to both Montessori and Steiner, but it also had very much its own approach, in many ways rather more disciplined than its more famous counterparts, but it had achieved some remarkable results in what were often highly complex cases.

By the age of eleven, Alice was well aware of her status as a "problem child" and she did genuinely want to be cooperative in the matter of her schooling, but she was apprehensive at the prospect of joining what she considered to be the "school for nutters". Margaret Huber, the principal of the school, was a woman in her late fifties who exuded kindness and competence in equal measure. There were no selective mutes at the school at the present time, she told Christian, but she had come across them, not infrequently, during her tenure at Herring. About 1 child in 140 children suffered from it to varying degrees, and she felt confident that Alice would find the school a positive, rewarding and transforming experience. Most importantly, however, she believed that Alice could be happy at the school, and that was what really mattered, both to the school and, of course, to Alice herself.

For the first month, Alice cried every morning as Imelda dropped her off at the school's front door, and then again for at least an hour each evening on her return home... just to make her point. After that, she seemed to settle in quite well, without showing the slightest sign of surrendering her silences, and without really attaching herself to any of the other children, but her behaviour was compliant and her academic progress satisfactory.

Then, after two terms, a problem arose that threatened to derail the entire strategy, though it was in no way related to the school itself. It was one evening, after Alice had gone to bed, Imelda informed Christian that she had received a letter from her brother in Manila, telling her that her mother was seriously ill and that she, Imelda, was required at home. She had no idea how long she may be away, or even if she would be able to return at all, but she would have to leave within a few days. Christian was devastated; he had come to utterly depend on his long-serving, long-suffering housekeeper-cum-nanny, and without her support he really had no idea how he would cope. Toby was coming up to GCSE exams and doing pretty well, and Isabel was remarkably mature for a thirteen-year-old girl, and seemed perfectly capable of looking after herself in most regards, but Alice... who would look after Alice... who would have the first idea how to handle a girl with her very particular difficulties?

Although she would never have admitted to having favourites, Miss Huber had taken a shine to Alice, and they often sat together at mealtimes, with the Principal carrying on one side of a lively conversation whilst her pupil responded with occasional nods and glances, which somehow seemed to suffice. She didn't officially have any boarding vacancies at that moment, but with a little rearrangement, she should be able to offer Alice a place in the Park Street accommodation, if the girl herself was happy to come. Christian took a week's leave, something quite unheard of, to supervise arrangements for Imelda's departure and Alice's instalment in the Herring Boarding House, both transfers taking place on a wet Saturday in late February on the very same day as the hurriedly arranged arrival at the school of Roberto Sanna, the troubled only son of the Italian Ambassador in London.

Vissenta Sanna, whose family came originally from Cagliari in Sardinia, had been appointed Ambassador almost three years ago, and it had been a difficult tour from the start. His wife, Lisa, the internationally acclaimed travel writer, had never been enthusiastic about her husband's appointment but had agreed to play her diplomatic role, so long as she was still able to continue with her own career. So play it she did, but with little enthusiasm and, some would say, even less grace. Vissenta's daughter from a previous marriage, Maria, was eight years older than Roberto and studying Philosophy at the Sorbonne, so only joined the family at holiday times, and often not even then.

In the three years since his arrival in England, Roberto had already joined, and then been asked to leave, four schools, and very expensive schools at that. Whilst his academic ability was not in question, and he never failed to keep up with his studies, his behaviour was erratic at best, and frequently totally unacceptable. His outbursts, both in the classroom and outside it, disrupted his fellow students and often frightened the teachers, who really had no idea how to control him. There seemed to be little rhyme or reason to these episodes; something would set him off, and then he appeared to lose all self-control, lashing out blindly and screaming obscenities that scarcely needed translating from the Italian. Herring was his very last chance; if he failed here, he would probably be sent back to the equivalent of a young offender institution outside Rome, where the regime would be far less tolerant of his behaviour, and where there would be very little opportunity to see his family. Roberto knew the score.

There was a small, nicely furnished, comfortable room at Herring which the staff called the Sanctuary. It was a place where students could be sent, or go to of their own volition, when it seemed like a good idea to be out of circulation. It was used infrequently by the staff and never as a place of punishment, so it retained a special atmosphere, a place where the norms of the school were temporarily suspended, where questions were not asked and judgements not made. There was no time limit to its use, nor record kept of it, and most of the students at Herring never felt the need to use it, though, on arrival at the school, they were all informed of its existence and its ill-defined purpose.

On the Monday of his fifth week at the school, having behaved in an exemplary manner since his arrival, Roberto felt something stirring in the pit of his stomach, and it made him nervous. He became aware that his fists were repeatedly clenching and unclenching and he was finding it hard to stay focused. Perhaps for the first time in his relatively short life, he consciously thought about what his next action should be. His decision to take himself to the Sanctuary was only half-deliberate, and even that thought made him angry; angry enough to rip the notices off the wallboard in the main corridor, angry enough to kick at every door he passed through on his way to the rear wing where the Sanctuary was located, angry enough to smash his fist into a tray of mugs sitting on a side table, waiting to be returned to the kitchen. When he finally stood outside the door of his destination, he wavered. He took several breaths to see if that would calm him down, but it didn't, so he kicked the door open with all the violence he could muster.

She had been sat quietly in the room for almost an hour when she heard the sound of his approach, but Alice's silent prayer that he would pass by the Sanctuary went unanswered. She was cowering on the sofa in the far corner of the room facing the door when Roberto burst in.

'What you do in here, Dumb Girl?' he shouted. Alice remained perfectly still, with her eyes fixed at a point on the floor.

'This is room for me... you hear?' Roberto was shaking visibly, and Alice could sense his fear.

'Why you stay in here?' he demanded. And then... there was a strange pause, a moment of readjustment. The boy took a tentative step towards her.

'Why... why... why is this happening again?' His voice was softer now, and he held his head as if to stop it spinning. Then he slowly sank to the floor in front of where Alice still sat huddled on her seat, and for the first time she dared to look at him.

'What do I do, Dumb Girl... you tell me?' It was a plaintive cry now. The boy seemed to reach out to Alice, who was slowly getting to her feet when he grabbed her violently around the waist and hung on to her as if his life depended on it. For a moment, they held the pose, as if doing so for a photo.

Then there was a flurry of whispered activity outside the room, and the familiar figure of Miss Huber appeared, framed in the doorway. The Principal looked anxiously at Alice, who felt suddenly and completely in control of the situation. With well-practised facial expressions, the young girl made it clear to her teacher that she was happy dealing with this situation herself and would like the two students to be left alone. Miss Huber was taken aback, apprehensive and impressed all at the same time. Nevertheless, as she closed the door gently behind her, she wondered if she was doing the right thing.

The best part of an hour passed and Miss Huber, having listened unsuccessfully at the door several times, felt she had to act. First, she softly knocked and waited without result; then she slowly and carefully turned the door handle and eased the door ajar. The two youngsters were curled up together on the sofa, apparently fast asleep, and the Principal found herself almost reluctant to disturb them, but as she stood there, Roberto opened his eyes and smiled. As he raised himself off the seat, Alice also woke up, and the two of them looked at each other, and then at Miss Huber.

'Are you okay, Roberto?' she asked in her kindest tone.

'Me? Sure. I am well, thank you, Miss Huber,' the boy said, as he moved towards the door.

'Now there is a friend for me in England,' he said, 'so I am well,' and with that, and a smiling glance back at Alice, he stuffed his hands into his pockets and sauntered out of the room.

'And you, Alice? How about you?' the Principal enquired.

Alice's response was a nod and a knowing smile, much as Miss Huber had come to expect, but as the girl was making to leave, she turned suddenly and looked directly at the Principal.

'Actually, I'm good, thank you, Miss Huber.'

UAIGNEACH

…Old Donal dies, after fifty years of living a life of isolated austerity on the tiny island with his son, so might the truth about Uaigneach now, finally, be revealed?

When Katie Mulligan stepped cautiously off the little boat on that bitter, blustery February afternoon, she was the first female to step onto the island since sweet Colleen O'Doyle had mysteriously disappeared from it, sick and wretched and without her babe, more than half a century earlier.

Donal O'Doyle had spent the last two and a half years caring for his father, also Donal, as best he could in the circumstances. The old man had lain in his bed resigned to the fact that his troubled life was slowly drawing to its close, and with little desire to impede God's will for him. Young Donal, who was fifty-two years of age, had no skill in ministering to the sick, but he had done what he could to make his father comfortable.

Uaigneach (lonely place) lay north east of the Brannock Islands that in turn lay north east of the Aran Islands that guarded the entrance to the bay of Galway. It was little more than a mile from end to end and half of that at its widest point. It was mostly bare rock with a small area of cultivable ground to its southerly end, in the centre of which stood a long, low two-roomed cottage where the father and son had lived a life of extraordinary, and quite unnecessary, austerity.

The O'Doyles had money; nobody knew how much, or what its source was, but they had money. An ancestor had purchased Uaigneach back in the mists of time, and subsequent generations had lived on, or visited, the island at irregular times and for various durations until Donal senior took up residence some fifty-three years ago. He had rarely left the place in the intervening period. Just six months into his residency, he did leave for five days, for an unknown destination, returning with a pretty young bride, Colleen Brady, who dutifully produced an O'Doyle male heir within a year – young Donal – but had apparently vanished from the island, without trace, within another twelve months.

Katie Mulligan had been born and raised on a small family farm at Ballycordell, just outside Cork. A bright girl, she had shone at St Teresa's Convent School and was expected to do well for herself. Her mother, Bridget, thought she would make a fine teacher, or perhaps a nurse, whilst Mr Mulligan secretly prayed that the girl might take the veil, becoming a nun at St Teresa's, and thus able to combine service to children at the school with service to God. In the end, it was nursing that Katie chose, and having trained at St Finnbar's Hospital in Cork, she became a district nurse.

She had been thought of as handsome in her day, rather than pretty, and had not been without admirers over the years, but somehow nursing had always come first, and her chances had slipped silently by. Her familiar figure, crouched at first over the handlebars of her sturdy bicycle, and then over the wheel of her somewhat dilapidated Morris Minor, was as much part of the countryside and villages to the west of the city as the local bars that occupied so many corners. When word spread that Nurse Mulligan had been suspended from her duties, pending a disciplinary hearing, the shock to the community she served was palpable. Surely there had been some sort of mistake; it would all blow over in no time. What people did not know was that Katie's offence could not have been more serious; she was suspected of assisting one of her elderly patients to end his life. To be honest, Pat Orr's life, which had already spanned eight decades, the last of which had been a relentless purgatory, was one kinder to end than prolong, but it was sinful to even think such a thing, let alone act upon it. The medical authorities would have no scope for leniency if the allegations proved to be well-founded. In the end, it was Nelly Feeney, old Pat's eldest daughter, who insisted to the panel that her father had been solely responsible for his own death, and that Katie had never shown anything but the utmost professional concern for his welfare. The charges were dropped, but the damage was done. Nurse Mulligan had made her last round, in County Cork at any rate. It was time to move on.

For three entire days following Colleen's unexplained disappearance from Uaigneach, old Donal sat in his ancient chair beside a cold grate in the cottage. He neither ate nor slept, nor did he tend to the tiny infant swaddled in the cradle in the other room. He was deaf to both the babe's pitiful cries and then to its ominous silence. When the numbness in his brain began to dissolve and the reality of his situation began to crystallise, his first thought was one of dread. He had no idea how long it had been since Colleen had gone, or what had happened during that time. He listened, waited, hoping to hear some sound of life, but was met only by silence, edged with the distant breaking of waves on the rocky beach. For the first time since he was a boy, Donal tried to construct a prayer, a despairing plea, a cry for forgiveness to a God whom he did not know. When he lifted the babe up, he was certain that there was no life in him, and then, as though by miracle, he sensed he had been wrong. Inching the baby back from death's jaws now became Donal's obsession, and he devoted himself to this task, day and night.

And so their life together, father and son, began again. For a long while, Donal convinced himself that Mother's instinct would draw Colleen once again to their cottage, and so he remained in constant readiness for her return, but as the years passed, the expectation faded, even as his devotion to her memory grew stronger.

On what old Donal thought might be his son's tenth birthday (these occasions were moveable feasts for the O'Doyles), he decided it was perhaps time to begin young Donal's education. The boy had received no formal teaching; indeed, the authorities in Galway were blissfully unaware of his very existence. However, his father had taught him to read, to sign his name, if ever that proved necessary, and to play chess. This had seemed more than adequate up until now. Donal did not want his son going off to some school in Galway, or anywhere else for that matter, lest he be teased for being different in some way from the other boys, or in case such a course of action resulted in a distance growing between the two of them. Donal feared this more than any other thing in the world. A tutor, coming to the island at regular intervals, might provide the answer, so Donal set Thomas Ellwood, his solicitor and only regular link with the outside world, the task of locating a suitable candidate for the role.

Four months of diligent research produced just one possible name: Roberto Rossi. Rossi, the son of Italian immigrants, had retired to Galway after a lifetime spent teaching Classical Civilisation in both schools and colleges throughout Ireland, though mostly in and around Dublin. At first, the atmosphere was tense each time Roberto drew up to the tiny pier in his launch (a retirement present to himself), and Donal threatened to curtail the arrangement on more than one occasion, feeling that he had made a mistake engaging the tutor. It was young Donal's pleading that Roberto should be allowed to continue that swayed his father, and in time, both father and son grew first attached and then devoted to the teacher, as he did to both of them.

The breadth of Roberto's knowledge was quite astonishing, from Physics to Astronomy, from Chaucer to Louis Armstrong, so it was an eclectic, if unconventional, education that Donal received. The lessons, which usually lasted about two hours, continued twice a week, regular as clockwork, for almost seven years, until Roberto became too unwell to manage the boat trip across to the island. He had been diagnosed with prostate cancer eighteen months earlier but had not told the O'Doyles. After that, it was young Donal who made the trip to the mainland each week, to see Roberto, ostensibly to continue his lessons, but in reality it was to check up on his mentor, ensuring he had everything he needed. The young man was, in fact, with him the afternoon he died, peacefully in his own bed in his own little cottage near the quay. Donal always felt that he had waited for him, to say goodbye.

Katie didn't really have a plan; all she knew was that she had to get away, far away, to somehow start again, if that was possible. New York sounded a long way away. London sounded a long way away. Even Dublin sounded a long way away. Her sister, Mary, lived not that far away, in Galway, alone, and would be happy to put her up for a few weeks whilst she sorted out what she wanted to do next. She and Mary had always got on well enough, though they hadn't seen as much of each other over recent years. Five years younger than her sister, Mary had always been the spoilt baby of the family, good fun but wilful, more interested in boys and clothes than achieving anything at school or getting a useful job. There had been the shadow of a great family disgrace when Mary was thought to be pregnant at the age of seventeen, suspicion falling on a travelling salesman who had stayed in the village a while before, but it turned out to be a false alarm, though the girl had mysteriously disappeared for a week to stay with an aunt in Sligo, just before the "all-clear" was sounded with such relief.

At twenty, Mary had married, unsuitably as her father had described it, and, just as he predicted, it had not lasted. By the time Michael, the ne'er-do-well husband, left, she was glad to see the back of him and his philandering ways, leaving her with a pile of empty dreams and a pile of Victorian terraced house that needed everything doing to it, and a mortgage she could ill afford. She had struggled along for a good few years now, so Mary was genuinely glad of her sister's company and a bit of help with the bills.

After a week or two, and almost unintentionally, Katie got a temporary job as an agency nurse, filling in for maternity leave, and to her surprise, the whole arrangement began to take on a more permanent feel. The two sisters found they liked each other more than they remembered, and despite having diametrically opposed views on a number of issues, they laughed a lot and agreed to disagree. New York began to feel a very long way away.

The years passed largely uneventfully on Uaigneach, though when Roberto had started his lessons with young Donal, his father decided to install a small diesel generator, and the advent of electricity to the island propelled them, albeit reluctantly in old Donal's case, into the twentieth century. On the first Wednesday of each month, not that either man knew what day of the week it ever was – so it always came as a surprise – a boat would arrive at the island with supplies; food, diesel and any hardware items that they had ordered the previous month. The account was paid in advance by Thomas Ellwood, who attempted on the rare occasion he actually met Donal to persuade his client to take at least a passing interest in his financial situation. 'Is there enough?' is all Donal would ever ask, and having been reassured that there was more than enough for all current and potential needs, he was satisfied, and would discuss the matter no further.

With the necessary supplies, there also came a regular, and not inconsiderable, flow of books. Initially, these were suggested by Roberto, but as time went on, young Donal would make his own choices. His reading was both wide and deep, and by the time his lessons were forced to finish, he had accumulated a considerable library on bookshelves that lined almost every wall of the cottage. In time, it became necessary for him to build a third room onto the cottage, largely to house his books.

Each day after breakfast, which was always porridge and tea, young Donal would read until midday, when he and his father would share a simple meal and then discuss some topic from the morning's study. Whilst his son read, old Donal would pack a few items into a small rucksack and set off on the ten-minute trek to the rocky north of the island, where he would remain for a couple of hours before returning to the cottage to prepare lunch. This routine was adhered to in all but the fiercest weather, and on those rare occasions when the elements did actually defeat him, Donal would breakfast as usual, returning to his bed where he would remain until summoned by his culinary duties. His son never once accompanied him on this daily pilgrimage, nor did he ever enquire as to its purpose. It was mutually accepted that this time was precious as well as private, and it was not until after his father's death that young Donal discovered the significance of the ritual.

In one of those strange twists of fate, it was Thomas Ellwood that first brought the two of them together, in the rather unpromising location of the dreary waiting room of Ellwood Solicitors. Katie and Mary had, after an interminable period of dithering lasting many years, decided to formalise their domestic arrangements by taking out a joint mortgage, providing funds which would enable them to complete the renovation of their Victorian monstrosity. The long-term intention was, in fact, to sell the restored house and buy somewhere more convenient and manageable for them, but they weren't going to tell Mr Ellwood that, in case he disapproved. The two sisters had drawn straws to decide who would broach the matter with their solicitor and Katie had lost, so now she perched nervously on the hard wooden seat, feeling as though she was about to be interviewed by a terrifying headmistress.

Two empty seats away sat young Donal, entrusted with the task of providing the annual signature on the West of Ireland Fuel Company agreement that ensured their supply of diesel for the year. Mr Ellwood was delayed, announced the unnecessarily aggressive receptionist, and she couldn't say when he would be available. Further enquiry by Donal elicited scant details beyond the facts that Mr Ellwood had had to go out unexpectedly, he apologised for detaining them, and he would return as soon as possible if they would be so good as to wait.

An hour and a half passed in awkward silence, punctuated only by Katie and Donal periodically glancing at each other and rolling their eyes, and the Gestapo receptionist answering the telephone three times with the same curt and unhelpful response to enquiries. Each time, the two clients had hoped it was Mr Ellwood announcing his imminent return, but alas it was not. 'Any chance of a cup of coffee?' asked Donal, without the least expectation of a positive response.

'I'm afraid we're out of coffee,' lied the receptionist brusquely, without looking up.

'Shall we grab a cup at the Starbucks over the road?' Katie found herself saying, to her own astonishment. 'If we sit in the window, we should be able to see Mr Ellwood when he comes back.'

Donal looked at her as if she had just invited him to have sex. This really was new and very exciting territory for him. 'Umm, yes. Why not? That would be...'

They sat in the window of Starbucks, looking like two dummies in some charity shop display, for the next two hours, at the end of which time something extraordinary had happened; they had become... well... friends at least. Mr Ellwood did not return, so at lunchtime they parted, Katie to meet Mary at the dentist's, and Donal to return to Uaigneach to give deep thought to the events of the morning. Before separating they co-ordinated day and time the following week, for a return visit to Ellwood.

And so began one of the most unlikely of courtships. Because, they decided, it was highly unlikely to come to anything in the long run, Donal chose not to mention the matter to his father, and Katie, fearing the ridicule of her sister, also chose to remain quiet about it. As it turned out, this secrecy proved to be one of the great charms of their relationship; they enjoyed the cloak and dagger nature of their meetings, the subterfuges, the assignations. It was quite like being in a novel, and they both loved it.

Months, and then years, went by; Katie carried on with her nursing, Donal carried on with his... well, with his reading, and neither of them felt the need for more than they had.

There were just two caveats to their agreement: Katie had eleven more years before she wanted to retire at sixty, and Donal was deeply conscious of his responsibility towards his increasingly frail father. They would wait until these two matters were resolved before contemplating any *further steps*.

On Christmas Eve, in the year that Katie finally hung up her nursing uniform, old Donal had a third and final stroke. His son tried to persuade him to go to hospital, but the old man was adamant. He would die in his own bed. He would have liked to make one final visit to the north of the island, but realising that was not possible, he charged his son to take a posy of flowers up there when the time came; he would see easily enough where they should be laid. Donal promised. The old man was cremated on New Year's Eve, and his son scattered his ashes across the island the following day.

For the next six weeks, Donal spent every minute of every day, bar one, preparing the cottage, and on a blustery 14th February, Katie Mulligan, now O'Doyle, stepped carefully off the little boat onto Uaigneach, and she and Donal made their way up to their new home together, as he pondered how he would broach the subject of what he had discovered on the north beach of the island.

ESAU AND JAKE

*...when she turned and saw the figure, the
scream that rose from her shattered the still
silence of the sombre little church*

As she sat tentatively in the front pew of the tiny medieval Church of the Blessed Virgin in Cordes, Constance du Merville was simply grateful that she had managed not to make a spectacle of herself, so far. She took slow, deep breaths, trying to prepare herself for the ordeal to come. She wanted to check that her eye make-up hadn't smudged during the emotional car journey to the church, but realised she couldn't. Louis, black-haired and blue-eyed like his father, had just celebrated his eighth birthday and sat on her left, with the five-year-old twins, Jules and Cecile, both blond like their mother, on her right, and they were all trying their best not to fidget, but it had been a long day for them already. When the organ announced the entry of her husband Esau's coffin, Constance sensed the blood drain out of her, and she clutched at her children, as much to steady herself as comfort them, glaring fixedly at the white lilies that decorated the altar.

It seemed to take an eternity for the pallbearers to complete their journey to the altar rail, during which time Constance experienced an almost unbearable desire to look back at the west door through which they had all entered, as though expecting... she didn't know what exactly, but something. The doleful organ ground to a reluctant silence;

the very young and clearly apprehensive Fr Gabriel, who was standing in for the ancient and venerable Fr Jean who was away on his annual holiday, made his way awkwardly to the pulpit, removed his biretta and coughed nervously before welcoming the congregation in a voice so soft that even Constance would have struggled to hear it in the front pew, had she been paying attention, which she was not. Instead, her mind was consumed with an urge to look behind her to the back of the church, and whilst she fought the temptation as long as she could, eventually there was no resisting it, and as soon as she turned, she saw the figure, and the scream that rose from her shattered the still silence of the little church into a thousand pieces, and she collapsed unconscious into the unready arms of her children.

But I have started my story in the middle... I need to go back... back almost thirty-five years, to the end of the Second World War, to a village outside Cordes, and to a young sixteen-year-old girl named Fayette Charbonneau. Her father, Gilbert Charbonneau, owned nearly forty hectares of the richest vineyards in the region and having had all his property confiscated by the Vichy Government during the occupation, it had now been returned to him, and he set about restoring his wine to its rightful place amongst the premier wines of France.

1946 was an outstanding year for the grape; the weather pattern was perfect and Charbonneau's workers, fired by their newly regained freedom, applied themselves with an enthusiasm they had rarely displayed prior to the war. The *"vendange"*, or grape harvest, began in mid-September, and by the end of the month the crop had been gathered and the winery was working at full capacity, whilst the celebrations that accompanied the harvest were, if not quite Bacchanalian, certainly lusty.

Fayette was young and pretty and naïve, and had no head for the wine, hidden away for the past five years, that now flowed so freely. By the middle of November, she realised, with utter horror, that she was pregnant, and with very little recollection of how it had come about. Gilbert was not only a pillar of his community but also of his local Catholic church, which dominated the lives of the Charbonneaus and their neighbours, and his daughter's condition threatened shame and disgrace on the family from which they could hardly expect to recover. Within an hour of confessing her guilt to her parents, the young girl was on her way to a convent outside Paris that cared for, if that can be said to be the right expression, girls in Fayette's predicament. The Convent of the Holy Rosary was run by an order of nuns – Daughters of the Cross –, who, as well as their work with "fallen girls" also ran missionary schools in the Third World and had a number of contemplative houses where the sisters observed a strict, but not absolute, rule of silence.

For the next six months, Fayette worked twelve hours a day, in the convent kitchen, or the laundry, or in the produce garden, which despite being the hardest work, she liked best, and this manual labour was punctuated by prayers, each hour on the hour, during which the girls were required to prostrate themselves on the ground for ten minutes, wherever they happened to be when the bell summoned them to their obligation.

At seven o'clock each evening, Fr Claud Faucher, the convent chaplain, would start to hear the confessions of each of the thirty girls resident at any given time. Girls were expected to find sins to confess on every occasion, as it was pointed out to them repeatedly by the nuns that girls of their type would have "sins of desire" to confess, even if circumstances had denied them the opportunity to enact their sinful wishes. The remainder of the evening was supposed to be spent in murmuring their prayers of penance, or in silent reflection on their worthlessness.

On 14th June 1947, Fayette went into labour, having experienced very few medical difficulties whilst at the convent, but now, suddenly, the pain of childbirth descended on her and held her in its grip for hour upon hour without relief. The nuns appeared to rejoice in her suffering, attributing her agony to the sin that had brought it about. For thirty-six hours, her distress was ignored as she writhed and cried out for help or comfort, and it was only when it appeared that she might actually die before being able to give birth that the sister in charge of the delivery relented and sent for the doctor. By now delirious with pain, Fayette remembered nothing of the emergency caesarean section, carried out without the availability of anaesthetic, through which she brought new life into the world. By the time she regained consciousness, she was alone in her cell, and, as had been made clear to her from the moment she entered the convent, she knew she would never lay eyes on her child. All babies born there were sent abroad for adoption immediately after birth.

The engine coughed and wheezed and spluttered like an old man who thought his time was up, but eventually it caught, and as Jake twisted the throttle on the vintage bike's handlebars it roared into life, filling the garage with clouds of white smoke. Motorbikes, especially old ones, were not his business, but they were his passion, and engines at least had been his passport off the New South Wales farm where he had grown up, and into the world of engineering.

It was on his eighteenth birthday that Martha and Luke Durrant had broken the news to their eldest son that he was, in fact, adopted, but that, as far as they were concerned, he was their son in every way, and the fact that they were not his natural parents made absolutely no difference to how they felt about him. The same could not be said for Jake. This news changed everything for him. A world beyond the strictures of the farm and a lifetime spent 365 days a year at the whim of Mother Nature suddenly seemed possible. And it wasn't that he was ungrateful to his parents for the care they had shown him over the years, and the encouragement they had offered when, for example, he told them he wanted to apply for college, though the choice of a farm management course was certainly designed to soften any resistance they might display, but now he felt entitled to make his own decisions, he sensed his destiny was, for the first time, in his own hands.

Farming was a hard life, and growing up on a farm was hard too. Luke had been a father of few words and many expectations; quick to criticise and slow to praise, never knowingly unkind or unfair, and just occasionally sentimental – though that never lasted very long. Jake knew it would be a huge disappointment to both his Ma and Pa, as he called them, when he announced his change of plans, because they would realise immediately that an engineering degree would not lead Jake back to the farm. Because of the fact that the Durrants had chosen to provide him with a home and a family, he knew he would always be in their debt; he would just have to find some other way to repay them.

The smoke in the garage began to clear and he suddenly realised that it must be nearly six months since he had visited the farm. It was less than two hours away on the bike and he had nothing planned for the weekend that couldn't wait. He went into the house, stuffed a few things into his rucksack and grabbed his helmet. Jake never rang ahead when he visited the farm; he liked to see the look of delight on Martha's face when he turned up unexpectedly, but on this occasion the pleasure at seeing him was clearly mixed with something else; the smile was almost forced and the hug tentative.

'Got this letter the other day, love,' she said. 'Told your Pa he needed to contact you. Just didn't get around to it yet.'

'What letter, Ma?'

'Come inside, son, on the table in the kitchen,' she said. 'Postmarked Paris.'

The great majority of the girls couldn't get away from the convent fast enough once they had given birth. Most felt that they had little option but to return to their families, with some elaborately constructed excuse for their absence, which neighbours inevitably saw through. Gilbert Charbonneau gave out the story that Fayette had gone on a mission of mercy, to care for an elderly aunt in Paris who was dying of cancer and needed constant nursing through her final days. She would receive a warm welcome home when her task was complete.

Fayette had not the slightest intention of returning home, warm welcome or not. She had spent eight months trying to sort out her feelings, which ranged from anger with her parents for abandoning her when she most needed them, to disgust with herself for allowing her situation ever to arise, to contempt for the hypocrisy of the nuns who spouted the love of God but displayed nothing but cruelty and callousness towards vulnerable girls, and to a feeling of utter hopelessness, as though her life no longer had any meaning.

The night before she was due to leave the convent, she was sitting on a bench in the kitchen garden wondering what the next twenty-four hours might bring, when she became aware that she was not alone. Sister Marie-Josef was in her eighties and it was clear that life had taken its toll on her; well, on her body at least. She was wizen and bent and riddled with arthritis, but her eyes sparkled and her face lit up as she spoke, and whether she wanted to or not, Fayette had little alternative but to listen. The old nun told her she had spent most of the past fifty years teaching in missionary schools in Africa and now, not wishing to be morbid about it, she had come home to die, though not necessarily immediately. Fayette had to smile.

'And what about you, young woman, what is your name?' asked the nun.

'Fayette Charbonneau,' the girl replied.

'Well, Fayette Charbonneau, tell me about yourself.'

For a moment, Fayette remained silent; she was stunned. In the past eight months, nobody, not a single soul, had asked her that.

'To be honest,' started Fayette, 'there's very little to tell.'

'Stuff and nonsense,' chided the nun. 'You wouldn't be here if there was nothing to tell.'

Which, of course, was true.

'Well...?' urged the nun. 'Where were you born? Start there.'

And so began the friendship which, whilst not long in years, shaped the rest of Fayette's life.

'So, was he handsome then...this boy of yours?' Marie-Josef chuckled.

'Nuns aren't meant to ask questions like that.'

Decades later, as she sat in the Prioress' office in the order's Mother House in Paris, Mother Mary Agnus, formerly Fayette Charbonneau, reflected on that conversation, and it still made her smile.

It was only Fr Gabriel's third funeral, the previous two being regulation affairs both involving octogenarians ready and willing to meet their Maker, and Fr Jean had been in attendance anyway to ensure fair play. This was an altogether different matter. A healthy, successful married man with a young family cut down "in the prime of life" as they say, by an inebriated delinquent youth on a stolen motorbike, in broad daylight. And now the distraught widow, having first gone hysterical, had passed out and seemed unlikely to play any further part in proceedings. What, considered the bewildered cleric, was the appropriate course of action? Was there a protocol for such occasions? Should he continue with the ceremony, or postpone, or delay for an hour to give the widow time to recover, or perhaps just cut to the interment and finish things up quickly?

In the event, matters were more or less taken out of his hands when a nun came swiftly forward, with an air of authority and a face long since scarred with disease, yet glowing with kindness, who immediately assessed the situation, organised the transporting of the unconscious widow and her children back to their home, and instructed the acquiescent priest to complete the funeral service in a prompt but suitably dignified manner. The nun agreed to accompany the grieving family to explain what had happened when the widow recovered her senses. If he was honest, Fr Gabriel was far too frightened of the nun to do anything but agree to her proposals, and was actually rather relieved that someone else was making the decisions.

By the time Constance and her children had reached home, a doctor had been summoned and was there waiting for them. She was still in deep shock from the extraordinary events of the day, and said nothing as she was helped into bed, where she remained, semi-conscious, for several hours, whilst her children ate sandwiches and watched television in the living room, and the mysterious nun waited patiently in the dining room.

In one way, it was a spur-of-the-moment decision, and yet, in another, Jake felt the letter simply provoked him into an action which had an inevitability about it. After university, he had joined a highly regarded civil engineering company specialising in major infrastructure projects, bridges in particular, and he had done exceptionally well, rising from a very junior position to an assistant project manager in an unusually short time. If he stayed with Protheroe and Spinks, he would almost certainly be offered a junior partnership within the next five years, and his financial and professional future would be assured, but the prospect really didn't excite him. Then, of course, there had been the site accident. Not his fault in any way; not anyone's fault according to the accident investigation, but, nevertheless, three workers had lost their lives, three families were devastated, and it had profoundly affected Jake for months afterwards and caused him to reassess his own life.

He had devoted all his energies to his work, but he now began to realise that it had been at the expense of his private life. There had been girlfriends, of course, one or two near misses in the marriage stakes, but here he was, at thirty-three years of age, a successful career, a smart out-of- town house and three beautiful vintage motorbikes, but it wasn't the same as a happy marriage and three beautiful children.

Since the age of eighteen and that announcement by his adopted parents, he had been searching for who he was, and he still didn't have the answer. So what did he really have to lose? He would go to Paris, but not just take a plane and arrive sixteen hours later the same person. No, he would go on his favourite bike, overland as far as was possible, a sort of odyssey, in the hope that he might discover "something" along the way. He estimated the journey might take him eight months. It was probably a ridiculous idea, but then some of the best ideas started out like that, didn't they? What he couldn't possibly have anticipated was the news that greeted him when, eleven months later, he did finally arrive in France's capital city.

When Constance finally felt sufficiently herself to face people, she called out from her bed, expecting a response from her younger sister, Therese, who had been staying with them since the accident; but it was not Therese who appeared in the doorway.

'May I come in?' asked the nun, in a tone that did not really brook refusal.

Constance shrunk back against her pillow, half afraid and half indignant at this unwelcome intrusion. The nun stepped into the room.

'My name is Mother Mary Agnus, Constance, and we have a connection, indeed the most painful of connections,' she said softly.

'I'm sorry, I have no idea who you are. Do you mind leaving at once.' Constance was outraged by this woman's impertinence, and at such a time.

'Therese!' she shouted, first glaring at the nun and then turning her whole body away from this intruder.

'Constance,' said the nun, and her voice was now raw with emotion. 'You have lost your husband, and I have lost one son.'

And these words were spoken with such heartfelt sincerity that despite everything she thought she knew about her husband, and everything she did not know about the woman in front of her, Constance could not fail but to believe her.

And so Fayette Charbonneau told her story; of her pregnancy at sixteen, the Convent of the Holy Rosary, Sister Marie-Josef, her own missionary work in Africa, including in the school for leper children, and of her return to Paris just as the new laws on the access rights of adopted children and natural parents were being passed in the French parliament.

'And did Esau know that you were his natural mother?' asked Constance.

'He did,' replied the nun, 'but he chose to keep the past in the past, as he put it, for the time being anyway, and I respected that decision.'

'So why have you come forward now?' asked Constance. 'What do you want?'

'I would not have done so, Constance, had there not been someone I felt you were entitled to meet.'

At which the nun rose and went to the door.

'There was something that the nuns at the Holy Rosary failed to tell me,' she said as she opened it. Constance gasped. The slim figure; the dark hair; the blue eyes. It had not been Esau's ghost she had seen in the church after all.

THE PRIEST HOLE

…there's a priest's hiding hole behind the great fireplace, thought Marian, but she had no idea where that thought had come from… or what it meant

'Do as you please,' said Marian, in her most emphatic tone of voice, 'but I'll tell you this for nothing, Doug, if you stand again, that's it, I'll leave you. I mean it.' They both knew this was an idle threat, but it made her feel better anyway.

'It's not so much that endless campaigning nonsense,' she continued. 'It's the inevitable disappointment at the end of it all that gets me... seeing you so predictably... defeated.'

'Nothing's inevitable, Marian,' offered Doug, though, to be honest, he hardly sounded convinced himself.

'Why don't you let someone else have a go this time, Doug?' Marian pleaded. 'You've done your bit, haven't you, over the years? Why not let one of the younger ones have a go, eh?'

'No one else is willing to stand, I'm afraid.' Even Doug realised that this was a weak argument, but it was all he had to offer, and it happened to be the truth.

'Well then, maybe nobody should stand, if that's how they feel.' Marian began to scent victory.

'No one represent the party? That's unthinkable, Marian.' Poor Doug was sounding desperate now.

'Well, Doug, I've said my piece. You'll have to choose... your wretched party or your... wretched marriage.'

Wendelborough Council Offices had a colourful history; a rather splendid late Victorian Gothic edifice, actually mentioned by Pevsner, was erected in the 1870s and had stood proudly at the centre of the town until 1963 when it had been "claimed" that necessary repairs and alterations to the building would cost far more than pulling it down and building a new one. So down it came, and in its place a monstrosity of 1960s so-called *modernist* design arose; square, featureless, concrete and glass, destined for the scrapheap before the paint was dry. By the 1980s, this new building was already beginning to fall apart, afflicted with something called concrete cancer, and whilst the application of various remedial solutions forestalled its demise, by the end of the century, for reasons of public safety if nothing else, there was no alternative but to demolish it.

Since then, and in the absence of sufficient council finances to erect a new building, council business had been conducted in the former Town Museum, ironically a far older building dating back to the 1660s, and significantly less suitable for this new role than the late much-loved red brick Victorian creation. There were, of course, plans, updated and revised at five-yearly intervals, but no one was holding their breath on that one.

It is probably worth mentioning at this point that the 1960s were also notable for the exponentially rapid growth in the architectural reclamation business, a matter we will return to in due course. Whilst the major portion of the museum's collections was reluctantly placed in storage, supposedly awaiting restoration when new council offices were eventually built, a significant number of items of particular interest to the town remained in the museum, dotted around the place as a sort of reminder of its former status.

Doug and Marian Black had lived in Wendelborough all their married life, twenty-eight years in August, and their three children, Peter, Michael and Sally had gone to the local schools, then on to university, and now all three lived, disappointingly unmarried, in London.

Doug had been an engineer at Hughes and Webbs since he left school, surviving the major redundancies that followed the firm's takeover by a German company in the 1980s. His loyalty to the company was only exceeded by his commitment to the Wendelborough Liberal Democrat Party of which he had been Treasurer now for fifteen years, and for whom he was one of the regular Borough Council candidates at local elections. The Tories had held the town for as long as people could remember, up until the last elections, that is, when the Labour Party suddenly, and quite unexpectedly, gained a dozen seats, putting them neck and neck with their opponents, so close, in fact, that there was no overall majority and the two major parties had formed an unhealthy and unpopular alliance. Minor parties took eight seats, of which the Lib Dems gained two seats, taking their total to… two, of whom Doug was not one. But now the Borough elections were due again.

Marian taught History at the Wendelborough College of Higher Education, until it metamorphosed into the University of the North Midlands, a development with which she profoundly disagreed, so, rather than becoming sad and bitter, she took early retirement and looked for new and exciting opportunities. When the post of Senior Curator for the Wendelborough Museum Collections was advertised, despite being rather surprised that such a job still existed, Marian decided she'd apply; nothing to lose, she thought. There wasn't an avalanche of applicants, to be honest, but she did beat off a stiff challenge from Mrs Willows, who had been the Assistant Curator at the museum some twelve years previously but was still a very lively septuagenarian. It was a part-time appointment, two days a week, and apart from regularly checking that the museum collections in storage remained in a satisfactory condition, her other role was to oversee the items still on display in the temporary council accommodation. This was the part of the job she enjoyed most, getting to know the various pieces and almost establishing a relationship with them in a way.

Carwyn Thomas was the leader of the Conservatives on the Borough Council, and had been for many years, having also served a term as the town's mayor. He ran a construction company, MT Holdings, but this was really little more than a fig leaf to cover a whole raft of other business connections that preferred to remain "incognito". Thomas' father, Mervin, who founded MTH, made his money in the 1960s in the architectural reclamation business. At a time when fine old buildings were being demolished at a positively criminal rate, there were rich pickings for a man with an eye for what might be worth saving. Whenever a Victorian school or an Edwardian public baths was due for demolition, MTH would put in an enticingly low bid to do the work, knowing that the real profit was to be made in stripping it of fireplaces, staircases, windows, doors, roof tiles, hand basins and lavatory pans, to say nothing of the brick or stone and all the timber and anything else that had a resale value. The company became known nationwide and MTH flourished for many years, but inevitably other companies began to muscle in on the trade, so Mervin decided to retire, leaving Carwyn to try to revitalise the firm. Local politics proved to be the answer for Carwyn, and he always made sure that he did enough high-profile local charity work to quell any concerns that he might be using his position on the council to feather his own nest.

Having stood in the Great Hall at Wendelborough Manor, later to become the town's museum and then the temporary council offices, for some 400 years, Sir Richard Hayward, or at least his suit of armour, was feeling aggrieved at the state of things in the town. In his day, he had been not only the major landowner in the county but also the town's principal benefactor, endowing schools, building alms houses, and so on, and thus was still revered by the townsfolk. In her role as guardian of collections, Marian came to know Sir Richard pretty well. She researched his family thoroughly and whilst she herself was a fully paid-up and seriously active member of the Church of England, she was happy to recognise, and even admire, the Hayward family's historical fidelity to the "old religion", and interestingly, it was this Papal connection that instigated a remarkable and extremely useful "inter-period" conversation.

She happened to be in the Great Hall one Friday afternoon, giving Sir Richard a much-needed dusting, when a thought came to her, both unsolicited and somewhat disconcerting. *There's a priest's hiding hole behind the great fireplace,* the thought said. Marian's first response to this strange intervention was to wonder where she had read this, if indeed it turned out to be true. Of course, she knew about the so-called "Disappearing Passage" with its concealed door in the panelling behind the top table dais, where the Chairman's desk now stood, which led down to the back hall and the rear exit, but this priest's hole story was all completely new to her and, she imagined, anybody else.

Feeling slightly foolish about it, she started to examine the huge opening which measured nine foot wide, six foot six high and about three foot deep. The fireplace was fairly typical of the Tudor period; huge oak supporting timbers, each about eighteen inches square, clearly hadn't been moved since the place was built and felt solid as rock. The herringbone brickwork to the sides and back was also in remarkably good condition for its age, with no evidence of repair or alteration at any stage; and finally the massive cast iron fireback, with the Hayward coat of arms in proud relief, looked as if it would take a small army of workmen to move it. So, a dead end sadly.

She wasn't in again until the following Tuesday, but she had spent some of the intervening time looking through all the notes she had on the Manor, but nothing about a priest's hole... and then it happened again.

On this occasion, she had quite deliberately stood beside the suit of armour facing the fireplace hoping for something... she didn't really know what... nothing... and then just as she dismissed the whole idea as nonsense and turned to go... *eyes right* popped into her head.

Eyes right, she thought. *What does that mean?* She examined the fireplace again, very carefully this time, but the only thing she could find was the smallest of gaps between the right hand upright and the main wall; less than a quarter of an inch, hardly wide enough to get your fingers into, though she did try. *Is this worth exploring?* she wondered. In the caretaker's cubbyhole she found what she was looking for... a crow bar. She had never handled one before and was amazed at how heavy it was; if there had ever been any crow barring to do at home, Doug would have done it. The angled end of the tool fitted snugly into the crack, but Marian was apprehensive about yanking it very hard for fear of doing damage... she needn't have worried. With the gentlest of pressure, the huge beam began to rotate, probably on some sort of hinge mechanism, she assumed, and within seconds an eighteen-inch gap had appeared, just about wide enough for a person to squeeze through.

Marian just stood and gazed in amazement... then with torch in hand, and feeling extremely intrepid, she inched her way into what turned out to be a passage. They must have been very thin priests, she thought to herself; certainly no space in here for portly prelates. After a few steps, the passage took a sharp left turn and... there she was in a tiny chamber, less than six foot square, with a vaulted ceiling and the only furniture being a low, narrow bed.

There was a crumpled heap on the bed, and for a terrifying moment Marian thought it might contain a skeleton, but closer examination allayed her fears. There also appeared to be a hole drilled into the wall, at about five foot from the ground, which must correspond with the back of the fireplace, but it was impossible to tell how deep it was. Rather conveniently, the hole was just slightly greater in diameter than the crowbar, which had provided the key to her discovery, so Marian now inserted the tool into the opening to gauge its depth, and just as she thought she was about to run out of crowbar, she felt the rod hit some soft resistance and then, a second later, she was through to the other side.

The drilling of this ancient peep hole had been done with impressive precision because as she put her eye to the opening, she had a clear view, albeit a limited one, directly to the dais at the end of the Great Hall, where the incumbent master of the manor would have been seated. All this was simply too much for the ardent historian to take on board; she carefully made her way out again, retracing her steps, and stood in the great opening in utter bewilderment, staring at Sir Richard. *Mum's the word.* The thought came insistently to her mind, and she realised immediately that this should remain her secret, for the time being at least. With some effort, she managed to return the beam to its original position, and decided she needed a cup of tea.

The next borough election turned out to be even more extraordinary than its immediate predecessor. As the count progressed on that evening, at the temporary council offices, excitement grew. Was there going to be another upset?

Rumours were rife about a Tory routing, which turned out to be wildly misleading or over-optimistic, depending on the colour of your rosette. However, when the results were announced, it was a shocked Wendelborough that had to come to terms with a rather different political landscape. The Tories had lost numerous seats, as had the Labour Party, whilst the minor parties had all done remarkably well. The Greens, the Ratepayers' Alliance, the Real Socialist Party and even the more dubious independents had all gained seats, but it was the Lib Dems who were the undoubted "victors of the hour" with twelve seats... TWELVE.

It was a truly astonishing performance, and it meant that Douglas Black, veteran campaigner, had been elected to the council on his fifth attempt. This new distribution of seats meant that the Lib Dems now held the balance of power; whoever they chose to ally themselves with would form the majority and therefore take control of the council. After a good deal of horse trading, which Doug found thoroughly distasteful, it was finally agreed that the Lib Dems would form a coalition with the Tories, as they had the largest number of seats, just. The upside of this was that the Lib Dems could now demand some major positions in the council cabinet, and with his long experience as treasurer of his party, Doug was appointed Chairman of the Finance Committee, a position of great power and influence. He replaced Archie Fairbrother, who had held that position for as long as Carwyn Thomas had been leader of the council, and that was no coincidence. Archie had been one of the more high-profile Tory casualties of the election. Carwyn retained his position as Chairman, but with a much weakened grip on council business.

It didn't take Doug long, looking back through the council accounts, to see that there had been financial shenanigans on an epic scale and over many years, but he also realised that to challenge the previous administrations, claiming mismanagement or even illegal misconduct, would be to court danger. Carwyn Thomas was not a man to take kindly to any sort of criticism, let alone accusations of wrongdoing. He would really not be a good enemy to make, so Doug would have to play a clever game if he was contemplating going public with his suspicions. The only person in whom he felt safe to confide his concerns was Marian, as if she was likely to be interested. Well, much to Doug's surprise, and delight, his wife was interested.

'I have to take my hat off to you, Doug,' she smiled. 'When they were giving out tenacity, you got it in bucketloads.'

'You mean you'll help me,' he said, sounding like a small child struggling with his maths homework.

'Any wife would be proud to, Doug,' she said. 'I was the one of little faith, but now, Doug, I'm behind you all the way.'

'It might get nasty, Marian. You know what Thomas is like.' He felt he should warn her.

'Then let battle commence,' she proclaimed, without really having the slightest idea of what that might mean.

I gather someone's set the cat amongst the pigeons, said Sir Richard's thought in Marian's head, as she was passing through the Great Hall on her way to lunch, one Tuesday about two months after the election.

This was the chance she had been waiting for... *So what have you heard then?* Marian thought, wondering if she might get a reply.

Oh, I have my spies, the thought came back.

Your spies? enquired Marian. How good was this?

Oh yes. There's Lady Margaret Hayward's portrait on the main staircase. She picks up a lot of passing gossip. The two brass firedogs in the library are excellent at keeping ears pricked for tittle-tattle. Then of course there's the ormolu mirror in the back hall. It's amazing what people will tell a mirror that they wouldn't dream of telling anyone else.

Marian was astonished. Conversation was a completely new development.

So what have your spies told you then? she thought deliberately.

Of course, back in the old days of the Manor, when the house was still lived in as a home, we had the tapestries, especially the bedroom tapestries... oh, the stories they told us.

Yes, thought Marian, *very interesting but...*

And don't get me on to the statues in the entrance hall. Spare their blushes. Midnight assignations were almost commonplace.

Do you think we could get back to the current situation? thought Marian, slightly irritated by now.

Sorry, was I rambling? Don't get much chance to chatter these days. Anyway, I'm reliably told that your husband is not flavour of the month with Mr Thomas and his associates.

Not flavour of the month, thought Marian. *What's he done to upset the Chairman?* Marian thought.

More, what might he do? So my sources tell me.

What might he do? What's that supposed to mean?

Apparently, "the Knot" are seriously worried he'll find out something politically embarrassing from the past and "drop them in it" as they say.

The Knot... what Knot?

Mr Thomas' inner circle, and according to the firedogs who overheard them plotting in the library, your husband is far too clever for his own good.

So what are they planning to do to him?

Well, Mr Thomas was preening himself in front of the Ormolu the other evening, when he suddenly pointed at the mirror in a very threatening manner and hissed... 'I've got my eye on you, Black, just one false move and...'

And what...? thought Marian desperately.

He was interrupted by the caretaker at that point... but you get the gist.

Oh my God! What am I supposed to do? Marian was starting to panic.

Well, the Knot always hang about after the council meetings here in the Great Hall have finished, and have their own strategy sessions as they call them, sat around the Chairman's desk. That's where you'll find out what they're up to.

So how am I supposed to do that? Marian thought hard. The priest's hiding hole, of course, of course. She already had a plan forming in her mind.

The first council meeting she spied upon was a very dull affair. Much of it was taken up with Doug laying out, in excruciating detail, plans for the following year's council expenditure, and Marian knew that her husband was being so circumspect for fear of arousing suspicion. He had told her he intended playing a very straight bat until he had sufficient evidence against Thomas to make a decisive move, possibly involving the police at that stage. For her part, Marian had not told him anything at all about her secret plan, or the priest's hole or Sir Richard, as instructed.

The meeting ended and the council members began to disperse in dribs and drabs, until only three councillors were left standing, rather furtively, by the main door to the Great Hall. Once the coast was clear, they returned to the front of the hall, gathering around Carwyn, who had remained seated at his desk. All four conspirators were beautifully held within the circle of Marian's peep hole. If she put her ear to the hole, she could just about make out what they were saying, but if she chose to look through it instead, the sound was too indistinct to hear, so she alternated her senses and managed to get the general drift of what was going on.

It was clear from their animated speech and their nervous body language that the Knot was very unhappy with the situation, and it took all of Carwyn's oily charm and cunning to persuade them that he had matters under control.

'I need to pull in a favour from a surveyor friend of mine,' he explained, 'and then there will be plenty of goodies all round,' he added teasingly.

'But what do we do about Black?' asked Councillor Grimshaw, owner of Grimshaw's Coaches, a nasty little piece of work.

'Leave Black to me,' Carwyn reassured them. 'I know how to deal with upstarts like him.'

'So what is this plan of yours then, Carwyn?' insisted Councillor Patel. His string of retail outlets was going through a rough patch and he really could do with a bit of a boost to his cash flow.

'Funnily enough, it's a bit of an old trick.' Carwyn chuckled to himself. 'Yes, it's something my old dad used to specialise in.' He left them wondering what he was on about as he stood up. 'More details later, gentlemen,' he said, by way of a closing remark.

Interesting, thought Marian.

Very interesting indeed, thought Sir Richard.

It was two months in between full council meetings, and neither the Chairman nor Marian had been idle during the break. Marian assumed that the actual meeting would be uneventful, so having secreted herself in plenty of time behind the fireplace, she took out her book – Hilary Mantel. She had kept putting it off but now felt she had to embark upon the Tudor epic out of a sense of duty. Prior to the meeting, she had spent that afternoon rigging up a small microphone, skilfully concealed directly under the crossbeam of the fireplace, with the wire dropping down into, and through, the peep hole, then connected to her ancient cassette recorder, which she had extricated from a box of electrical rejects in the loft. Fortunately, the almost antique piece of equipment still contained a cassette – goodness knows where she would have acquired one otherwise – and she had been delighted to discover that everything still seemed to work. She recorded herself singing *Tie a Yellow Ribbon Round the Ole Oak Tree* just to make sure. The meeting ended, the councillors departed, the Knot reassembled and the record button clicked down.

'I'm very sorry to report, gentlemen,' began Carwyn, in his most sarcastic tone, 'but the building in which we are now gathered will very shortly have to be condemned.'

'What?' Councillor Patel sounded astonished. 'The museum? But it's been here for hundreds of years.'

'Structurally unsound apparently,' said Carwyn. 'Even the most historic of buildings eventually reach the end of their lives. My surveyor tells me that there's nothing we can do about it, short of dismantling it brick by brick and then rebuilding it, and that would cost millions, literally millions.'

They were all totally stunned.

It was Councillor Patel that first came to his senses. 'So where's the profit in that for us?' he asked.

Marian smiled to herself. She knew the answer.

After explaining his plan in detail, Carwyn finished with a flourish.

'I intend to announce the decision to the next full council meeting, with a tear in my eye and a crack in my voice,' he said. If anyone could pull this off, it was Carwyn Thomas.

Marian clicked the record button off.

Over the next eight weeks, Doug spent a good deal of his free time collating, referencing and rechecking his information. When he felt he had enough positive evidence to indict Thomas, he contacted the local constabulary and between them they decided to confront the Chairman at the next council meeting. Do it publicly, thought Doug, then there's no wheedling or bribing his way out of it. Marian had her own back-up scheme. By eight o'clock, everyone was assembled in the Great Hall and the Chairman called the meeting to order.

'Ladies and gentlemen,' he started, 'I regret to tell you that I have some distressing, I might even say tragic, news to impart to you all this evening.' He felt he was on good form. 'No one is more devastated than me when I have to tell you that this wonderful building in which we are meeting this evening, and which has played such a significant part in the history of our town, has been condemned by a specialist surveyor as unsafe and, even worse, irreparable. In short, ladies and gentlemen, our beloved Town Museum will have to be demolished.' The shock in the hall was almost tangible. And it was at this precise moment that Doug decided to spring his trap.

'Ladies and gentlemen,' Doug was on his feet, 'I have indisputable evidence that Councillor Thomas has...'

'Sit down, Mr Black,' shouted Carwyn. 'We are discussing important matters here.'

'But I have...' Doug tried again.

'Sit down, Black. If you have matters you wish to raise, I will consider them fully after this meeting.'

He was very scary when his blood was up. And now the Knot came to his aid.

'Yes, sit down, Mr Black,' chorused the Chairman's henchmen.

This was not going to plan when suddenly from large speakers on either side of the dais came a muffled but audible sound of a conversation, or more of a monologue, in fact. Carwyn recognised it immediately and his blood ran cold. Everyone in the hall was stunned into silence as they strained to hear what was being said, and the nature of the words they were hearing gradually dawned on them.

'Stop that recording immediately,' shouted Thomas. 'It's completely... inadmissible. It's... it's... unconstitutional... stop it at once.' He was standing up waving his arms like a man drowning, which was really quite appropriate, and then he noticed a group of uniformed policemen had appeared at the main entrance to the hall. He spun round and more officers were entering through the side door. The game did appear to be up when, quick as a flash, Carwyn had the secret door to the Disappearing Passage open, and was down the corridor like a rabbit down its hole, before anyone had time to react. He reached the rear hall leading to the exit when, passing the ormolu mirror, he happened, out of habitual vanity, to glance sideways into it... nothing there... what... he looked again... all he could see was the reflection of the hall itself... he placed his hand directly on the glass... nothing... a sudden dread filled the fleeing chairman, when he heard footsteps and voices not far off. Coming to his senses, he bolted for the back door, but some idiot had moved the suit of armour which now blocked his escape route, and in shoving it out of his way, he tripped up over the knight's left leg, which was arranged at a very unusual angle. The collision rocked the armour, which then collapsed on top of the would-be escapee, successfully pinning him to the ground until the pursuing arm of the law arrived. Carwyn Thomas cursed under his breath.

It was Easter weekend. Doug had accompanied Marian to church for one of his two annual appearances there. All three children had arrived to share the Sunday lunch, a most unusual and very welcome change, and now Doug stood at the head of the table in his best bib and tucker, carving a handsome leg of lamb.

'So what's been going on here, Pa?' asked Michael. It was a loaded question.

'Oh, nothing much,' replied Doug casually.

'Come on, Pa,' said Peter. 'Wendelborough's new political enforcer. We've heard all the chat.'

'Well, perhaps you know more than I do,' his father said.

'You tell us then, Ma... what's the old fella been up to?' Michael wasn't going to leave it alone.

'To be honest,' said Doug, 'what I still don't know is where your mother got all her information from. She's the one with the answers, I think.'

Marian just smiled. 'So what's the news from the big city then?' She wanted to change the subject.

'Actually,' said Sally, 'I do happen to have some news.' All eyes were now on her. She looked down at her spring lamb and new potatoes and cabbage and peas, then took a deep breath.

'I'm pregnant,' she said.

(But that story is for another day.)

THE SWITCH

…when Aidan eventually plucked up the courage to get out of bed and look in the mirror, he was literally struck dumb, and he wasn't the only one

Before he even opened his eyes, Aidan knew something was wrong. It felt wrong somehow. When he did eventually brave the glare of the morning sunlight, it was less than a second before he shut his eyes again in panic, took a deep breath and assured himself that it was just an aberration. His second peep from under the bedclothes only served to confirm the incomprehensibility of the initial look; he didn't recognise anything – not the room, not the furnishings, nothing... but there was worse to come... so much worse. Aidan tried rubbing his face in an attempt to clear his head... oh my God... he didn't recognise the feel of his own face... and his chin... it was... smooth... no early-morning stubble... and his hair... he had long hair... what the hell was happening?

He screwed himself up into a ball under the duvet and tried to tell himself this was just the end of a bad dream... a nightmare. He should count to ten then start again. But he hadn't even managed to get to his target when he realised that he wasn't wearing his usual pyjamas. In fact, they weren't pyjamas at all... he was wearing... a nightie, a woman's nightie... and there was a reason for that... a reason... Aidan wasn't prepared to contemplate. A voice came from outside the bedroom door.

'Gone eight o'clock, Mattie... you awake?'

Who on earth was Mattie? He was staring at the door in horror, when it sprung open and a face appeared.

'You getting up, or are you gonna lie there all day?' said an attractive girl in running clothes, early twenties, short blonde hair, whom he had never laid eyes on before in his entire life. 'Good night, was it?' said the girl. 'I'm in the shower first. You better get a move on, though.'

There was a long mirror on the door of the wardrobe on the far side of the room. When Aidan eventually plucked up the courage to get out of bed and look in it, he was literally struck dumb.

When Mattie woke up, her head was splitting and she was dying to go to the loo. With her eyes still almost closed, she threw off the bedspread and got to her feet... then she froze. Her mind, till then struggling to get into focus, was now racing... she couldn't move... she wildly looked around at her totally unfamiliar surroundings... then she looked down slowly at herself... or whoever it was that was standing there... she wanted to scream... to wake herself up... 'STOP IT,' she shouted to herself, without any response... she sank slowly back down onto the bed, waiting for this madness to end. Then she realised that she was still dying to go to the loo.

She couldn't quite work out why, but half an hour later, Mattie had almost become used to the insane idea that she had taken over some man's body. She wasn't panicking for the time being; she believed all situations had an explanation, and all problems had a solution. But why on earth was she so calm? She guessed the storm was still to come. The bathroom had been an... interesting experience... as had dressing, though she was used to wearing trousers most of the time.

Nervously, she explored the flat where whoever-it-was lived; there were books everywhere, and files and a desk with a MAC and an iPad and loads of serious-looking techie stuff... this guy was clearly a weirdo or nerd or something. Eventually, she found a surprisingly well-stocked kitchen, where she calmly made herself some coffee and toasted a couple of slices of rather nice multi-seed bread. She was in a daydream surely... all of this would resolve itself at some point.

Ten minutes later, Jen, that was the flatmate's name, appeared around the door again.

'God, you haven't moved, Mattie. Are you okay?'

'Fine,' said Aidan. It was the first time he had heard his, that is, her, voice.

'You don't look fine,' said Jen.

'Honestly,' said Aidan, immediately aware of the irony.

'Well, you look like you've seen a ghost to me,' said Jen. 'You going in?'

'Perhaps I'll have a morning in bed then,' said Aidan, playing for time.

'D'you want me to ring in for you?'

'That would be great, thanks.' He rolled over and pretended to be going back to sleep.

As soon as he heard the front door slam, Aidan was up, dressed – not without difficulty – then dared himself to look in the mirror again. *Not bad,* he thought to himself, quite his type, then it struck him, the bizarre thought that he might be fancying himself. He had been working at the Government

Institute for Medical Experimentation, and he had been part of a team researching MT, or memory theory. It was all very blue-skies stuff and ridiculously hush-hush, but basically they were working on the idea that memory was medically treatable, in much the same way as your heart or lungs or, perhaps more significantly, your brain, even though it wasn't actually an organ. The idea was that this might be useful in the treatment of Alzheimer's or similar conditions. It doesn't take a genius to understand that all the elements of a person's personality are encapsulated within their memory, but isolating that in some way, and then treating it, was still in the realms of "suck it and see" experiments. But could something… somehow… have happened in the lab? And then the obvious occurred to him; if he had someone else's body… then they must have his. It was all too fantastic to think about, but a switch of bodies, however unbelievable, should surely have resulted in a switch of memories; but that clearly hadn't happened. There must be someone… this Mattie, he supposed… out there somewhere… walking about in his body… and probably not too happy about that either.

The mobile phone rang and she almost jumped out of her skin. She didn't recognise the tone, but then she wouldn't, would she? She let it ring, waiting to see who it was. Maybe they'd leave a message.

'Look,' Aidan started, 'I've no idea who I'm speaking to… but if it's Mattie… then could you call me back…?' It was her voice… her own voice; you can recognise your own voice. Then there was a long pause whilst Aidan tried to think what to say next, but he gave up and rang off.

There was an inexplicable and massive sense of relief as Mattie realised that at least someone else was in this nightmare with her. She, or was it he, sounded okay; normal would be going a bit too far, but in the circumstances... it was so weird... none of it made any sense.

Before she could decide what to do, the phone rang again. She snatched it up quickly, determined to say something this time, though God knows what.

'Aidan, where the hell are you? The Director's going ballistic. There's something up at the lab, and he's terrified there's been a breach of security. Aidan...? Aidan...? Are you there? Aidan ...? Aidan...?' The line went dead.

Bloody hell, thought Mattie. *What is going on?*

The mobile rang again.

'Hello... hello... please pick up... if that's Mattie, please pick up.' Aidan's voice was more urgent this time.

'Hello,' said Mattie, very apprehensively.

'Hello... hello, is that Mattie?' Aidan asked.

'Yes... I'm Mattie.' It was all very tentative, and her voice sounded ridiculous.

'Look... I'm just guessing...' Aidan began.

'How did you get this number... who are you?' Mattie began to feel queasy.

'I guessed I'd got your phone... so I just rang my own number.'

'Just tell me who you are... and...' She didn't know how to begin to ask him what it was all about.

'If you don't tell me, I'll ring off,' she threatened. It was beginning to freak her out now. The storm was starting to hit.

'Don't do that... listen... Mattie... I know how this must be freaking you out... me too, actually.'

'What's happening?' Mattie managed to splutter out as she began to cry.

'Look, I'm so sorry.' Aidan was wondering how to deal with this. 'I can't really explain it myself.'

'Explain what?' sobbed Mattie. 'What's going on, for God's sake?'

'We really can't do this over the phone,' said Aidan. 'Do you think we could meet up?'

They ended up talking on the phone for ages, whilst Aidan, sounding like Mattie, tried to explain as much as he dared to about what might have happened, and Mattie, sounding like Aidan, fired question after question at him, desperately trying to make any sense of it. In the end, she agreed to meet up, though not without massive trepidation; the local Starbucks providing a safe and suitably public venue. Of all the strange things one might experience during a lifetime, meeting up face-to-face with yourself, even if you know it isn't really you, would certainly take some beating.

On his way out of her building, Aidan had bumped into a couple of Mattie's neighbours, who were very friendly and didn't even notice anything untoward. The two strangers sat at a table in the window and just stared at each other in silence for several minutes, but once they started talking, there was no stopping them. And what was extraordinary was that they quickly forgot they were in their wrong bodies. They talked about themselves, their families, their jobs – she was a post-grad student, working as a waitress to pay her way through her studies in Renaissance Music. He was... well, that was part of the problem, wasn't it, and all supposed to be so highly confidential. He did try to explain the general area in which he worked, without compromising his position, but it really wasn't easy, especially since he did feel there must be some link with their current situation.

Perhaps the strangest thing of all, when you think about it, was that they found that they liked each other... liked each other... very much, in fact.

When the Director was told that two people were waiting to see him in his office, and the codename, Exodus, for the MT project had been given as proof of identity, alarm bells began to ring in his suspicious old brain. His obvious annoyance on seeing Aidan, with some strange girl, was swiftly superseded by horror when their situation was explained to him. It didn't take more than a few moments, and one or two simple questions, to verify their story, but even he had no idea how such a thing could possibly have happened, nor had he the slightest idea how to resolve matters. What the Director did know, however, was that nothing of this story could ever become public knowledge. A complete news blackout was the first imperative; even family and friends had to be kept totally in the dark about this. *Well, that's easy to say*, thought Aidan, and just about impossible to do, even in the short term. As for the long term, well, no one was thinking long term right now, but sooner or later they might have to.

'Go away somewhere for a while,' suggested the Director, though when the Director "suggested" something, it wasn't usually a suggestion as such.

'The department will pay, obviously, whatever it costs. We can do all the arrangements. Temporary identities, distant isolated location, that sort of thing. Tropical island, if you like. Think of it as a vacation, paid holiday, whatever you want to call it.' The Director's brain was in overdrive.

'I can't do that,' said Mattie, 'just drop everything and go.'

'We do have to be practical, Director,' suggested Aidan, but he sensed the tide running against being practical, at least in his terms.

'I do appreciate the difficulties this will cause you, Miss...?'

'Henshaw.'

'...Miss Henshaw,' said the Director in a more conciliatory tone. 'But be assured, we will do everything necessary to ensure that you and Mr Banks are properly looked after.'

'But how long will this be for?' asked Mattie, not unreasonably.

'Hard to say,' said the Director. 'As long as it takes, I imagine.'

'But as long as "what" takes?' she pleaded.

'Whatever has to be done to resolve our, that is, your, dilemma,' said the Director firmly.

And that was that. There wasn't any arguing, even if they had tried, which, in the end and after a good deal of discussion, they didn't.

Tinakula is a delightful island, one of the Solomon group. Very small, very unknown, very exclusive and the destination of choice for special people that the Government needed to disappear in comfort. To that end, a cluster of about half a dozen charming executive residencies had been erected some twenty years earlier, with all conveniences, including house staff and weekly food deliveries of whatever one chose to order. There actually did appear to be no limit on the lengths to which the authorities would go in order to keep their ex-patriate guests happy.

Mattie's cover story had involved an unexpected and utterly wonderful opportunity to do some hands-on research into indigenous music that might have influenced European developments in the Middle Ages. The original researcher had suddenly dropped out for personal reasons and Mattie had been given this unique chance at a moment's notice, as long as she was prepared to take up the offer within twenty-four hours. Her family and friends were astonished at the speed of events, but delighted for her if it was what she wanted. Not sure how long she'd be away. Half a dozen phone calls and "*bon voyage*".

Aidan was joining an international research group expedition, studying memory patterns amongst the native tribes of the Amazon. It was planned as a six-month tour in the first place, but the timeframe might need to be flexible. What family he had were indifferent to his comings and goings; he had always been a bit of an oddball, so this really didn't surprise them. His friends were simply green with envy.

Arriving on Tinakula, Aidan and Mattie felt they had died and gone to heaven. The six days it had been since waking up in each other's bodies had flown by, and it had all seemed like an extraordinary dream, but a dream, not a nightmare. About halfway through the flight, the plane hit some rather nasty turbulence which frightened Mattie much more than she would have expected, and Aidan, aware of her distress, gently placed his hand over hers as it lay on the armrest. It was only a passing gesture, but it calmed the woman's nerves, after which she immediately fell asleep, as did he, both remaining unconscious until just before touchdown.

Once established in their salubrious hideaway accommodation, the couple soon found that they got on incredibly well and felt remarkably easy in each other's company, so they decided to make the best of the situation. Since they had time on their hands, they did try to work out what connection they might have had with each other previously. "Valentino's", the Italian café that Aidan frequented and where Mattie had just started working, turned out to be the link. Not only that, but they were both in there at about five thirty the evening before things happened. Aidan remembered bumping into a waitress on his way out, knocking a stack of menus out of her hands, then stopping to help her pick them up. Mattie remembered, too, because she felt very odd afterwards and when she got back to her flat after her shift, she had gone straight to bed.

Over the next few months, the Director was in touch on a very regular basis, checking how the exiles were coping, and they always gave the same response – no change in their condition, they were managing okay, no need to take any further action for the time being. As their first anniversary on the island loomed, the Director was feeling more and more guilty about the banishment of these two young people, wracking his brains to think how they could be safely returned home, yet Aidan and Mattie seemed strangely stoical about it all, assuring the Director that they were prepared to sit it out until it was okay to return. By eighteen months, Aidan's boss had resolved to bring them home, no matter what the consequences. He'd think up some explanation; he had a duty of care and should not impose any further on their steadfast and loyal natures.

So the Director was the only person there to greet them at Heathrow Airport, and as they passed through the arrivals lounge, Aidan placed a very suntanned hand on the old man's shoulder.

'We're back, sir,' he said.

'I can see that, Aidan, and I am delighted you are both here safe and well,' said the Director.

'No, sir, I mean we are back to being ourselves.'

'What?' asked the Director in astonishment.

'It happened on the plane, sir. No explanation. Like before.'

'On the plane? What do you mean?'

'We were both asleep, but when I woke up... I knew I was myself again.'

'Just like that?'

'And when I woke Mattie up... she was herself again... obviously. Isn't it wonderful, Sir?'

'Wonderful... of course... just like that... and both of you are...?'

'Ourselves again. We can hardly believe it, Sir... after all this time.'

'It's like a miracle, Sir,' said Mattie, feeling she should contribute to the conversation.

'On the plane, you say?' said the Director.

'On the plane, Sir,' said Aidan. And strictly speaking, "on a plane" was true.

THE LIBRARIANS

...not all librarians are the same... which is just as well as it turns out, because it takes all sorts to defeat the powers of darkness

Not all librarians are the same. Many are quietly competent, helpful, responsible, undemonstrative sorts of people... and some are not. Olivia Harrison was not; she was young, attractive, frighteningly intelligent, ambitious and thoroughly good fun. Her problem, and it was one that she would not allow to stand in her way, was that she was an *assistant* librarian. Primrose Meadowbank, sixty-three, was the librarian, and all she longed for was the return of the golden days, when libraries were full of books and silence and an air of genteel enqury. The County Council's library sub-committee were well aware of Primrose's many strengths but sadly they did not include an embracing of innovation or modernisation and certainly not anything approaching digital competence, and so it was that Olivia Harrison, with her spanking new English degree from St John's College Cambridge, arrived at Broadhaven Public Library.

'All right to call you Prim, is it?' asked Olivia brightly at their first encounter following her appointment.

'I would prefer Miss Meadowbank if you don't mind,' replied the librarian coolly. 'At least until we know each other rather better.'

'That's fine. Miss Meadowbank it is,' offered Olivia, thinking that "Prim" did maybe sound a bit judgemental, in fact.

'So, shall I show you how we do things here in Broadhaven, Miss Harrison?' said Primrose, rather formally.

'That would be great, thanks, but do feel you can call *me* Olivia, Miss Meadowbank.' Olivia was making her point.

The battle lines were already being drawn.

Broadhaven only had a population of about 15,000, but Ron Parks was a big fish in this small pond and, what's more, Ron had serious plans to turn this little pond into a large and lucrative lagoon. So far, he owned the main supermarket; the only garage; one of the two pubs, the Jolly Brewer; the Clarence Hotel and the small, very run-down caravan park. But Ron had dreams; Broadhaven would become Dorset's holiday destination of choice, with a huge multimillion pound leisure complex, offering every convenience the discerning holidaymaker could wish for. Five hundred luxury family units arranged around a futuristic hub comprising shops, restaurants, cinema, swimming pool, night club and anything else on which the gullible visitor could spend his hard– earned money.

And Ron had something else as well. He had influence; friends in high places, or on the County Council, if you prefer. Over the years, Ron had done "favours" for a good many people in Broadhaven, and backscratching was definitely a mutual activity in his book. But for every "friend" Ron had in Broadhaven, he had three enemies: toes he had trodden on, backs he had put up, arms he had twisted a bit too often. He was a man who needed to be careful, and so he had people for that too. That to one side, Ron knew he could access the necessary finance for his plans. All he needed was the right location for "Paradise Parks" to become a reality, and twelve months ago, he had thought he had it in hand, though he had had to up his offer when Alexi Uranov, the millionaire owner of Poole Holiday Village, had made a counter offer for the land in question.

Western Downs was a vast undeveloped area of coastline that ran from the village Little Knotgate right down to the outskirts of Broadhaven itself, and with the assistance of his friends on the planning committee Ron had managed to obtain permission to develop 130 acres of it, sweeping down to its own beach... subject to a land stability assessment. That part of the coastline was exceptionally vulnerable to erosion, and all planning consent had this condition, but Ron had done his homework, employing his own surveyor to produce a report that suggested that Western Downs was indeed suitable for his proposed development. So it was a huge blow to the would-be holiday magnet when the plans were refused in the light of the county surveyor's report. Ron then spent some £25,000 oiling the wheels of the appeals process, but to his astonishment, without success; his dream was starting to go up in smoke.

Lorraine, Ron's trophy wife, was from London, which as far as Broadhaven folk was concerned was on another planet, and she was fed up with Broadhaven and Dorset and not living in London, to be honest, and when Lorraine was fed up, that was not good news for Ron. Having a wife almost twenty years his junior, and a looker at that, was flattering for a man like Ron, but it was also bloody hard work. Their house wasn't big enough, the cars weren't flashy enough, the shops were "shit", to quote the lady. Where was the flat in Fulham he'd promised? Or the apartment in Majorca? And the two weeks in Bali the year before last, which admittedly she only remembered very vaguely, were wearing pretty thin now. Ron's friends were boring and unless something changed pretty soon, well... Ron knew what that meant. Paradise Parks would solve all his problems in one stroke; somehow he had to make this development happen... whatever it took.

To be honest, Primrose didn't have much else to occupy her, so she took a very close interest in local matters, and had done for the past forty years. There was certainly little went on in Broadhaven that escaped her attention. She scrutinised every word of the weekly *Broadhaven Gazette*, she was either chair or secretary of most of the local societies, from the Ancient History Society to the Broadhaven Amateur Dramatic Group, of which she was a "non-acting" member, most of which used the library reading room for their meetings, and she attended all the parish, district and county council meetings without fail. She had even stood for the parish council in the local elections many years ago, as an independent, but had not been successful. So Primrose's detailed grasp of council business was unmatched, as was her knowledge of all the councillors and the various committees and sub-committees on which they sat. Had she been of a more Machiavellian temperament, what power she might have wielded.

Olivia Harrison, by contrast, liked to think on her feet,

act on instinct and damn the consequences. The really irritating thing about Olivia, and this was according to her friends, by the way, was that she was invariably right. She would get a feeling about something, ignore any sensible advice going, chance her arm on a whim and somehow come up smelling of roses. It was both annoying and comforting at the same time. To give you one example, Olivia was, shall we say, Bohemian in her appearance; a wild mane of red hair was generally worn loose, occasionally with a purple chiffon scarf laced through it, then there were two or three layers of orientally patterned tunics and waistcoats and jackets, sometimes over huge baggy trousers, finished off with what looked like hand-sewn moccasin boots. Nothing could have been less appropriate for a librarian to wear, and Primrose was not slow in telling her just this. 'You'll frighten the locals away dressed like that,' she warned, but she couldn't have been more wrong. Everybody loved it; and youngsters, who hadn't darkened the doors of the library for years, suddenly appeared just to get a look at the weird new librarian, and then even stayed to have a look around.

To say that Primrose and Olivia were like chalk and cheese would have been to suggest that they were closer than they really were. Whatever Olivia suggested by way of developing the facilities at the library, Primrose opposed; whether on principle or not it was difficult to say, but the result was the same anyway. And Primrose's insistence on retaining traditions that had clearly long had their day – like the Wednesday evening reading group with its membership of four, including Primrose – was terribly dispiriting for the newcomer, who desperately wanted to launch exciting initiatives aimed at reinvigorating the rather tired institution. 'Libraries are about books, first and foremost,' was Primrose's mantra, though she probably wouldn't approve of the idea of mantras, and that meant books monopolised every prime location in the building.

Olivia's view was that modern libraries were primarily about information, and whilst books were an important part of that, they were not its sole concern; the digital library could not be ignored if libraries were to survive at all. The two women differed on almost every detail of librarianship, but on one matter they were in complete harmony: libraries were an important part of the community, a vital element in a civilised society, something to be protected at all costs. And it was this common ground that eventually drew the two protagonists together, when the thing that they both valued most suddenly came under threat.

Whilst he planned the next move in his strategy to build his holiday Utopia, Ron Parks needed a stopgap project to keep things ticking over, a little money-spinner to provide some spending power for his rapidly wilting flower of a wife. There was a promising piece of land on the eastern side of the town that had been a "Fun Park" in its day, which had been more or less derelict for years but could possibly provide an improved location for his caravan park. With a relatively small investment, the area could be redeveloped to create up to forty pitches, with an amenity block and, most importantly, direct access to the beach. Ron wondered why the site had stayed vacant for so long, then he saw the problem. Access to the area was very limited and there would certainly be traffic flow issues, which could be overcome but would require the removal, or resiting, of the town's library. This didn't seem like much of a problem to Ron... who cared about the library anyway these days?

Primrose spotted the planning application the day it went in, and she knew perfectly well that if the plan was given approval, once the library was knocked down, it would never be rebuilt; there would always be more pressing projects demanding the Council's attention. She also knew that the arguments for a smaller scale holiday development, providing much-needed visitor appeal for the town, would be likely to garner support amongst many Council members, even those not necessarily in Ron's pocket. And whilst the enormous Paradise Parks, and the impact it would certainly have on the character of the town, provoked horror amongst many of the locals, a modest development, improving a very shabby area of the town and injecting welcome visitor income, might be seen as a blessing. The fate of the library would probably come fairly well down on people's list of priorities. So, if the library was to be saved, Primrose knew it was up to her to do it, and she thought she knew whom she could count on to help her.

'I know we've had our differences, Miss Harrison,' began Primrose, 'but perhaps now is the moment to put them behind us; to unite in a greater cause.'

'My word, Miss Meadowbank, that all sounds rather terrifying,' replied Olivia.

'The very existence of the library is at stake, Miss Harrison, nothing less.'

'They're not closing us down, are they, Miss Meadowbank?' asked the assistant.

'Knocking us down, more like, Miss Harrison, if that appalling man Parks has anything to do with it,' spat Primrose, and she proceeded to explain the dire nature of the threat under which the library laboured. She also gave her assistant a quick, and appropriately unflattering, resume of the man and his various Broadhaven projects over the years, including the aborted Western Downs fiasco.

'Can't have this, Miss Meadowbank,' said Olivia, much to the delight of her senior. 'What we need is a plan.'

'A plan, yes, of course, a plan, that's exactly what we need.'

It took Olivia approximately five minutes to formulate one, and whilst Primrose considered it to be daring in the extreme, in the absence of an alternative she hesitantly agreed to it.

'So does this mean we are partners now, Miss Meadowbank?' asked Olivia, rather presumptuously.

Primrose was torn, but in the end necessity took precedence. 'In a manner of speaking, Miss Harrison, I suppose we are.'

'So how about calling you Primrose then?' Olivia ventured.

Primrose took a deep breath. 'If we succeed in our campaign, Miss Harrison, then we may celebrate... on first-name terms. Would that satisfy you?'

'You're on, Miss Meadowbank,' said Olivia, failing to suppress a wry smile.

The lounge bar in the Clarence Hotel was about the only respectable place in Broadhaven where ladies could take a drink without causing gossip. The members of the Wednesday evening reading group regularly adjourned there after their meeting, and it was not unusual for Ron Parks to be propping up the bar of his hotel with a few of his cronies. On the evening in question, he was sat on a stool alone, looking somewhat down in the mouth, which Primrose thought might well suit her purpose. When her fellow readers had finished their drinks and made ready to leave, Primrose loitered behind, with distinct intent.

'Good evening, Mr Parks,' said Primrose as she approached the bar, not without trepidation.

Ron found it hard to disguise his astonishment at being approached like this.

'Miss Meadowbank! Good evening to you too. Is there something I can do for you?'

'Well, actually, Mr Parks, there may be,' Primrose began.

'Fire away, Miss Meadowbank. Always happy to assist a lady in distress.' Ron was attempting humour, but without success.

'It's the library, Mr Parks. I'm very concerned about the library.'

'Aren't we all, Miss Meadowbank,' said Ron cheerfully. 'How may I help with that?'

'I believe there is a planning application going before the Council which would involve the removal of the library, and that it's in your name, Mr Parks,' said Primrose.

'You're very well informed, as usual, Miss Meadowbank,' said Ron, 'but my hope, indeed my understanding , is that the library would be relocated at some new and convenient situation in the town.'

'Mr Parks, let's not beat about the bush. You and I both know that if the library is demolished, there is very little chance of it being rebuilt anywhere else, in the current economic climate,' Primrose was in full flow now, 'and the only possibility of a new library is if you somehow manage to incorporate it into your proposal.' She took a breath to steady herself.

'Miss Meadowbank, I would really like to help you, and the plight of the library is certainly dear to my heart, but I fear my hands are tied.' Ron almost sounded sincere.

'Perhaps if I were to offer you something in return, Mr Parks, you might reconsider?' Now she was teasing, surely.

Ron smiled patronisingly. 'I can't quite imagine what you could possibly offer that—'

Primrose cut him off. 'Information, Mr Parks, council information that may well be of interest to you.'

'Council information, Miss Meadowbank?'

'Of a planning nature, Mr Parks,' Primrose added, and watched to see the man's reaction.

'What planning matter would that be then?' Ron was always interested in planning matters; the librarian had hooked him.

'Information not yet in the public domain, Mr Parks.' Primrose found herself actually enjoying herself.

'But what exactly do you want from me, Miss Meadowbank, for this secret information of yours?'

Ron's problem was that he knew Primrose's reputation for knowing things before anyone else, and he really didn't want to risk missing out on something that might just turn a profit.

'Your assurance that you will do everything in your power to ensure a new library is part of any development plan. What I want is your word, Mr Parks.' Primrose smiled to herself. All this was going even better than planned.

'I think I'd need a bit more information than that before I could make any sort of commitment, Miss Meadowbank.' Ron was now struggling to work out how to handle this situation.

'If I said to you... Western Downs, Mr Parks...' said Primrose.

'Western Downs ?'

'And if I said to you, Mr Uranov...' Primrose could see the reaction in Ron's face.

'What do you know about Uranov and Western Downs, Miss Meadowbank?' Now there was panic in Ron's voice.

'Your word, Mr Parks, about the library?'

'Yes, yes, of course. You can have your... library.'

'I have your word that the library will be included in the planning application?'

'You have my word, Miss Meadowbank. Now, what's all this about Uranov?'

'Well, if you care to check the preliminary list for forthcoming planning applications, you will find the name Uranov there, and whilst it does not yet specify that Western Downs is the subject of the application, I have it on indisputable authority that that is the case.' Primrose had gone to the bother of persuading Mrs Gilson in the planning office to enter Uranov's name onto the said list, on the understanding that she would remove it within a couple of days, and well before any of the councillors had bothered looking at it.

'That's all very well, Miss Meadowbank, but what about Mr Thomas' report ? The county surveyor had stated quite clearly that the land had stability issues that precluded any planning permission being granted.' Ron felt there must be more information the old bat wasn't telling him.

'Well, Mr Parks, this information must remain strictly between ourselves,' said Primrose.

'Strictly between ourselves, of course,' gasped Ron.

'Well, officially, Mr Thomas has decided to take early retirement—'

'So?' interrupted Ron.

'The actual reason seems to be more about a large sum of money that somehow appeared in Mr Thomas' bank account soon after your Western Downs application was rejected. Nothing provable, of course, but enough to encourage Mr Thomas to retire rather sooner than expected, to his splendid new villa on Crete.'

'You mean that Thomas was in league with Uranov?' Ron actually sounded shocked.

'Same golf club apparently,' quipped Primrose.

'And now he's going to buy up Western Downs, knowing that any future land survey would clear the land for development?' winced Ron.

'Already made an offer to the farmer, who apparently is delighted to get the land off his hands.'

'I don't believe it,' said Ron. 'The scheming bastard... excuse my French, Miss Meadowbanks.'

'But as far as I know, the deal hasn't gone through yet,' hinted Primrose.

The trap was set.

Ron's financial backers took a lot of persuading to recommit to the Paradise Parks scheme. They demanded every bit of security he could lay his hands on; the house, the cars, all his various properties in Broadhaven, even Lorraine's "rocks" as well as every penny of his savings, but it was going to be worth it. Ron was like a man possessed; nothing was going to stop him this time. This, at last, was his big break. First, he checked Primrose's story about the planning application, then he spoke to the farmer who owned Western Downs, and the man pretended not to know anything about another bid, but that was clearly just bluff, so Ron made him an offer ten per cent higher than the one he had made before, on the understanding that they would exchange contracts in ten days. He was on a roll.

'What if the plan doesn't work?' Primrose asked Olivia plaintively.

'It'll work,' replied Olivia with sublime confidence.

'But if it doesn't?' pressed the librarian.

'Plan B, I guess,' Olivia said breezily.

'What Plan B?' Primrose was totally confused now. 'We don't have a Plan B, do we?'

'There's always a Plan B, Miss Meadowbank.' Now Olivia was grasping at straws.

'Involving what, if you don't mind me asking?'

'Off the top of my head... the honeymoon suite at the Clarence, some sexy black underwear, a mobile phone switched to camera mode under the pillow and a scribbled note to Lorraine Parks. How does that sound?' and Olivia laughed.

'Utterly appalling, Miss Harrison. You wouldn't really, would you?' Primrose could feel herself blushing acutely.

'Might be fun,' said Olivia, and Primrose couldn't tell if she was joking or not.

'Not even for the library, Miss Harrison,' said Primrose. 'Even I draw the line at that.'

'Well, let's hope it doesn't come to it then.' Olivia's tone was more assuring now.

The lounge bar at the Clarence Hotel was unusually crowded and noisy when the ladies of the Wednesday evening reading group arrived, somewhat earlier than usual. *The Satanic Verses* had been a brave choice for discussion, but perhaps just a tad ambitious for Broadhaven tastes. They ordered their usual drinks and found a table, even if it wasn't in what you'd call a quiet corner. Ron was in exuberant mood; laughing, joking, backslapping, buying drinks all round and generally celebrating…something or other. When he spotted Primrose with her friends, Ron could not resist the temptation to share his good news with the library lady.

'It's thanks to you, Miss Meadowbank. It's all thanks to you,' he roared, with a face red with triumph and drink.

'Me, Mr Parks, what can you mean?' said Primrose with a little smile of anticipation.

'You may congratulate me, Miss Meadowbanks. You are now addressing the proud owner of Western Downs, soon to become the holiday jewel of Dorset, "Paradise Parks", continued Ron.

'Indeed, Mr Parks. How wonderful for you. So, does this now mean that the library is safe from the bulldozers?' she quizzed him.

'Ah. The library. Yes, the library. Well, I'm sorry to say that despite my very best efforts, Miss Meadowbank, I have been unable to save... the library,' and he smirked in mock apology.

'Oh dear,' said Primrose. 'That is a shame.'

'You win some, you lose some, Miss Meadowbanks.' Ron chuckled. 'Best be a good loser, eh?' and he turned to rejoin his chums.

'Just before you go, Mr Parks, I should probably clear up one or two things,' said Primrose.

'Clear away, dear lady.' Ron was barely listening now.

'Actually, it's about Western Downs.'

'Or Paradise Parks as it's soon to be,' added Ron.

'Quite. Well, I'm rather afraid I may have inadvertently misled you regarding that matter, Mr Parks.'

'Misled? On the contrary, Miss Meadowbank, you led me very well, madam.'

'It's just that Mr Uranov never did intend to put in an application for Western Downs. In fact, he lost all interest in it when the county surveyor's report condemned the land,' Primrose continued.

'What?' Ron exclaimed.

'All a bit of a misunderstanding, I'm afraid,' said Primrose.

'A misunderstanding? What about Thompson and bank accounts and villas in Crete?' You could hear the panic creeping into Ron's voice.

'My sources seem to have got all that wrong as well,

most unusual for them, so reliable on the whole.' Primrose was having difficulty controlling her delight at Ron's discomfort.

'But what about…?' Ron was close to tears now.

'No buts, I'm afraid, Mr Parks. Still, as you say, you win some, you lose some, eh?' Primrose's triumph felt complete.

Just for a moment, Ron pondered the possibility that Lorraine would stand by him, but it was only a fleeting thought, then he dragged himself off towards the bar to contemplate life as a bankrupt. At which point, Olivia appeared in the doorway, smiling broadly; she had gathered the news. 'Well, your plan worked, Miss Harrison, worked like a dream,' said Primrose. 'Will you excuse me for a moment?' and she made her way towards the bar. The other reading ladies were still congratulating Olivia when Primrose returned with a bottle of Champagne and flutes. 'We must celebrate properly now,' she said, and when the glasses were charged, the two librarians stood and faced each other.

'To you… Olivia,' said Primrose Meadowbank.

'And to you… Primrose,' said Olivia Harrison.

'And to the library,' chorused the reading ladies, and they all drank to that.

THE CODICIL

*…with a name like Houseman, Brian was
predestined for his profession; now at sixty-nine,
he had reached the end of the road, as it were, but
he had just one more house to sell…*

There was just something about the place; Brian couldn't put his finger on it. It wasn't unpleasant, but there was something. Old Mrs Luscombe had lived in the house for most of her married life, but since Mr Luscombe died, about ten years ago, it had been rather neglected. And now that Mrs Luscombe had also passed on, the house would come onto the market for the first time in over forty years.

"Far Horizons" was a desirable detached Victorian villa, in an enviable location, in need of some updating. So read the advertisement in the window of Houseman's Estate Agents. With a name like Houseman, Brian was predestined for his profession, but at sixty-nine he really should have retired several years ago. Rita, his long-suffering, if rather unpredictable, wife, had been pressing him to sell the business, which he had himself founded, for at least the last five years, but Brian had always prevaricated, claiming that it wasn't quite the right time to do so. In truth, there wasn't going to be a right time; the business, once a flourishing and profitable concern, had been on its last legs for years, and Brian, unable to accept the inevitable, had continued to convince himself that things weren't as bad as they seemed. The departure of Trevor Ainsworth, somewhat flatteringly described as his junior partner, for a job in Bristol, had left just Brian and Muriel Butler, the part-time secretary-cum-receptionist, to run the office. They only had a handful of properties on their books at the moment, of which at least two would never sell, except at a knock-down price at auction, so when the solicitors for Marjorie Luscombe's estate rang him up one Friday afternoon to ask if Houseman's would handle the sale of Far Horizons, Brian was understandably delighted.

Second bedroom, he scribbled onto the sheet of graph paper attached to his long-serving clipboard. 'Twelve foot eight… by…' he strode across the room and held his end of the tape measure under the window sill, whilst an unenthusiastic Muriel Butler, press-ganged into being responsible for the other end in the absence of young Mr Ainsworth, shuffled reluctantly into her position on the opposite wall '…by ten foot… eleven… call it eleven foot. Twelve foot eight by eleven foot.' Brian had steadfastly refused to abandon the wind-up tape measure in its leather casing that his father had presented him with when he first opened the doors of Houseman's Estate Agents. Laser tape measures weren't for him. He didn't trust technology, and he told Muriel that it was good for her to get out of the office sometimes.

When he got home that evening, with all the relevant measurements, he would have to concede defeat as he handed them over to Rita who, for all her faults, was a bit of a whizz-kid on the computer. He had had to purchase a programme that somehow, magically, converted his figures into spankingly modern-looking floor plans for the printed details and to go on Rightmove. And don't talk to him about Rightmove; that was another thing he had issues with. How he missed those happy hours he had spent drawing floor plans.

The office telephone rang. 'Houseman's Estate Agents, Muriel speaking, how may I help you?' Brian winced; why did she have to say her name? Just 'Houseman's Estate Agents' was always good enough before. Ghastly American business-speak, he thought.

'It's Mr Devlin, the Headmaster of Castlehope Academy for you, Mr Houseman,' Muriel barked. She always took into account Brian's suspect hearing.

'Ask him what he wants, Muriel.'

'Putting you through now, Mr Devlin,' said Muriel firmly.

'Ah, Mr Devlin, what can I do for you?' said Brian in his breeziest voice.

'Mr Houseman, sorry to bother you. I've got this lad, Charlie Goode, thinks he wants to be an estate agent when he grows up, if he ever does grow up, that is. Don't like to discourage the boy, rather leave that to other people, so I was wondering if he might do a bit of work experience with you, month or so, something like that.'

There was a significant pause whilst Brian tried to quickly weigh up the advantages of another pair of hands, e.g., on the tape measure, against the presence of an almost certainly annoying and possibly disruptive youth disturbing the tranquillity of his office. 'How old is the boy, Mr Devlin?'

'Seventeen coming up eighteen,' said Mr Devlin. 'He's a goodish lad. Clean and polite. Not very bright. Ideal for an estate agent, I'd say,' he added, without the slightest intention of being rude.

'Why don't I give him a couple of days' trial, Mr Devlin? Then if the lad shapes up, we'll see about extending. How would that do?' Brian said eventually.

'Excellent,' said Mr Devlin. 'Wonderful. Starting next Monday?' You could hear the relief in his voice.

'Next Monday it is then.'

At twenty past nine, and abject in his apologies for being late on his first day (it was his mum's fault for not getting him up in time, he thought), Charlie Goode stood in front of Brian's old leather– topped oak desk . His ill-fitting suit, which presumably had been handed down from a significantly larger donor, hung limply on his shoulders like something in a charity shop. The shirt was at least clean, if untucked, but the tie knot left a great deal to be desired. The image was crowned by an eccentric arrangement involving a three-inch wide central strip of floppy blond locks flanked by two shaved areas that reached down to his protruding ears, with their faux diamond-studded lobes. Brian pondered whether, at weekends, the said locks were sprayed purple and encouraged, with the aid of some sort of starch, to stand on end in the style of a Native American Indian. All that said, Charlie had an engaging manner about him; a ready smile accompanied an evident desire to please. 'I'd be happy to make it up after five o'clock, Mr Houseman,' he offered.

'That won't be necessary, Charlie,' said Brian in his most magnanimous tone. 'Just make sure you're here by nine o'clock sharp tomorrow.'

Charlie promised.

Sat at Mr Ainsworth's old desk, Charlie felt very important. His duties, as outlined by Mr Houseman, included keeping the office tidy, running errands as required, making the tea – a task delegated to him by Mrs Butler, as he was to call her – various clerical tasks such as stuffing envelopes and using the franking machine for local advertising campaigns, and, most excitingly of all, answering the telephone but only if it rang three or more times and nobody else picked it up. 'The correct form for answering our telephone is, "Houseman's Estate Agents," said Brian in a hushed voice that he hoped Muriel wouldn't hear. 'Then wait for the enquirer to speak.'

Charlie hadn't had the opportunity to practise his telephone manner before his services were required in a more demanding role. Brian was away in Bristol at Slowbottoms Solicitors discussing the details of the late Mrs Luscombe's estate, when Muriel took a call from a Mr Billings, of Billings Developments, wishing to arrange a viewing of Far Horizons.

'I'm terribly sorry, Mr Billings, but our Mr Houseman is unavailable for viewings today. Would tomorrow suit you?' said Muriel apologetically.

'No,' said Mr Billings. 'That would certainly not suit me, young lady.'

Muriel flushed girlishly behind her hand at the description, and then, regaining her composure, added, 'I'm awfully sorry, sir, but there's nobody available.'

Nathan Billings was not a man accustomed to having his requirements frustrated. 'There must be someone capable of unlocking a door and then relocking it ten minutes later, surely?'

Muriel was flustered. 'There's only young Charlie Goode, but he's—'

She was cut off by Mr Billings. 'Tell him to meet me there in forty-five minutes,' he barked. 'I suppose he does know how to get there?' And he slammed the phone down.

The 2005 reg. Jag pulled up outside Far Horizons an hour and a half later. It had taken Charlie about twenty minutes to walk the mile or so from the office, and he had spent the intervening time on his mobile phone to his girlfriend, Shelly Grainger. In junior school, Shelly had been given the nickname Shelly Tubby on account of her shape. This had been shortened at secondary school to Tubs. Her friends, and that obviously included Charlie right now, called her Shell. It was generally agreed that Shell was the number one fifth-form nympho, and this in a year where promiscuity was far more popular than netball. This situation was fine by Charlie (it was his turn). Shell had been through just about every other boy in his year, and was running out of options. Having been "bonny" as a baby, "cuddly" as a child and "over-developed" as a young teenager, she was by now "curvaceous" and would almost certainly end up "voluptuous". Apart from what Shell described as "just nookie", her other main passion in life was her mobile phone. When it was suggested that young people spent up to eight hours every day on their phones, Shell thought she probably spent eight hours *not* on hers, and most of that was when she was asleep.

'Got to go,' said Charlie. 'Duty calls.' He thought that sounded pretty cool. Mr Billings was not in the least apologetic for being late, and was extremely impatient when

Charlie experienced great difficulty in opening the front door. He really should have tried the key during the three quarters of an hour he had been at the property, but other things had taken his mind off the job. Eventually, Mr Billings, who was clearly more experienced in these matters, wrenched the key from the dithering boy's grasp and eventually managed to get the door open.

'You wait here, lad,' said Mr Billings as they stood in the rather gloomy hallway, 'whilst I have a look around.'

Being rather green, Charlie saw no problem with this arrangement, sat himself down on the wooden chest in the space under the stairs and took out his phone. 'Hi, Shell,' he said.

Having spent some fifteen minutes or so poking his penknife into skirting boards and window sills, peeling corners of wallpaper away and lifting up the edges of fitted carpets, Mr Billings returned to the hall. He needn't have bothered with the shaking-the-head-and-tutting routine. 'What a state, eh!' was all he said by way of comment before he disappeared down the front path and into the Jag, without even offering Charlie a lift back to the office.

Muriel had her third mug of tea of the day in her hand and a mouthful of Garibaldi when Mr Billings strode in. 'Houseman back yet?' he demanded rudely. His florid complexion, bulging bloodshot eyes and irregular breathing gave the impression of a man on the verge of coronary failure.

'I'm afraid not. Mr Billings, is it?'

'Listen, I don't know what clown did the valuation, but I'm willing to offer three hundred and twenty-five thousand pounds for Lost Horizons and not a penny more. Cash, of course, quick completion.'

'It's "Far" actually, Mr Billings,' said Muriel, a stickler for accuracy.

'Far… far…far what?' said Mr Billings.

'Horizons,' said Muriel. 'It's "Far Horizons", not "Lost".' Mr Billings stared at the receptionist in bewilderment, then took a deep breath to steady himself.

'Just tell Houseman three hundred and twenty-five, that's my final offer, and I want a reply by this time tomorrow.'

At the offices of Slowbottoms in Bristol, Brian sat opposite Edward King, or King Edward as the office girls called him behind his back, sipping a tepid beverage. He had been offered a cup of tea but had been presented instead with a *mug* of ditchwater, and a rather coarse mug at that. Another sign of the times, Brian thought to himself. King was a pompous, self-regarding solicitor, so at least some things didn't change.

'I suppose you've come across codicils before,' he said patronisingly. Brian smiled an acknowledgement. 'Well, this one's quite extraordinary, never come across anything like it in thirty years of dealing with wills.' Brian was intrigued. 'Marjorie Luscombe had no known surviving relatives. In her will she made various bequests to friends, charities, the ladies who cared for her over the final months of her life, and so on. These bequests cover all her assets with the exception of her house.'

'Far Horizons,' interjected Brian.

'Far Horizons, quite so,' continued the solicitor. 'And this is where the codicil comes in. Mrs Luscombe instructed us, through this codicil, not to reveal the beneficiary of the sale of the property, until the sale was completed.'

'How extraordinary,' said Brian. 'But you know who the beneficiary is, I suppose?' said Brian, thoroughly intrigued by now.

'Well, yes… and no,' said Mr King enigmatically. 'All will be revealed after the sale is completed,' he said, adding only that the property needed to be sold within three months or it would have to go to auction. Brian returned to his office that evening really none the wiser for his Bristolian foray.

There was no denying that Far Horizons was a fine double-fronted residence. Red brick with dressed stone quoins under a Welsh slate roof. It had a substantial stone pillared porch with castellated parapet, flanked by two single-storey bays also in dressed stone. The two front first-floor windows had arched stone lintels, giving the impression of eyebrows. Across the stone beam directly above the solid oak front door was evidence, barely decipherable now, of the house's origins. The 18 was fairly clear, then what looked like "Laurel Villa" followed by 67, or it may have been 61. The house's original name and year of construction. Despite it being in a rather poor state of repair, or possibly because of that fact, the property had excited considerable interest locally. Mr Billing's opening salvo of £325,000 would fall well short of the mark; indeed, Brian began to think that his guide price of £400,000 had been rather too modest.

Over the next three months, a number of noteworthy things happened in Brian Houseman's life. Firstly, the persistent Rita finally persuaded her reluctant husband to agree a date for his retirement; the commission on Far Horizons would be a useful supplement to his retirement funds that were based principally on an insurance policy that had matured when he was sixty. It was with some trepidation he informed Muriel of his intentions, fearing a resentful response after such long service, but in the event, his stoical secretary seemed almost relieved. 'If I'm honest, Mr Houseman, I only stayed on after Mr Ainsworth left out of a sense of loyalty. I wasn't sure how you'd manage,' she said with admirable dignity.

Charlie was proving to be absolutely invaluable. With Brian uncharacteristically busy bringing thirty years of Houseman's Estate Agents to an orderly conclusion, Charlie was promoted to the position of Junior Negotiator, which in reality meant he was responsible for accompanying viewings. And it has to be said that those viewings of Far Horizons were, not to put too fine a point on it, quite extraordinary events.

After Mr Billings' rather cursory inspection of the property, Mr and Mrs Jenkins, a local couple with two small children, spent the best part of two hours going over every inch of the place. Mrs Jenkins talked incessantly whilst the mute Mr Jenkins made copious notes on his iPad. Mrs Jenkins bombarded poor Charlie with questions to which he could only reply that he would try to find out the answers for her when they got back to the office. At about four o'clock, with all other areas of the house exhausted, Mrs Jenkins said, 'Better pop our heads into the loft, just to make sure there are no holes in the roof.' Charlie sighed, and then disappeared off to the garden shed where he'd spotted a stepladder earlier. Mr Jenkins said he wasn't good on ladders, so it was his indomitable wife that teetered precariously on the top step of the ladder before disappearing into the roof void, a feat she achieved without once interrupting her own running commentary.

There was forty years of accumulated memorabilia piled into every corner and crevice of the space: travel trunks, cardboard boxes, even discarded items of furniture, but with nothing of any interest to Mrs Jenkins, and concerns about the integrity of the roof allayed, she turned to commence her descent. It was then her eye caught sight of the old low-slung dressing table with its cheval mirror, and that was when she screamed. The ragged little girl in the mirror, clutching her naked doll, was looking directly at poor Mrs Jenkins and shaking her head despairingly. It was an image of terrifying wretchedness. And that was the end of Mr and Mrs Jenkins.

Buoyed by her success over the retirement question, Rita moved on to further plans. They had lived at 23 Western Road for eighteen years, ever since their son Reg had moved away to take up a job in Liverpool. It was a nice enough house but not the one she wanted as a final resting place, as she put it. She thought they could afford to go upmarket a notch or two, and if they didn't do it now, they never would. Actually, she wouldn't have said no to somewhere like Far Horizons, but that was probably a step too far, and it needed a mountain of work. She'd keep her eyes open.

There were no further viewings for about a fortnight and then two applicants showed interest on the same day. Mr and Mrs Patel wanted to know if the property would be suitable for a small guest house. It did have four good-sized bedrooms and three reception rooms, as well as a sizeable outhouse with water and electricity. 'So that might provide six bedrooms and a dining room,' said Mr Patel excitedly.

'But what about you and Mrs Patel?' asked Muriel curiously.

'I thought you said there was an outhouse,' Mr Patel replied, as though stating the blindingly obvious.

Muriel shrugged and arranged an appointment for them to view the house the following Friday. She had hardly put the phone down when it rang again. Dr Lipinski was moving into the area with his wife and five children, and wanted to know if Houseman's had anything suitable on its books. Far Horizons was the only four-bedroom property they had available, and, of course, it did need some improvements, but Dr Lipinski was undaunted by that, and another viewing went into the book.

At 10.30 on Friday, Charlie was stood outside the house, having already taken the precaution of unlocking the front door to avoid another embarrassment. Mr Patel drew up in an ageing Volkswagen campervan, and his wife emerged tentatively from the rear door carrying a large basket with what appeared to be a Thermos flask protruding from the top. Charlie prayed that this didn't suggest a long appointment. As it turned out, he needn't have worried.

'You do upstairs, Shami, I'll do down here,' instructed Mr Patel, and off she went obediently, but within a couple of minutes she was back.

'There is a spirit residing in the back bedroom, Papa,' she announced calmly.

'Good or bad?' enquired Mr Patel.

'Not good, Papa, definitely not good.' Mr Patel nodded graciously towards Charlie as he ushered his wife, still clutching her basket, towards the front door.

'Thank you for your trouble, sir,' he said, 'but this house will not suit our purposes.'

'Oh dear,' said Charlie, 'I'm sorry about that.'

'However,' Mr Patel continued, 'I can recommend an excellent Holy Man who could come and decontaminate your house for a modest fee.' Charlie took the telephone number, just to show willing.

Dr Lipinski seemed a more promising prospect. For starters, he was a cash buyer, always a big plus, and he seemed to know exactly what he was looking for. Charlie was getting the hang of this viewing business and accompanied the applicant through the house, pointing out various advantageous features. He then left the doctor to take a wander around by himself whilst he answered an urgent call on his mobile phone. Shell's calls were usually *urgent*.

Dr Lipinski's second circuit of the house proved rather more problematic. 'I think it's always better to be upfront if a property's got issues,' he announced accusingly to Charlie as he reached the hall.

'Issues?' asked Charlie. 'We did make it clear that the property needed updating, Dr Lipinski.'

'Updating?' The Doctor laughed. 'More like pulling down and starting again, I'd say.' Just for the young agent's benefit, he then enumerated the causes for concern for which he had discovered evidence, which included beetle infestation in three of the four bedrooms, woodworm in the staircase and rising damp in the kitchen extension, added to which the property was clearly overrun with rats.

'Rats, Dr Lipinski?' Poor Charlie was horrified, and if he was honest, terrified as well.

'Don't pretend you didn't know,' sneered the doctor. 'There are droppings everywhere, and when I went into the dining room just now, there was a huge one sitting up in the fire grate, bold as brass.'

After Dr Lipinski's less than cordial departure, Charlie decided to take another look around. He hadn't seen any evidence of rats, or any of that other stuff, so what was it all about? As he moved cautiously from room to room, Charlie become ever more perplexed; there were no droppings anywhere, no damp stains, no rickety stair spindles, nothing.

For the third time since his initial visit, Mr Billings was on the phone. On each previous occasion, it had been to improve on his first offer for the house; 325 had turned into 350, then 380, but, he had announced, that was absolutely his final final offer. Now he was on the phone again, and Brian was hopeful the estimated £400,000 might be reached.

'Word's out, you've got a sticky one on your hands, Houseman,' said Mr Billings, making little attempt to conceal his pleasure. 'Look, I'm a fair man, Houseman, and I'm still interested in Long Horizons, so I'll tell you what I'll do. I'll honour my initial offer of three hundred and twenty-five, if we can come to an agreement, and you'll take it off the market today.'

After all the goings-on of the past weeks, Brian had to admit to himself that he was tempted; agree the sale and be done with it. And if Mr Billings hadn't foolishly overplayed his hand, the property would probably have been his, instead of which he took a chance, which he very quickly regretted. Whilst Brian was taking a moment to consider the situation, Mr Billings jumped in aggressively. 'Listen, Houseman, I haven't got time to shilly-shally around. Do we have a deal or not?'

It was enough to jerk Brian out of his complacency; he wasn't going to be pushed around by some two-bit property developer. 'I'm sorry, Mr Billings,' crooned Brian, 'I'm afraid your offer will still be unacceptable to my client. Of course, you are at liberty to make a further offer, but it will need to be very close to the guide price. Otherwise, we will be very happy to see you if and when the property comes up for auction.' He heard an expletive, and then the phone slammed down. Brian was pleased with himself.

The next month yielded no further offers for Far Horizons, not once the notice for the auction was posted. The sale would be held in the function room of the White Hart as usual, on the first Monday in June. Two other agents would be involved, with Houseman's offering Far Horizons and one other property, a repossession, which would probably struggle to reach £200,000. The sale would start at midday, and Brian, who was kitted out in his rarely worn best suit for the occasion, estimated that, with eight lots coming up before his, it would be around two o'clockish by the time they got to Far Horizons.

House auctions only came around four times a year, so they were a big occasion for the agents involved. They could usually rely on a good crowd turning up, mostly regulars, but always a few unfamiliar faces. Several people had expressed interest in the property, but Brian had received no "offers prior to sale", and that made him nervous. Mr Billings had requested an auction brochure, so he would be there, determined to get his hands on the Luscombe lot and hoping to pick it up at a knock-down price. Charlie had asked if he could attend, as it was his last week, and he'd never been to an auction. Muriel would, as usual, be left to hold the fort, which she certainly didn't mind, and even Rita had surprised her husband by expressing the wish to attend "Houseman's Last Stand" as she referred to it. Mr Featherstone of Millard's Auctioneers would conduct proceedings with his customary panache (everyone knew he was really a frustrated actor), and Edward King would be in attendance to represent the Luscombe estate. Rather unusually, Mr King had rung Brian on the morning of the sale to say that he should not put any reserve price on Far Horizons; they didn't want it failing to sell.

On the stroke of twelve o'clock, Arthur Featherstone gave a firm rap of his gavel on the auctioneer's desk to bring the gathering to order, and after a few words of welcome and an outline of the day's proceedings he moved swiftly on to the first lot, some rather unprepossessing commercial premises in the centre of town. 'Right, ladies and gentlemen, what will someone offer me for this highly convenient property? Who will get me started at... let us say one hundred thousand pounds?'

Derek Gower's hand shot into the air. This was not a surprise to anyone, simply a part of the regular ritual of auctions at the White Hart. Dear Derek was not a serious buyer; auctions were actually just a hobby for him, but he did love to feel involved, so he invariably made the first bid, without the slightest intention of buying, and then, when other parties joined in the bidding, he dropped out. One day, of course, he might be caught out, if nobody else was interested, but that was part of the thrill of it for him. And so the day progressed, mostly predictably, with properties going for something close to their estimated price, but with the occasional surprise, good or bad depending on whether you were a buyer or seller.

At twelve fifteen, Mr Billings set off for the White Hart, which he estimated would take him around three quarters of an hour to reach. He knew how to get there, and that the Houseman lots wouldn't come up until well after one thirty, but he had allowed himself plenty of time. At ten to one, he hit roadworks, which took about fifteen minutes to clear, but he was still fine for time, he thought. With only a couple of miles to go, the traffic slowed down, and then ground to a halt. It couldn't be more roadworks surely, or an accident; Mr Billings' concern grew.

By half past one, with no sign of matters improving, he realised he might well not make the auction in time, and his blood pressure began to rise. By two o'clock, Nathan Billings was on the point of boiling over when on the seat beside him he noticed the auction brochure, and there, listed with the names of the Agents were their telephone numbers. Perhaps he had a chance, he could at least put in a phone bid, and if he made it generous enough, Lost Horizons could still be his.

The phone rang on Muriel's desk; one, two, three, four rings – if Charlie had been there he would have been allowed to answer it, but he wasn't there – had Muriel been at her desk she would certainly have answered it, in her usual efficient manner; but Muriel wasn't at her desk either. She was in the little back kitchen having a quiet cup of tea and listening to Radio Two, blissfully unaware of Mr Billings' growing anxiety. In a moment of uncharacteristic efficiency, Muriel had decided to include Mr Houseman's mobile phone number in the brochure but had sadly typed in Charlie's number by mistake. Had Mr Billings managed to ring that number five minutes earlier, he would have been greeted by Charlie's cheerful voice. However, the line was now occupied by who other than Shelly Grainger. 'I've skived off school,' she was boasting. 'Told Miss Piggy [the Deputy Headmistress] that I had really bad PMT.' Charlie wasn't sure what PMT was, but it sounded serious. 'Meet us down the park.' Charlie knew what sort of invitation that was. Was he really needed here? 'Tell 'em you're feeling sick,' Shell suggested, and Charlie wondered if he could tell Mr Houseman that he was suffering from really bad PMT.

'Lot 9, Far Horizons. A fine detached double-fronted Victorian villa, presented in sound structural order, with scope for improvement,' announced the auctioneer, as if it were top of the bill at the Palladium. It was ten past two. Muriel had finished her refreshment and just returned to her desk but hadn't as yet listened to her messages; Rita had found a seat in the hall in the back row; Charlie had crept in by a side door and still had his mobile phone to his ear – he wasn't actually saying anything, but then that wasn't usually necessary when talking to Shell; Brian had taken over the job of recording the sales, so was sat beside Mr Featherstone standing at his lectern; Mr Billings had decided he would try to walk to the White Hart, an activity with which he was startlingly unfamiliar, but was still a good ten minutes away.

'Who's going to start me off with this excellent property?' cried Mr Featherstone. 'Do I hear three hundred thousand pounds?' He left a dramatic pause. 'Two hundred then. Who will start me off with two hundred thousand?' Still, silence from the floor. 'Come along, ladies and gentlemen, who's going to say two hundred thousand?' A long silence.

'A hundred and fifty thousand,' a voice shouted, and all eyes turned to Derek Gower, beaming, with his right arm thrust in the air.

'Thank you, Mr Gower,' said Mr Featherstone patiently. 'The bid is one hundred and fifty thousand. Who'll give me two hundred?' He scanned the hall. This was going to be hard work, he thought to himself. 'Come along, ladies and gentlemen, do I hear two hundred thousand?' There was an ominous quiet. Even Derek began to look a bit nervous. Word about the problems that Far Horizons was said to have had clearly spread. Now there was a note of desperation in Mr Featherstone's voice. 'The bid stands at one hundred and fifty thousand pounds with Mr Gower. Do I hear two hundred? Do I hear… one hundred and seventy-five thousand?'

Brian was sweating by now; this was a disaster. How could this situation get any worse for him? And then it did. 'I'll bid one hundred and seventy-five thousand, Mr Featherstone,' came a very nervous voice from the back of the hall. If Brian hadn't known better, he would have sworn that voice belonged to his wife.

'Do I hear one hundred and seventy-five thousand from the lady at the back?' There was the beginnings of relief in Mr Featherstone's voice.

'Two hundred thousand,' came a new voice from a portly gentleman sporting an Astrakhan hat and with a Roman nose that looked suspiciously like what was known in his family as the "Luscombe Hook", sitting in the front row. This was a turn-up for the books.

'Thank you, sir,' said Mr Featherstone. 'I have two hundred thousand from the gentleman in the front.'

Brian breathed a sigh of relief. Poor Rita had obviously experienced some sort of mental aberration, but fortunately the Astrakhan man had saved the day. 'Two hundred and twenty-five thousand,' yelled Rita. She had absolutely no idea what she was doing, but suddenly she knew she had to have that house, and it was still going for a song.

'Thank you, madam. We have two hundred and twenty-five thousand pounds. Do I hear two fifty?' enquired the auctioneer cautiously.

'Two fifty,' said the man.

'Three hundred,' said Rita; the occasion now going totally to her head. This was a complete disaster, thought Brian, what was the woman thinking of? He saw his comfortable, carefully planned retirement slipping away before his eyes.

'Three fifty,' said the man. There was a growing air of excitement in the room now.

'Three seventy-five,' gasped Rita breathlessly. There was something gloriously gladiatorial about two people desperate for the same property, prepared to fight to the death for it.

'Do I hear four hundred?' asked Mr Featherstone, looking directly at the man in the front row. There was a long pause. 'The bid is with the lady at the back. Do I hear four hundred? Are we all done then? At three hundred and fifty thousand pounds. I am going to sell at three hundred and fifty thousand pounds. All done.'

'Brian couldn't bear to listen anymore. He was past praying. 'For the first time then, at three hundred and fifty thousand pounds. Are you quite sure, sir? For the second time, at three hundred and fifty thousand.' He raised his gavel. 'For the final time of asking, at three hundred and fifty thousand pounds,' and just as the hammer was about to fall…

'Four hundred thousand,' said the Astrakhan man.

'Four hundred and one thousand,' jumped in Rita, before Mr Featherstone had had a chance to react. The tension was unbearable, but the man in the front row had reached his limit. The auctioneer looked at him questioningly, but he shook his head.

'For the first… for the second… for the third time of asking.' The hammer came down theatrically, just as Mr Billings burst into the room. 'Sold to the lady in the back row.' The room erupted into spontaneous applause. Rita's heart was pounding as crowds gathered around her, offering their congratulations, whilst Brian's head slumped hopelessly onto the recorder's table.

It was about fifteen minutes later, when the crowds had dispersed and other successful buyers had paid their ten per cent deposits to the auctioneer, that Mr King sauntered up to Brian Houseman. Brian was still in a daze; it was all a bad dream. Rita had tried to explain her behaviour, but to be honest she really didn't understand it herself.

'I'm glad I've caught you, Mr Houseman,' said Mr King. Brian looked up at the solicitor rather as a lost child would look up at a policeman. 'There's the matter of the codicil, you see, Mr Houseman. That needs dealing with.'

'Oh. The codicil. Of course,' muttered Brian, who genuinely could not have cared less about anything.

'I've got the document here with me,' continued Mr King. 'Shall I read it to you?'

'If you must,' sighed Brian, just wanting to get everything over with. By now, Rita had rejoined her husband and was trying to console him, but with little success.

'As I indicated to you when you came down to our offices, Mrs Luscombe's will included this very unusual codicil. I won't read you the whole thing. There's a good deal of rather sentimental stuff about how much she and her late husband had loved the house, and so on, wanted it to be passed on to someone who would treasure it, that sort of thing. Anyway, the condition she stipulated in the codicil was that the net profits from the sale of Far Horizons should go to—'

Brian interrupted him. 'That's right, I remember, some strange mystery beneficiary.'

'Indeed,' said Mr King. 'The net profits, after legal fees and so on, go to... the person who purchased Far Horizons. It was, in her own words, her gift to them.' Brian and Rita looked at one another in disbelief.

At precisely the moment that Mr Featherstone's hammer had fallen, a young mum was walking up Tudor Hill on the opposite side of the road to Far Horizons, with her five-year-old daughter in tow. She paused at the top to catch her breath, and the child suddenly tugged at her arm. 'Look, Mummy,' she said. 'That house over there – it's smiling.' The mother looked at her daughter, and then at the house. She was quite right; the house was smiling.

THE FAMILY PORTRAIT

...you need to get under the skin of a portrait to really find out what's going on, and sometimes that can take a very, very long time

Despite the small fortune spent on her education, a fact her father, Lord Lavenham, never missed the opportunity to point out, Cissy Lavenham was not a success at school. She enjoyed Lacrosse, at which she did excel, and Art, by which she was utterly fascinated without the least corresponding practical ability.

She somehow managed to scrape through most of her GCSEs, and then rather surprised everyone by achieving three A-Levels, albeit with modest grades. She then proceeded to astonish and delight both her parents by announcing she intended to go to university to study Fine Art. It was the start of what would prove to be a lifelong passion for the history of painting, and her journey started very close to home.

It had never been George Lavenham's way to lay down the law to his would-be wife. To be honest, it wouldn't have done him much good if he had. The reason for George's excursion to America in 1925 had been quite simply to come back with a rich bride in order to secure the future of the Lavenham estate in Norfolk. Had he returned with the ubiquitous New York heiress, all might have been well, but... a highly strung, self-willed, albeit outrageously rich and beautiful, Hollywood starlet was quite another matter. Lilly-May Rosewell, or Mary

Browning as she was born, came from gentle Mid-West farming stock, and at the tender age of seventeen had been spotted by a canny producer in the fledging moving pictures industry, called Leyton Adell. Two things had struck Adell on first seeing the girl; firstly, her quite extraordinary looks – her oval face, with its huge, innocent eyes and Cupid's bow mouth would be a gift to the camera, to say nothing of the twinkle that promised and warned in equal measure. The second thing that struck him was her clenched fist.

'Don't get fresh with me, mister,' she barked, turning round quickly to receive the applause of onlookers.

Adell was on one knee, wiping away the trickle of blood from his nose. He had noticed the girl flirting playfully with a group of lads in a drugstore in Shipshewana, and had innocently suggested going to the hotel next door, where he was staying… in order to sign her up for the studio he represented. He fumbled in his jacket pocket and produced a card: Leyton Adell, Executive Producer, Galaxy Studios. Mary roared with laughter as she pulled him to his feet.

'Well, why didn't y'say so sooner, mister?' was the nearest he got to an apology. It may have been an inauspicious start, but it precipitated a glittering future for the simple country girl.

Eighteen months and a dozen or so films later, the now renamed Lilly-May Rosewell was one of the hottest properties in Hollywood. She and George Lavenham met at a New York society party, following the premiere of her most recent film – *The Cossack Bride* – in which she co-starred with Rudolph Valentino, thereby enraging Mary Pickford, who had been expecting the part herself. The rather gauche

English aristocrat was quickly and firmly in the sights of the newly proclaimed Queen of Hollywood, who was now used to getting everything she wanted. Poor George, what chance did he stand?

It wasn't the fact that the picture was so large, all of ten feet by six; nor was it the exquisite beauty of the sitter, which was indeed undeniable; nor even her fabulous silver gown, reputed to have been commissioned specially from Coco Chanel at the height of her powers; it was none of these. It was the pose that was so intriguing. It was that provocative posture that caused the sensation when the portrait was first revealed. Had the censorious observers of the time known what secret the picture really concealed, how much greater their outrage would have been. The portrait was to be Lord Lavenham's wedding present to his eldest son and future daughter-in-law, and had he but realised the unimaginable storm his gift would provoke, he would surely have thought again. Whilst there were numerous acceptable, even talented, English portrait painters who could have executed the commission, Lilly-May insisted on her own choice of artist, and as with pretty much everything the lady did, this initially ruffled feathers and then rapidly provoked establishment scorn.

Alexi Grigoriev had been the toast of St Petersburg in the 1890s. Having studied at the city's Academy of Arts, he rapidly established himself as the leading portrait painter to the aristocracy and was soon gaining an international reputation. However, leading up to, and after, the Revolution, Grigoriev's work was first frowned upon and ultimately denounced as decadent by the authorities, so the painter fled to Paris, where he once again enjoyed considerable success.

At the outbreak of war in 1914, he decided to move again, this time to America where, from the outset, he was viewed with some suspicion, except in Bohemian circles and in the celebrity world of the movies. What concerned polite New York society was not his ability as an artist, which was beyond question, but his reputation as an utterly unscrupulous womaniser. It goes without saying that amongst the Hollywood stars, this was hardly seen as a problem. All that said, when the question arose as to who should be entrusted with the task of immortalising the future Lady Lavenham, Lilly-May was adamant – it would be Alexi Grigoriev or no one at all.

The Russian sailed into Southampton a month later, and was driven by Rolls-Royce to a delightful cottage on the Lavenham estate, where he took up residence and was treated as an honoured guest throughout his stay. The commission took over three months to complete, during which time rumours were rife about the nature of his relationship with the sitter, based, unsurprisingly, on the amount of time the two spent in each other's company. George, his father and the entire family did their best to ignore the society tittle-tattle and breathed a collective sigh of relief when the work was finally finished. At Lilly-May's insistence, nobody was allowed to see the portrait until its official unveiling, which was to happen at a specially arranged grand dinner at Lavenham Court.

Three hundred guests, comprising the great and good of Norfolk, plus the cream of London society, filled the

Great Hall, and as the focus of the occasion drew close, an air of excited anticipation permeated the room. When, in a moment of sheer theatrical drama, the scarlet velvet cloth covering the painting was removed, there was an audible gasp from the assembled crowd. And there it was; the pose that gave the lie to all the weak excuses and proffered explanations. Her elegant head, with its fashionably short cropped hair, was in profile, the chin lifted as though in disdain. Lilly-May lay draped languidly across a white Art Nouveau armchair, in her shimmering silver gown, a black velvet diamond-studded choker the only embellishment to her naked neck and shoulders. One arm lay casually across the back of the chair, the hand clasping a long silver cigarette holder, the other arm dangling limply down the front, almost to the floor. The fullness of the gossamer-fine skirt allowed her right leg to be suspended across the arm of the chair, whilst the left leg sprawled towards the viewer in an attitude of shameless abandon. The image was one clearly designed to shock, and it achieved its intention with spectacular success, though perhaps with unforeseen consequences for the provocateur.

The society wedding of the season, due to take place in London the following month, was postponed indefinitely, and Lilly-May dispatched back to the New World, ostensibly to visit her slowly dying father. And that, most people assumed, would be the end of the Lilly– May story. *However,* fate sometimes intervenes to thwart the gods of common sense. Within three months, George's father was dead, of what some people decided was a sadly predictable heart attack, and the new Lord Lavenham had, inexplicably, rushed back to America to beg his former fiancée to revive their original plans. Now, once again, holding all the cards, Lilly-May was persuaded to return, but with a list of conditions to which the desperate George was more than happy to comply. He made but one request, which was that the now infamous portrait be destroyed, to which Lilly-May reluctantly agreed, and yet... and yet... somehow, some seventy years later, her great-granddaughter, Cissy, would sit in the basement of the National Portrait Gallery in London, spellbound by this portrait and determined to discover its story.

Having gained a respectable degree from Norwich University, Cissy was subsequently accepted on a postgraduate course, offered in conjunction with the National Portrait Gallery, to train as an art restorer specialising, in her case, in paintings. It was whilst she was down in the vaults beneath the gallery looking through some unframed canvases on which to practise basic restoration techniques, that she came across it, tucked in a remote alcove with other long-neglected paintings that the gallery owned but had no intention of ever displaying again. It was in a sorry state of repair, and yet, through the accumulated grime of years, it still managed to radiate a brilliance, an almost mystical quality, that transfixed Cissy the moment she laid eyes on it.

She didn't recognise it, of course. How could she? She didn't even know such a portrait ever existed, let alone its history. However, the painting captured her imagination, and although she couldn't really explain why to herself, she really felt a connection somehow. Even seventy years after the date neatly displayed in the corner of the canvas, the picture still exuded a sensuality that was intoxicating; the quality of the composition, that outrageous pose; the treatment of skin – soft, lustrous, inviting the touch; and even the brushwork of the glittering evening gown still seemed impossibly fresh, as though it had been painted only yesterday. Indeed, it was the almost spontaneous quality of the brushstrokes that the artist had employed in realising the dress that fascinated the student, almost as much as the subject herself. What was it about that dress? And then Cissy noticed something even more interesting; the model's right foot was hidden beneath the hem of the dress as it puddled on the floor in the foreground, but the left foot... the left foot was exposed... and it had no shoe on it. No delightful silver slipper to enhance the vision, not even a stocking apparently. Just the hint of a pretty foot, peeping out shyly on the far right of the picture. It probably didn't mean anything, just a Bohemian touch, and yet it bothered Cissy... why no shoe? The initials AG in the left-hand corner above the date, 1926, gave her something to investigate at least.

The deception had been easily achieved. Alexi had produced a number of full-sized sketches on canvas, as preparation for the final piece. Indeed, it had been an altogether unnecessary number of studies, designed to extend his residency at Lavenham Court more than anything else. Whilst the portrait itself was miraculously spirited away to safety, one of the more developed sketch canvases, carefully rewrapped in the original velvet cloth, was taken into a courtyard and ceremonially burnt in front of an unrepentant George. Decency was satisfied, and the family reputation at least partially restored. Exactly where the authentic portrait resided over the next five decades is a mystery that may never be resolved, but in 1977, appropriately the year of the Silver Jubilee, the portrait of the lady in the silver dress re-emerged at an auction in Norwich, from whence it eventually made its way, doubtlessly by nefarious routes, to the basement of the National Portrait Gallery.

After Lacrosse, sleuthing had been Cissy's favourite pastime at school, so now she delighted in the prospect of reactivating the "little grey cells" in pursuit of the story behind the beguiling painting. The gallery records gave her, at least, the name of the artist, and a little more research revealed something of the character and reputation of the man. Further searches online produced a wealth of information; lists of significant dates, influences, the complete diaries that his estate had released after his death in 1934, international galleries that held his important works and a comprehensive catalogue of all his known works.

The trouble was that nowhere could Cissy find any reference to "her" portrait; it simply seemed not to exist, or at least not to be attributed to Alexi Grigoriev. She took photographs of the picture on her phone, which probably wasn't strictly allowed, and emailed them to anybody she thought might be able to help, but despite sustained and valiant attempts to solve the mystery, Cissy had to eventually admit defeat, and she moved on to other things.

It was about three months later that she was visiting her mother at Lavenham Court, always more of a duty than a pleasure, when to fill the time, she decided to show her some photos of the work she had been doing. They were both going through the motions of being interested in the little screen when suddenly her mother grabbed her arm. 'Stop,' she whispered with a panicked urgency. 'Go back one… one more… oh my God.' Her grip tightened. The poor woman looked as if she had seen a ghost… and, of course, she had.

Back in the gallery basement, Cissy renewed her acquaintance with the portrait, but now how differently she viewed the canvas. Her mother had told her as much of the story of Lilly-May, Lord Lavenham's own grandmother, as she herself knew. It was the stuff of family legend really; a whiff of scandal, a fabulous portrait in an exquisite gown, seen once and then never again, Lilly-May's tragically young death in a motor accident, and the sense that, in the end, it was an episode that the family had preferred to firmly sweep under the carpet. Cissy pulled up her research and, of course, once you know what you are looking for, things suddenly fall into place, and there it was – a gap in the dates, from mid-1926 to early 1927, and for a man fastidious in his diary-keeping, this had to be significant.

Now, suddenly, she noticed the great ormolu mirror in the picture's background; surely that was the same one that still hung in the ladies' drawing room at the Court? Even the Persian carpet seemed to resemble the rather tatty one that now loitered in the back hall. Cissy was beside herself with excitement as she garbled out the story to Dennis Westerman, the gallery's technical director. He was the man responsible for all the clever stuff that restorers can now do to reveal the history of a painting, and Cissy was desperate for him to give her great-grandmother the technical "once-over".

Now it was fortunate for Cissy that she had inherited something of Lilly-May's charm, and those big innocent eyes implored the overworked technician to take a look. After a good deal of "umming and ahing", he eventually relented, telling Cissy to get the painting to his lab at five o'clock, and he would record it as overtime. That was easier said than done with a ten-foot canvas, so more outrageous flirting with a couple of the porters was required, but she got it there. However, it was another two days before the technician contacted her, and when he did, he warned her that she should prepare herself for a shock. Cissy's heart sank; was the painting a forgery, in fact? A recent fake? What was the problem with it?

In his lab, Westerman explained some of the processes through which he put a painting, one of which was called sequential X-raying, involving taking three separate X-rays to establish the different layers of paint. He then went on to say that he had stopped the process after the first X-ray image had come through, as he thought Cissy might want to see what he had discovered. He handed an A4 printout to her, and there, in that now familiar pose, lay the late Lady Lavenham... naked as the day she was born, bar a diamond-studded choker around her neck. Whether the dress had really been an afterthought or not didn't really matter; the truth about the artist's true relationship with his subject was now, all these decades later, beyond doubt. And those peeping toes on her left foot had just been there to tease.

As promised, Cissy returned to the Court a couple of weeks later. Her mother was anxious to learn of any details her daughter had discovered about the painting, and even more keen to actually see the portrait for herself. At the same time, she was clearly a little apprehensive about dragging out any skeletons from the family cupboard, albeit so long after the events. There were so many questions to be answered. What had happened to the painting after its disappearance? How did it come into the hands of the gallery? Would they sell it back to the family? What sort of condition was it in, and was it still suitable for public display?

'There's something you need to know, Mama,' said Cissy nervously, 'about the picture.'

'I'm sure there is,' said her mother. 'Quite a lot, I expect.'

'No, something rather shocking, I'm afraid,' the girl added. She was in such a quandary. She would love the picture to be back on display at Lavenham Court, where she felt it rightly belonged, but she had two real concerns about it. Should the portrait be restored to its "naked" originality? And what would the family actually feel about having such a picture decorating the walls of their ancestral home? She had the printout stuffed in her bag, but should she show it to her mother or not? She pretended to be searching for a tissue as she felt the piece of paper brush against her hand, and it was then that she could swear that she heard a little voice in her head – *Let's keep it our secret,* it said.

'So what is it that's so shocking then?' her mother asked. 'I'm dying to see Lilly-May in all her glory.'

'Well, that's it, Mama… I'm afraid… I'm afraid…' she agonised. 'It's… a fake,' she finally blurted out.

'A fake? A fake?' Her mother's disappointment was almost heartbreaking. 'But you said…'

And then it came to Cissy in a flash. 'No, not the portrait... I didn't mean the portrait... the dress... I meant the dress.'

'The dress?' Her mother was now even more confused.

'It's supposed to be by Coco Chanel, but it's not at all.'

'It's not?' said her mother.

'No. I've researched all her formal designs for 1926, and it's not there... it must be a fake.' Cissy was delighted with her own cunning.

'Well,' said her mother, with a huge sigh of relief. 'That's easily resolved then,' adding with a laugh, 'if it's just the dress... why don't we simply remove it?'

RAGGLE TAGGLE

…NanaVera had told her granddaughter, Kezia, that she would marry Django Lee and bear him many children. For Gypsies, things must be as they must

S uddenly a great fist exploded into the side of his face, and then, as he hit the ground, the first of many hefty boots drove into his groin, and then his chest, and then the small of his back, and that was the last thing that Django Lee remembered, until he came to, in the A&E Department of Gloucester Royal Infirmary. Four of his fellow Travellers also needed medical attention, as well as two police constables, but none had his life-threatening injuries. A broken arm, a dislocated shoulder, temporary concussion and dozens of stitches didn't really compare with Django's hit list; a ruptured spleen, a fractured cheekbone, damaged kidneys, five shattered ribs and a punctured lung were his rewards for leading the protest against the Travellers' eviction. There would, of course, be the predictable police enquiry into the incident, with the equally predictable exonerating conclusions. Nothing ever changed, but the days of "bashing and coshing" were over for this young Gypsy lad.

'Pens... down,' ordered Mrs Elliott, 'and please ensure that your answer sheets are properly numbered.'

Thank God that was over.

'Remain seated until all the papers are collected and you are told you may move,' the teacher intoned dryly.

That was the last one, and the same sodding waste of time as all the others. Sally Mitchell hated exams; she hated school; she hated all the teachers, except maybe Miss Evans 'cos she usually let her off Games without a note; she hated Dursley; she hated her dad, who she lived with; and she just about tolerated her mum, who she only saw once a week anyway. She'd definitely fail all her exams, leave school, get a job at Morrisons, then, with a bit of luck, some gullible bloke would get her pregnant and be stupid enough to marry her... and they'd live miserably ever after. Or, maybe, she'd win the lottery, buy a massive house, marry a footballer, have three amazing kids and become an A-lister. You had to be optimistic, didn't you?

When she was six years old, Kezia Codona's grandmother, NanaVera, told her that she would one day marry Django Lee, and bear him many children. NanaVera followed the "old ways" in how she dressed and how she spoke and what she believed in. She was still a fearsome woman, almost six feet tall at seventy-three, and nobody messed with her; not Travellers, not Gorgios, not even the police, not if they knew what was good for them.

Kezzy was just a tiny chavvie when her mother died in a trailer fire, and NanaVera had brought her up. She taught her how to cook the Traveller way, to sew, to play the fiddle and even how to fight. The story went that one day, a strapping Gorgio lad, being the worse for drink, followed Kezzy's mother, Imelda, back to the hatchitan, and tried to have his way with her. NanaVera heard her daughter's cries, and by the time she had finished with him, the lad had a broken arm and several missing teeth. To be fair, NanaVera had a five-inch gash on her forehead from a smashed bottle, the scar of which she hid under her headscarf for the rest of her days. When her neighbours asked how an ambulance had arrived so quickly, NanaVera admitted that she had made a precautionary 999 call *before* she set about the "bashing". Kezzy loved that story, like so many that her grandmother told, and despite her meagre five foot seven, she always wanted to live up to NanaVera's reputation.

Django and Kezzy were exactly the same age, and they had known each other all their lives. Whilst their families had not always travelled the same roads, they would regularly meet up, maybe half a dozen times a year, sometimes at Appleby or Stow or one of the other horse fairs, or sometimes their paths would simply cross on one of the familiar Gypsy routes. So it was more by luck than design that the Codonas were passing through Gloucester when they heard about the eviction and the brawl and Djanjo being in hospital.

Kezzy had been sitting at his bedside for nearly three hours when Django hesitantly opened his eyes, and thought maybe he was dreaming.

'How d'you feel, Champ?' Kezzy asked, with a smile.

'Cushty,' the boy replied, but the sharp pain in his face made him wince. His head was splitting.

They didn't speak much after that, but the girl held his hand as though it were something precious, and an understanding began to grow between them. Hours dissolved into days, and days into weeks, and then months of convalescence, with Kezzy always at his side. As Django healed, their understanding turned into wedding plans, and eight months after his leaving hospital, the two young Gypsies made their vows, with NanaVera giving her granddaughter away. They made their home in a trailer on a permanent site just outside Hereford, and the first part of NanaVera's prediction came to pass.

Since the eviction fight, Django was no longer strong enough to do many of the hard physical jobs that were a Gypsy's natural way of earning a living, but he could turn his hand to many a trade: carpentry, plumbing, even simple electrics, so there was usually work to be had for a handyman. But whenever the fair came to Hereford or even Gloucester, he would be there to pick up some casual work on the rides or stalls. Everyone knew him and liked him and was happy to take him on. But Kezzy dreaded the fairs, because although they meant extra work and extra money, they also meant extra drinking with his mates and her husband sometimes away for days on end. She knew he couldn't hold his drink anymore, and she feared both his temper and his passion getting the better of him. And Kezzy had another worry: three years married and no babies. Perhaps NanaVera would be proved wrong in that.

Up and down the country, all the Gypsy families knew NanaVera, and not just for her warrior spirit. She had brought eight of her own children into the world, Imelda being the last, and midwived scores of others. If a young girl was having a hard time in pregnancy, it would be to NanaVera that she would turn if possible. Or if a newborn was not thriving, NanaVera would have a remedy, if anybody did. She was sometimes referred to as the "patron saint of babies", but more commonly she was simply called MamaVera.

So it was not a complete surprise when one morning she opened her trailer door to find a bundle deposited on the step; the babe was about three months old, poorly dressed and underweight with a shabby toy rabbit tucked into its blanket. This was not the first time such a thing had happened, but there would often be word on the grapevine, and usually the distressed mother would eventually contact NanaVera, and a solution to the girl's problems would somehow be worked out. This bundle was clearly different. There was just an old envelope pinned to the blanket. It contained a five pound note – probably all the money the mother had in the world, NanaVera thought, but it was what was written on the outside that turned the old lady's blood cold… Django.

It was the same old row as ever. If United were playing away, long distance, Jed would travel with the lads, they'd get wasted after the match, crash out somewhere and he'd be back, bleary-eyed, Sunday afternoon. What was her problem? But Sally had had enough. It wasn't just Saturday matches, it was almost every night, and she was sick of waiting around for him, sick of washing puke out of his clothes, sick of being ignored, sick of having no fun. She thought about it all day, then finally plucked up the courage and rang Tina, her best mate from schooldays, who she hadn't spoken to for yonks.

'Fair's on in Gloucester,' she said tentatively, already feeling guilty. 'Fancy going?'

'You've got to be kidding.' Tina was astonished.

'Be a laugh, Teen,' Sally teased. 'Like when we were at school.'

'Yea, like a hundred years ago, Sal.'

'So what's the difference?'

'Like I've got better things to do with my time now, Sal.'

'Well, I'm going anyway… just for a bit of fun. Come on, Teen.' She was almost pleading now.

'No way, Sal. Don't mind going out for a drink sometime, if you fancy it.'

'Thanks anyway. Think I'll take a spin on the old dodgems.'

'Watch out for them Gypsy lads.'

'Yea, see'y then.'

'Yea , see'y.'

So Sally went on her own.

All she could remember the following morning, when she woke up in a tatty, freezing cold trailer, was hanging out with a lively bunch of lads, and having way, way too much to drink. When her head cleared a bit, she did remember one bloke in particular, Jimbo or Jambo or some stupid name. She remembered getting off with him when his Rifle Range closed for the night. He gave her something… a cuddly toy or something. She looked down and saw the rabbit on the floor. God knows why, but by the time she made it home she was feeling riddled with guilt; three weeks later, when she missed her period, it all fell into place. Test proved positive, and she knew perfectly well that Jed wasn't the father, so now she had some serious thinking to do. Tell Jed? Keep the baby?

Keep quiet? Get rid of the baby? In the end, she just waited a couple of months before telling Jed she was pregnant, He was a bit surprised, but by then it was at least a possibility, though he'd thought she was on the pill.

'It's not one hundred per cent, Jed,' she'd told him.

It was a terrible pregnancy. She felt sick and weak and weepy, but most of all she felt lonely. Jed wasn't interested. Woman's stuff, he thought. It was pretty clear what sort of dad he was going to make. By the time Sally decided that the whole thing was beyond her, that there was no way she would cope with a kid on her own, it was already too late to do anything about it. So she'd have it, then have it adopted. It wasn't until that idea fixed itself in her head that the name Jango, or was it Gingo, came to her again. Maybe he'd be at the fair when it came to Gloucester again. Worth asking around.

By the time the baby arrived, Sally had done quite a bit of homework. She knew about Django, that was his name, and he was married but had no kids. She knew about Nana Vera, "Patron Saint of Babies", and she had a sort of plan. When she got the baby home from hospital, she knew she had to tell Jed that it wasn't his, and he hardly even seemed to care. Unbelievable. But the next day, he'd packed up and moved out, and that was the last time Sally laid eyes on him.

She had almost three months to wait before the fair was back in Gloucester, and they were really hard months. She couldn't work because no way could she afford childcare. She'd lost touch with her mother, who wouldn't have been much help anyway, to be honest, and her father had hitched up with a new girlfriend and moved to Swindon. Her benefits barely paid the rent on her tiny flat, which was cold and damp and depressing, so she hung on to the idea that baby Joey, that's what she called him, would be so much better off with his real dad, and then she might have the chance to start again.

When it came to it, though, actually leaving that bundle on the trailer doorstep was painful beyond belief. She stood there, at six o'clock on a cold Wednesday morning, because she didn't want the baby outside for long, and she agonised about her decision, changing her mind, then changing it back again. In the end, she thought if she stayed any longer she would be discovered. She tucked the rabbit inside the blanket, kissed the baby's forehead, gently laid the bundle down, and then with tears streaming down her cheeks she turned and ran as fast as she could, until her lungs burnt and her heart felt as if it would burst. She sat in Starbucks for about two hours, with a cold cup of coffee in front of her. Then she stood up, took a deep breath and headed home. She knew she had done the right thing for Joey, and as she passed a newsagent's, she stopped, went back inside and bought a lottery ticket.

The rabbit was one of the prizes off the Rifle Range; Django recognised it at once. He had tried to forget the girl at Gloucester Fair, and what had happened, but every time he looked at Kezzy he felt wretched. He told her he was giving up working at the fairs, which, of course, delighted her, though she was very surprised. It was a link with his past; it was part of their culture. But NanaVera was adamant; he had to be straight with Kezzy or he would lose her for certain when she did discover the truth, which was bound to happen eventually.

'Perhaps it would be better coming from you,' Django pleaded. 'At least she wouldn't be angry, and you could explain how it was all just a terrible mistake.'

'You explain, Django,' the old lady said. 'Your problem – you solve it.'

'So what d'you expect me to say, Django?' was her first response. He didn't know.

'And what about this baby?' He didn't know that either.

It was so much to take in. Kezzy knew, without even asking him, how her husband felt. What she felt was betrayed and dishonoured, and he knew that too. Most of all, she felt the emptiness of her own childlessness. She told him she'd go stay with NanaVera, to give herself some space.

Three days passed. Django phoned every day, sometimes twice, but she wouldn't speak to him. Her grandmother was looking after the babe whilst it was decided what to do, and at first Kezzy wouldn't even look at it. On the second day, she did have a peek into the cot, and after that, the baby slowly wheedled its way into her heart, so by the fourth day, NanaVera felt she could ring Django and tell him he could come round.

'I've got conditions,' she said.

'Of course, Kezzy… whatever you say.' He was just pleased that she was speaking to him again.

'You need to hear them first… before agreeing, eh?'

'Okay.'

'No trying to get in touch with whoever she is… the mother.'

'To be honest, I wouldn't know where to start anyway.'

'But if she tried to get in touch with you.'

'She's not going to, Kezzy.'

'But if she did… no contact… no access… nothing… right?'

'Right.'

'No more boozing, and I don't mean no drink at all, just no stupid binges, right?'

'Right… I'm done with that.'

'And you have to take your share of the responsibilities… with the baby, I mean.'

'You mean… if we keep him?'

'If we do.'

And they did keep him.

There was no way the baby was going to be called Django, even if that was what the envelope suggested. When they told NanaVera they had decided to name him after Grandpa Joe, her face lit up. Her husband had died in a motorcycle accident thirty or more years before, soon after Imelda had been born, but not a day went by that she didn't think of him. Just his name, Joe, made her smile.

That evening, they sat around together in the old lady's immaculate trailer and talked about the past, and the present, and even a bit about the future, and by ten o'clock NanaVera looked really tired.

'I'm away to my bunk,' she said, as she slowly stood up and stretched before coming over to Kezzy, cupping her granddaughter's face in her great hands and bending down to kiss her on the forehead, as she always had done.

'Bless you all,' she said, as she gently closed the door to her bedroom.

Just for once, NanaVera was not first up the next morning, and when Kezzy went in to see her, she found her peacefully asleep, but not a sleep from which she would awake again.

Once word spread, people from all over began to gather. It would be a proper Gypsy funeral, legal or not. Django made the arrangements. Her home was made ready, NanaVera dressed in her finest traditional clothes, and on the evening of the second day the celebrations began. There was drinking and singing and dancing and endless storytelling and as midnight approached, it was Kezzy who solemnly put the torch to the trailer in which she had grown up, sending her beloved grandmother on her final journey.

It was almost three o'clock in the morning by the time the blaze had died down and Django carefully settled his wife and son into their car to return home. It was then that Kezzy felt it, the thing that she hadn't dared to believe, that she hadn't even told her grandmother; a life moved inside. Amos, as he turned out to be, was the first of Joe's three brothers, and then, ten years after the Gypsy funeral, finally a daughter, who they named... well, you can probably guess, can't you?

THE OCTET

...everyone who went on retreat had a need; that's why they went. Identifying that need was invariably easier than finding the solution

'So... we have Eugene... Martha... Chris... Nathan... Milly... Andy... Abbie and Bev.' Each individual acknowledged, as their name was read out.

'Dean and Ali weren't able to make it for some reason, so we have... "an Octet", which is great.'

People nodded awkwardly to each other by way of greeting. 'So, welcome to you all. I hope you enjoy your stay with us here at Cranmore, and that each of you benefits from your experience here in your own particular way. I'm Brother Dominic, and I'll be your retreat leader over this weekend.' He paused, looked around reassuringly and then added, 'Shall we begin by offering each other the Sign of Peace?'

There was another pause, reluctant this time, then the women tentatively embraced each other... then dutifully embraced the men... and then the men... shook hands.

Cranmore Castle had been built around 1540, and although it did look a little like one, it was never intended as any sort of military defence. For almost 400 years, it was owned and lived in by the Catholic Cranmore family, who never displayed the slightest desire to improve its domestic comforts. When the family could no longer afford its upkeep, it was sold, in 1929, to the Order of St Alban, or the Albanian Friars as they were known, for a fairly nominal figure, on the understanding that it would be used as a retreat house.

Some piecemeal improvements had been made to the fabric of the building in the intervening years, but still the accommodation could scarcely be described as comfortable, especially in the winter, when draughty corridors, bleak reception rooms and freezing cold bedrooms were the order of the day. The exception to this chilly welcome was the Great Hall, situated in the very centre of the castle, where a huge log fire burned continuously from October to March, day and night, providing at least a warm heart to the community. All meals were taken here and although there was an ice house of a chapel, the hall was also used as a space for collective worship during the winter months.

Despite ever-shrinking numbers in the order, there were still seven brothers who called Cranmore their home, as well as a loyal domestic staff of three to care for visitors, and it was not unusual to find an ancient insomniac friar nestled into one of the short oak settles that lined the sides of the enormous inglenook at two or three o'clock in the morning, deep in private prayer, or possibly asleep.

Brother Dominic was not a permanent member of the Cranmore community. He had arrived unexpectedly, with a letter of introduction from the Vicar General of the order, having apparently spent several years studying at the English College in Rome. He was probably in his early fifties, but he was one of those people who seemed ageless, always full of energy and endless good humour. Comfortingly portly, he had a mop of curly silver hair, but only one of his pale blue eyes ever looked directly at you.

When Brother Aloysius, at the age of eighty-two, had a mild stroke and was unable to continue in his role, Brother Dominic seemed the natural choice to succeed him as Director of Retreats. This proved to be an inspired move by the friars, as numbers applying to go on retreat at the castle, which had been steadily falling for many years, suddenly picked up. Brother Dominic was a hit, it seemed, and not just with the mature ladies of the Union of Catholic Mothers, nor the annual Catenian get-together, but with young people as well, whether Catholic or not. So Cranmore rapidly became, if not a destination of pilgrimage, at least a popular place for spiritual renewal, open, as the saying goes, to those of any faith or none.

The Octet was an unusual group. Most retreats were made up of people who had something in common, usually some kind of church connection, so they tended to know each other before they arrived, which naturally allowed for a more relaxed atmosphere. None of the eight individuals in this particular cohort had ever met before, and they could scarcely have been more diverse.

Perhaps the only thing they had in common was a need of some sort. Everyone who went on retreat had a need. That's why they went. The only religious amongst them was Martha. She was twenty-eight and had been a novice nun since leaving university. Whilst studying, she had consciously kept herself separate from the social life of the other students, praying instead of playing, and now she realised how little she knew of the world she was relinquishing. What she didn't know was whether that mattered.

Of the rest, Milly had been an exemplary, devoted wife and mother to three well-adjusted children, but when, after a seven-year gap, a fourth child appeared unexpectedly, her world had completely fallen apart, whilst Eugene's ever more successful import business had never compensated for the failure of his marriage and the loss of his cherished daughters.

It was his third retreat with Brother Dominic at Cranmore. Alcoholism had cost Nathan, a master carpenter, more jobs than he cared to admit, and whilst he was now in recovery, it was early days and it was fragile.

Perhaps the two people with the most in common were Chris and Abbie; both were young secondary schoolteachers, Chris teaching Music in an leading independent school, in which he felt thoroughly out of place, and Abbie, RE, in a rough, albeit thriving, inner city comprehensive that she loved. Both had struggling marriages they wanted to save.

The Octet was completed by two late-teenagers, Bev and Andy, who seemed the least likely participants on the retreat, and yet who proved that age was a poor yardstick by which to judge anything in these circumstances.

At five o'clock, with introductions and a brief tour of the castle over, the group retired to their rooms (originally, they had been called cells, but nowadays that sounded a bit too penal) to unpack, freshen up and wait for the supper bell, which was rung at six o'clock precisely. Everything was done precisely.

Lunch was the main meal of the day, so now they sat down, rather unenthusiastically, to fish fingers, chips and beans, with a cup of tea or coffee and a slice of Battenberg or a Mr Kipling Bakewell Tart. As they had expected, the meal was accompanied by the reading of a passage from scripture by one of the brothers; otherwise, silence was observed.

Vespers followed the evening meal, but this was optional for those on retreat. From eight o'clock to nine, the Octet had the first of their four meditations that provided the structure of the weekend together. They sat in a semi-circle around the Great Hall fire and Brother Dominic started the session off with a short prayer asking for God's guidance in their retreat. The expectation then was that most of the hour would be passed in silent contemplation, but also that at some point each and every participant would say something, however brief; a question, a statement, an observation or even, occasionally, a request. On one infamous occasion, an overzealous retired prioress had launched into an extended poem, in Latin.

On this first evening, the contributions were generally conventional expressions of hopeful anticipation and mutual support; only Andy's intervention provoked much response – 'All I can say is thank God my mum and dad aren't here' – and was greeted with genuine laughter and a palpable relaxation in the atmosphere. At nine o'clock, Brother Dominic withdrew, reminding them that Matins was at six o'clock the following morning and that they were very welcome to join the community if they wished. The remainder of the evening was their own to organise as they chose; no bed times or lights out. There were hot drinks and biscuits provided in the kitchen, which was the only other warm room in the castle, courtesy of the enormous AGA, so that was where they regathered to chat over their initial reactions to the place.

Already certain dynamics had begun to emerge; one group evolved into three – Milly had teamed up with Eugene and Nathan – whilst Martha attached herself to the youngsters, Andy and Bev. This left Chris and Abbie thrown together, perhaps unfortunately. After about half an hour, Milly's group were the first to bid the others goodnight, but the two teachers were still talking well after midnight.

The following day, Saturday, passed largely predictably, with discussions, silent meditations or prayer, and some instruction, interspersed with frugal, and to be perfectly honest rather unappetising, meals and occasional short, but very welcome, breaks. When the group split up for personal reflection, Brother Dominic spent some time with each retreater... "being beside them" as he put it. In reality, he and Martha seemed to have rather more to discuss than the rest of the group, which was perhaps unsurprising.

By the time the evening Meditation came round, however, there was the distinct feeling that the group had opened up; some wounds had been exposed, some prejudices explored, some fears expressed, and if they were being honest, most of the group would probably have admitted that they had also experienced some sense of healing. Not bad for twenty-four hours' work. However, there was one thing that had bothered the members of the Octet, more than once during the day, and that had been the sound of a raised voice coming from the private apartments of the order.

On the first occasion it happened, Brother Dominic hurried off to investigate, returning to reassure them that all was well... 'Just a little misunderstanding,' he said. But when it happened again later in the day, and this time the voice sounded more desperate than angry, the group were told that one of the brothers was experiencing some "personal anguish" and that he was being well cared-for in his distress... nothing to worry themselves about.

It was when, after the evening meditation, the group had adjourned to the kitchen for hot chocolate and biscuits that the disturbance broke out again; only this time the sounds were still more alarming. It started with shouting, more voices than one, cries of anguish, and then things being thrown about, banging of doors, heavy items crashing, glass smashing, building to a crescendo of violence; and then silence. The entire episode had probably lasted only a few minutes, but it left the group stunned, rooted in the kitchen, unable to decide what to do.

Eventually, Brother Dominic arrived and attempted to explain, to apologise, to reassure them that everything was now calm and under control. Brother Aloysius had had a seizure, a sort of mental breakdown resulting in a wild outburst, which had become a kind of rampage. Brother Dominic did not suggest the cause, but the situation was now under control, and Brother Aloysius was calm and being looked after. So it was a very apprehensive Octet that then made their way to their individual rooms and, perhaps understandably, they did not all stay in them.

The fire bells went off at 3. 30 am. After the initial response, to see if it was just a false alarm, the group quickly emerged from whichever room they were in, realising that the fire was real. There was the smell of smoke and the sound of people shouting and running.

'Leave everything… just get out… quickly, for God's sake,' shouted Nathan as he tried to herd the now rapidly panicking group towards the Great Hall. Nobody had bothered to read the fire instructions on the back of their doors, so the most direct route through the Great Hall seemed obvious. They had no way of knowing that they were heading directly into the very heart of the blaze. The great oak staircase that rose out of the hall was starting to catch, but as they hovered at its head, they realised that there was no way back, and smoke was now beginning to catch in their throats. Nathan went first and, pausing on the half landing, urged the rest to follow. Martha, half coughing, half screaming, stumbled as she reached him, and he caught her, helping her down the remaining steps and pointing her at the great doors that Brother Dominic was holding open.

By now, the others were following in a state of shock that barely disguised their terror. Chris and Abbie were behind the rest, and halfway along the hall corridor, Abbie tripped and fell onto the burning carpet. Chris tried to pull her to her feet but she couldn't stand. He tried to get hold of her under her arms, but she sagged forward. Finally, he bent down, dropped his shoulder into her stomach and threw her over his own shoulder in a desperate attempt at a fireman's lift. When he staggered to his feet, he found he could just about walk as he made his way towards the burning staircase.

The banister was now fully ablaze and the flames were creeping across the treads, leaving just enough space next to the wall to walk down. Tentatively, he stepped onto the stairs, feeling the weight on his back shift awkwardly. Painfully slowly, one step at a time, he descended towards the half landing, but by the time he reached it, the flames were licking right across his path. Nathan was still at the foot of the staircase and was shouting encouragement. Chris stepped into the blaze, acting more on instinct than anything else, and as he reached the last three treads he stumbled with exhaustion, and his final fall, with his burden, was broken on Nathan's sturdy frame. Now Brother Dominic was there with another brother, and between them they dragged the teachers out, just as the flaming oak structure finally collapsed, bringing the timber roof beams down with it.

It took what seemed like an eternity for the fire brigade to arrive, and by the time they did, the entire castle was alight, a spectacular inferno lighting up the night sky. Now outside on the wide drive that swept up to the castle, the Octet were all accounted for, as were the live-in domestics, but only six brothers, who were stood in a tight circle, a picture of bewilderment and despair. Brother Dominic with another brother, Simon, and the apparently inexhaustible Nathan, had tried again and again to fight their way back through the flames, but to no avail. The ambulances arrived, and whilst nobody appeared to be seriously injured, they were all taken to A&E as a matter of routine.

Sixteen rooms were found for them in a local hotel, and by nine o'clock the next morning they were all in bed, albeit not asleep. Events like that night change people's lives. It changed theirs.

It took five fire crews the rest of the night to get the blaze under control. In their report afterwards, they suggested that the blaze was probably started deliberately, but in a statement issued by the police they said that they were not looking to charge anyone.

The Octet emerged later that day, in dribs and drabs, to find the Red Cross had arrived with boxes of clean, if mostly ill-fitting, clothes that they were grateful to rummage through for something to wear, and a message went round suggesting they all gather at one o'clock in the hotel reception room.

By ten past one, they were all there, with three exceptions; the firemen had recovered Brother Aloysius', body, which was now lying in the hospital mortuary. They had looked for, and waited for, but no one had seen, Brother Dominic or Martha since they had been dropped off at the hotel. So they sat around, not really knowing what to say, but somehow feeling like there was no going back for any of them. Chris and Abbie had exchanged contact details, and then both thought better of it and deleted them from their phones.

After awkward farewells, the rest of the Octet set off for home, not unchanged but thankful to be alive. The five remaining brothers were absorbed back into their order's Mother House in Durham, whilst their distressed staff were given generous redundancy payments, which would never begin to fill the holes in their lives.

Six weeks after the fire, Mr Dominic McAllister and Ms Martha Robbins were married, quietly, in the registry office in Dover.

DEPARTMENT 13

*...9th Dec 1939, Luttlange, Northern France, first
fatal British casualty of the war. 9th Dec 1939, Harold
Pinchin, pig farmer in Suffolk, is killed in a tractor
accident. Enter the somewhat mysterious Captain N.Emo
of Department 13*

Firstly, I was an only child – there couldn't be any more – and secondly, I was a girl. This was not good news for a struggling Suffolk farmer in the years after the Great War, with agricultural mechanisation still in its infancy. What Harold Pinchin needed was a son, preferably several sons, in fact, so how would he respond to his long-suffering wife, Mary, presenting him with a bonny 7lb baby girl? Well, logic out the window, he was "happy as a sandboy", as he put it himself.

I was christened Charlotte Louise, so he could call me Charlie, and I would be the son he never had, until the day he died. We kept chickens and geese and goats, and Ma had her produce garden, which was over an acre, and meant we were more or less self-sufficient for food, but the main business was pigs – what else would it be in that county?

The farmhouse, which my grandfather had built on land leased to us by Lord Walsham, was a Suffolk pink thatch, with the walls coated in whitewash tinted with pigs' blood. The farmhouse's huge kitchen, with its roughcast walls and sturdy pine furniture, unaltered for decades and forever offering the seductive aroma of baking, never held much appeal for me. As soon as I could walk, I trailed after my father whenever I could, and by the time I was five, he had given up sending me back to the house.

By the age of seven, I could already drive the tractor, though only round the yard, and by the age of twelve, I was an indispensable part of running the farm. It was just as well that I had inherited my father's physique; broad-shouldered and strong-legged, and with a will that was frequently too strong for its own good. I didn't know whether I was pretty or not, and I certainly didn't care. At school, they said I was bright, and I didn't care about that either. All I wanted was to be was on the farm, working with Pa, and happy to be up to my knees in pig shit.

9th December 1939, the village of Luttlange in Northern France – part of the Maginot Line

War Office Statement:

> *Report received of first casualties (1 killed, 4 wounded, 3rd Infantry Brigade, 1st Battalion King's Shropshire Light Infantry – SAAR Front) caused by a patrol leader losing his way in the dark and walking into one of our own booby traps. The ambush party unfortunately fired into the ensuing melee*

The first fatal British casualty of the war was named as Corporal Thomas William Priday (twenty-three years). A second soldier, who died of his wounds three days later, was named as Private Harold Baines Walsham (twenty-one years).

He was in the stables of Weatherbeck Castle discussing, with a stable lad, one of his hunters that had gone lame the previous day, when a breathless footman rushed up to Lord Walsham with the telegram. He hadn't even known that Harry was in France; his last communication had been barely a month before, when the lad was still in training, somewhere in Kent. The peer read and reread the notice, which robbed him of his eldest son, but somehow he was unable to take in its meaning. It didn't seem to make sense.

He was still standing, motionless, in the yard fifteen minutes later when his wife, Rebecca, arrived, alerted to the telegram by the butler. He handed her the piece of paper and then, as though drained of all hope, sank to his knees, onto the cold cobbles, whilst his wife read the words with trembling hands and, failing to suppress a harrowing wail, collapsed onto the stones beside him. The dank stone walls of the stable yard began to close in on them as the first bitter drops of a thunderstorm started to fall. And so they stayed, for the best part of half an hour, until Grainger, the indomitable butler, organised a car to carry the distraught couple back to the castle. It was several days before Lord Walsham was again seen in public, and more than two weeks before his wife could summon up the courage even to leave her bedroom.

The winter of the Phoney War was over and I was busy repairing the roof of one of the sties when the thunderstorm hit, out of nowhere. I cursed, threw a tarpaulin over the half-finished work, and made my way back to the barn, where there were sacks of feed that needed stacking. Pa was over on the far side of the farm, clearing ditches round one of the fields, when the downpour erupted. He knew he should stop the tractor and wait till the worst was over, but, like me, patience was not one of his strong points, and so he pressed on, hoping to get the job done before lunch. There was no warning; the bank that was supporting his right-hand side wheels just gave way and the machine toppled over like a ninepin, into the water-filled gully.

It was highly unusual for Pa to be late for his lunch, and unheard-of for him to miss it completely, so by two o'clock, the alarm bells were ringing loudly in the farmhouse.

'He said he was clearing ditches this morning,' Ma said.

'Which field?'

'Beet, I think he said.' There was a tremor in her voice, as if she had some sort of premonition.

The first thing I saw from the far side of the field was the back end of the tractor rearing up, threateningly, from the ditch. As soon as I reached him, I knew. I was frozen to the spot, not even daring to touch him to check that I was right. I was nineteen years old, and the man who I had looked up to, almost worshipped really, all my life, was gone; gone forever. It was the 9th of December 1939.

Nobody seemed to know why Lord Harvey Walsham was always referred to as "Pinky" – to his face by his friends and behind his back by everyone else. Various theories circulated, including reference to his fresh complexion, which reddened rather quickly when he had taken a drink; something to do with the colour of the cottages in the villages on his estate, and even the position of his little finger when holding his cigar. Anyway, he clearly didn't object to the nickname which had followed him through school, through university and through a distinguished army career, culminating in the awarding of the Military Cross for outstanding bravery in the bloody trenches of Ypres. But now the colour had left his Lordship's cheeks, he took no interest in his estate and no pleasure in cigars. The effect on him of Harry's fate was devastating; he had always seen himself in his eldest son, and the boy's loss, so sudden and so wasteful, was like a living death to him.

The peer, who had been a war hero, a major figure in Suffolk life, lord lieutenant of the county, was a broken man, a mere shell, shuffling about his stately home, looking for something that could never be found. By the spring of 1940, Lady Bex, as she was happy to be called, realised that she needed to get a grip on matters, since her husband showed little sign of recovering from their son's death. The Walsham estate, covering some 55,000 acres of Suffolk and stretching into Norfolk, comprised twenty-three tenant farms, nine villages and a thirty-mile stretch of North Sea coastline. Lord Walsham had always been a very active landlord, taking a keen interest in every aspect of the estate's management, the day-to-day running of which rested in the capable, if occasionally somewhat slippery, hands of Phil Meadows, and had done for the past twenty or more years. Meadows was certainly a canny operator, knowing exactly how far he could exploit his position, which was one of not inconsiderable power, to his own advantage, whilst ensuring the estate always ran smoothly and, perhaps more importantly, profitably.

He was a man more feared than respected, and more than one tenant had come to grief attempting to outwit him. His Lordship was well aware of his overseer's reputation and was happy to play the gracious lord, whilst his servant applied the thumbscrews when necessary and took the resulting flack. Unlike her – now absentee – husband, Lady Bex was totally ignorant of this arrangement, and naive as to the "nature of business", so her introduction into the world of estate management was a shock, to say the least. Matters were complicated still further with the intervention of her middle son, Robert, still at university studying Modern Languages, but who now felt, with his elder brother gone and his father "indisposed" as it were, that he was entitled to assume a new measure of influence in the family business. Had Robert been of a more sanguine character, wanting only to assist his mother, offering support and occasional suggestions, it would indeed have been helpful. Instead of this, the young man was arrogant enough to believe that it was his place, indeed even his right, to take over the reins himself, because, as he said, it wasn't a woman's place to run an estate.

The youngest son, George, the brightest of the three boys, was in the Upper Sixth Form at Framlingham College, but usually managed to get home at weekends. He could see exactly what Robert was about, and it was George, with his easy charm and his extraordinary passion for the novels of Jules Verne, who provided the sole solace to his mother as she struggled to hold everything together. The fact that Meadows saw Robert as a serious threat to his comfortable lifestyle meant that, to some extent at least, the two sort of cancelled each other out.

The tenancy on the Pinchin farm had passed from my grandfather's into my father's name almost twenty years before this, but now, on his death, the lease became void, no provision having been made for its possible transfer to another member of his family. Meadows had been quick to issue the notice terminating the tenancy, seeing an opportunity for a little lucrative business to come his way. However, it seemed insensitively quick to Lady Bex when she discovered the fact in a letter from Ma pleading for the tenancy to be continued in her daughter's name. Change of tenancy was always an opportunity to increase rents, so unless the Pinchins were willing to meet new terms, Meadows was adamant that we should go. For once, Robert and the manager were in agreement, but Lady Bex stalled them, saying she wanted to speak to us first before making a final decision. It seemed like a small thing at the time, and yet its ramifications proved to be enormous.

I accompanied Ma to Weatherbeck Castle early in April. It was the first contact I had had with the family at the big house since one long-ago but fondly remembered summer when as a little girl I had played with the youngest son, George. He was a mischievous lad, an "imp", Ma used to call him, who delighted in teasing and bamboozling the farmhands and running rings around "ol' Meadows". After we had had some tea, we would go out into the fields and lie back in the stubble and he would thrill me with tales from Jules Verne and Alexander Dumas, for even at that young age he had acquired a passion for all things French, which would eventually lead to a distinguished academic career in French letters.

'Let me do the talking, Charlotte,' Ma said. 'You know what you're like.'

'It's our farm, Ma – we've worked that land for generations. We've got rights.'

'It's talk like that'll get us thrown off.'

'I'll not be quiet, Ma.'

'You'll do as I say.'

But nobody was going to stop me saying my piece, and once I was in full flow, it all came out in a torrent; the difficulties of farming since the war started, the struggle to pay the rent, even before it was raised, and Meadows... well, I had quite a lot to say about Mr Meadows. Poor Ma sank lower and lower into her chair, despairing of my usual tactlessness, and waited for the inevitable axe to fall. When I eventually ran out of steam, there was a strange silence. The three of us looked from one to another, nobody quite knowing what the others were thinking. It was Lady Bex who broke the spell.

'Well... thank you, Miss Pinchin. I think I probably learnt more about farming, and about this estate in particular, in the last ten minutes than in my previous twenty years living at Weatherbeck.'

It was the start of our extraordinary friendship.

For landowners and farmers alike, the next six years would prove challenging and rewarding in equal measure. The role played by agriculture in sustaining the country through the war years would be absolutely vital as imports dried up and home production needed to expand to compensate. Every scrap of useable land would be commissioned for food production; every sack of grain and every side of meat would have to be accounted for; yields would need to increase significantly, so artificial fertilisers would be introduced for the first time; and the tide of regulations spewing from the Ministry of Food would be enough to drown the poor old farmers. And preserving all this additional perishable produce, in the absence of widespread refrigeration, would require innovative techniques – bio-technology was employed on a wide scale, as well as simpler methods such as drying of milk and eggs, and salting meat. Farmers would not even be allowed to kill their own animals for their families to eat.

In theory, rationing was meant to apply equally to the entire civilian population, but in reality, people who lived in the countryside would fare very much better than their urban counterparts. But in the spring of 1940, much of this was still to come. My immediate concern was securing a new lease on our farm, and a growing sense of alarm that the continued absence of Lord Walsham would embolden Phil Meadows to expand his influence on the lives and livelihoods of all the Walsham estate farmers. And my fears were not without foundation; Meadows had paid unwelcome visits to most of the farms, warning the tenants that the war would mean tough times for them, and that they should expect a good deal of belt-tightening in the future.

To the annoyance of Robert, who complained that his inheritance was being altered without his agreement, and to the outrage of Meadows, who saw financial opportunities slipping out of his grip, Bex Walsham granted us a new lease in my name, but this was just the start of our ever-closer relationship. I was bursting with ideas that might improve and develop the management of the Walsham estate, to the benefit of both the landlord and the tenants, and Her Ladyship was eager to listen. These were very particular times and required special solutions to new problems, and whilst her husband was certainly improving in his spirits and getting about much more, he still displayed very little interest in the business side of things. He had taken to dressing in his old army uniform, complete with medals, and now Major Lord "Pinky" Walsham could be spotted riding around the nearby farms on his favourite black hunter, or occasionally further afield, scouting the outer reaches of the estate, driving the old Land Rover that was held together with wire and gaffer tape, and ran as much on prayer as diesel. It was generally agreed that the old boy had lost his marbles, but people still stopped to pass the time of day with him – he was harmless enough. In the meantime, Lady Bex and I discussed and researched and argued, and plotted the future of the Walsham acres.

On a glorious sunny morning at the end of April, Ma was in the kitchen, up to her elbows in bread flour, and I was sorting out the weak weaners in the nursery barn, when Lady Bex's Bentley roared into the yard. She was driving herself, which was most unusual, and she had an air of anxiety bordering on panic in her manner.

'I've had this letter,' she blurted out, 'from the Ministry of Food... and I don't have the first idea what to do about it.'

'Well, what does Mr Meadows say, Your Ladyship?' was my first, rather naïve, response.

'God, I haven't shown him the letter yet,' she said. 'He'll go completely mad about it.'

Poor Lady Bex was clearly in a terrible state.

'Come on inside and have a cup of tea, then we'll look at this letter.'

The Ministry of Food had been established at the very start of the war under WS Morrison. Now Lord Woolton had taken over as Minister, and the Lend-Lease agreement with the United States, supplying us with food and agricultural equipment, had just been signed, and there was talk of establishing a scheme recruiting single women to work on farms to replace the men who had been called up. The Land Girls, they were going to be called. So did the letter from the Ministry have something to do with any of this?

Lady Bex carefully replaced her half-drunk cup of tea in its saucer. 'Tell me what you think, Charlie,' she said, offering me the very official-looking letter. I liked her calling me Charlie.

Ministry of Food, Department 13, Sections A, B, C, D and E (Regulations applicable to multiple farm conglomerates)

It did sound a bit scary, I had to admit.

Section A applied to groups of five farms or less. Section E was for groups of fifty farms or more. The Walsham estate, with its twenty-three farms came into Section C. That seemed straightforward enough, so far. The letter went on to say that all farms in this section should be amalgamated for the duration of hostilities, for the purpose of maximising productivity, under the management of a joint committee, made up of representatives from each individual farm and under the chairmanship of the overall landlord, or his appointed representative. It then went on to say that all leases should be suspended indefinitely, to provide security to tenant farmers whilst emergency measures were in place.

I was beginning to see why Lady Bex was in a state about this. There were then several further paragraphs outlining specific details about the implementation of the new arrangement, including precise targets for productivity, yields per acre, livestock quotas and distribution timescales. The final paragraph was rather like a "call to arms". We all needed to do our bit for the war effort, willingly and cheerfully, but... failure to comply would be considered a grave dereliction of duty and result in appropriately severe consequences. The letter was signed by Cpt N. Emo, Co-ordinator for C Section, on behalf of Lord Woolton, Minister of Food. All communications should be addressed directly to him at Department 13.

It was a massive amount to take in. Poor Lady Bex seemed totally bewildered, and to be honest, I was struggling to get my head around it. One thing was certain – Meadows needed to be sidelined or it could spell disaster.

'Don't say anything to Mr Meadows yet, Your Ladyship,' I said. 'We need to think this through and work out how you are going to deal with it all.'

'You really will have to stop calling me Your Ladyship, Charlie.'

'But what should I call you then, Your Ladyship?' I said.

'Bex will do fine,' she said, 'but what do you think we should do first?'

That would be really strange – calling Her Ladyship "Bex", but if that's what she wanted, fine.

'I know nearly all the Walsham farmers,' I said, 'so I guess you need to call a meeting as soon as possible, and let them know the situation.'

One thing was certain: none of the farmers were going to object to having a say in running things, but, of course, there was one person who certainly would.

Meadows put up a half-hearted fight, complaining about every detail in the letter, but whilst he was happy to bully local Suffolk farmers, he clearly didn't have the stomach to take on Whitehall, and Cpt Emo gave the clear impression of a man with whom one did not meddle. Bex offered him a severance package, which was far too generous in my opinion, but he accepted it, without much grace, and disappeared from the area. Robert was a different matter. He would continue to be awkward, constantly complaining about his inheritance being eroded, but he knew he would have to bide his time until the war was over before anyone was going to take any notice. In 1940, and much to his displeasure, he was called up, and didn't appear again at Weatherbeck until after the armistice.

In 1943, I met Chip Brennon, a captain in the 95th Bomber Group of US Air Force, based at Halesworth. His plane had been shot down in a region north of Paris when returning from a night raid, and though he had managed to bail out, his parachute had failed to fully open and he damaged his back on hitting the ground. He was picked up by the French Resistance and cared for until they could smuggle him back across the Channel, arriving back in Suffolk five months later. But that was the end of Chip's flying career, much to his dismay. Instead, he was placed in charge of co-ordinating supplies to all the American bases across the UK.

Before the war, he had been a highly successful businessman, helping to run the fifth largest engineering company in the US, which is why he was given the job of supplying the almost 500,000 American Air Force personnel stationed at 200 bases, from Land's End to Shetland. That was a very big job. Supplying pork to US Air Force Base at Halesworth was a very, very small part of it – but that was how we met. A mix-up over an order might have meant "his boys missing out on their Saturday night pork chop barbecue", and no way was that gonna happen on Chip's watch. Don't ask me why we hit it off, but we did, and he remained at Halesworth for the rest of the war, so we saw quite a bit of each other as that Suffolk magic gradually got in under his skin.

At the end of the war, he proposed to me, and with my tongue firmly in my cheek I replied that since I had no better offers on the table... I'd accept. We tied the knot in the chapel at Weatherbeck Castle, and though it was a very small reception, the Great Hall made it look an amazingly posh one.

Throughout the war years, we had had a continuous flow of instructions from Cpt Emo, and the whole Walsham estate had flourished. One or two of the smaller farms had struggled to meet their required quotas, but the others had come to their rescue, and Cpt Emo was generally happy to leave the internal organisation to us. So the co-ordinating committee, under the benign chairmanship of Lady Bex, had functioned smoothly and profitably. Major "Pinky" continued his wanderings over the estate, though he did discard the uniform. He had metamorphosed into a rather lovable old sage, who had taken, once more, to permanently puffing away on his Havana.

Two months after the end of the war, Bex received a final letter from Cpt Emo, concluding the Ministry's direct involvement in the estate's management, releasing it from the majority of the special regulations, except those impacting directly on rationing, which would continue for several more years. To be honest, I am not sure how we would all have coped without the Captain's guidance and support during those difficult years.

1945 also saw the return of the two Walsham brothers. The younger had gone from Cambridge to a shadowy department in the War Office, where his job apparently involved frequent absences from Whitehall on "hush-hush" missions, something to do with the French Resistance. In the autumn of that year at a ceremony at the French Embassy, an extremely tall French general, with an enormous nose, bent to embrace and decorate the diminutive Englishman. It was not, presumably, for services to French letters.

Robert's war, by contrast, had been uncomfortable and occasionally dangerous, but more often tedious. He was older but, sadly, not much wiser. He was keen that the estate arrangements be returned to their pre-war status, and in particular that the suspended farm leases be reinstated, and the authority of the Castle be firmly re-established. As the undisputed heir to Weatherbeck, he now appeared to wield a more legitimate claim to a say in the estate management.

Without consulting his parents, Robert called a meeting of all the tenant farmers to inform them of the changes he intended to make, with particular reference to our leases. The meeting was arranged for Saturday 5th November, which did seem somewhat ironic, and both Bex and Pinky had reluctantly agreed to attend, albeit to fight the tenants' corner if required, but by twelve o'clock there was no sign of Lord Walsham, so, despite Bex's protestations, Robert started without him. It clearly wasn't going to be a long affair; Robert intended to state his intentions, perhaps allow fifteen minutes or so for the farmers to make any objections, before he would close proceedings telling all those involved that they would be informed of future arrangements.

By 12.30, there was uproar in the back room of the White Hart, where the meeting was taking place, and for a moment it did look as though things might turn nasty, especially as Robert had, rather foolishly, placed himself on a dais at the far end of the room from the entrance. His escape route was well and truly blocked off, and as the agitated crowd edged ever closer to their would-be prey, a shrill whistle pierced the din, at which everyone turned to look back at the open doorway only to discover the old peer standing, silhouetted against the midday sun as it streamed in through the door. He was frantically waving a piece of paper. The crowd hushed as Lord Walsham slowly made his way to the dais.

'I apologise for my late arrival, ladies and gentlemen,' he said, in a firm voice. 'I have been with my estate solicitors.'

The silence deepened.

'And I have today signed the document that confirms leases on all the Walsham estate farms for the period of… 999 years.' *Fait accompli* – as they say.

And what, you may ask, became of Mr and Mrs Chip Brennon? Well, I carried on running the Pinchin farm, as we continued to call it. We produced four fine Suffolk-cum-Yankee children, two of each, and Ma became Nanny May, which was very handy all round. Bex asked Chip to take over the role of co-ordinating the Weatherbeck estate, when Robert decided a comfortable life in the South of France, paid for by his mother, was infinitely preferable to the chill winds that caress the flats of East Anglia. In time, he would inherit Weatherbeck, but he would choose never again to make it his home.

On a trip to London to meet some agricultural machinery suppliers late in 1946, Chip decided to call in at the Ministry of Food and pay his respects to the famous Cpt Emo in person. After numerous blank-faced responses to his enquiries, he was eventually passed on to a Miss Midwinter, a Senior E.O. who had worked at the Ministry throughout the war, and coincidentally hailed from Ipswich.

'Department 13?' she asked quizzically. 'I don't recall there ever being a Department 13.'

'For multi-farm conglomerates,' he explained. The elderly official continued to look puzzled.

'Section C. Groups of more than twenty farms.' Now it was Chip that was struggling. Miss Midwinter smiled blankly.

'Well, what's happened to Captain Emo then? Which department does he work in? He must be able to help.'

'I don't recall any Captain Emo, but I can check the records if you like,' she offered helpfully, and disappeared, silently, down one of the endless corridors.

It was almost a quarter of an hour before she re-emerged, carrying a manila file but still wearing the same bemused expression.

'Any luck?' Chip asked tentatively.

'I have here the entire staff listings for those employed at the Ministry throughout the war...' she said.

'And?'

'Are you sure you have the correct name, Mr Brennon? Emo is an odd sort of name.'

'Emo, I told you, Captain N. Emo. Look, I even have his signature on this letter,' and he produced a crumpled correspondence which he had brought with him, for the Ministry's exact address.

Miss Midwinter's patience was clearly fraying.

'Look, see his signature. Captain N. Emo. I never knew what the N stood for.'

She took the letter and scrutinised the scribbled signature. Then slowly a wry smile crept over her habitually serious face.

'I think, perhaps, you should have another look at that name,' she said. 'Have a think about it,' and with that cryptic remark, she nodded politely and took her leave.

On the train back to Suffolk, Chip took the letter out again.

'Captain N. Emo... N Emo?' Suddenly the penny dropped... of course, Nemo. But what was that supposed to mean?

Back in Suffolk, Chip recounted all this to me in a bemused tone, but he was completely taken aback when I suddenly burst into laughter. What I could once again feel was the sun on my face, the prickly stubble on my back and the memory of a long-ago golden summer when mischief was in the air, and a young boy told tales of Jules Verne.

MY WAY

...if he couldn't hack it as a soldier and she wouldn't now make it as an Olympian, then perhaps they should try rowing round the island instead... there is a tide in the affairs of men...

At the end of the day, that's what it's about – willing to kill and prepared to die. They're the two indispensable rules of any army; all the rest is politics of one sort or another. Army families know the score, especially ones like the Barringtons, five generations of army men with General Sir John Barrington, former Deputy Army Chief of Staff for the last eight years of his illustrious career. So it was never going to be easy to buck the trend in that family. But the family had paid the price over the years, and whilst deaths were always a tragedy, they were never a surprise; they were the inevitable toll that sometimes had to be paid.

Sir John had had three sons, and it was his eldest, Harvey, that had continued the family tradition and was now a brigadier in the Welsh Guards, whilst he in turn produced two sons and a daughter: John, Charlotte and Timothy in that order. John had been a *"Boys' Own"* sort of chap, Head Boy at Marlborough, outstanding cadet at Sandhurst and then a commission, like his father, in the Welsh Guards; killed two days before he was due to finish his posting in Afghanistan. The family were all devastated, but none more so than Tim, because much as he had hero-worshipped his older brother, he had no desire to emulate him in his chosen career. To his father's and grandfather's horror, Tim's passionate desire, from the age of eleven, was to become a professional musician, a pianist. Now, in his Upper Sixth year and his musical career mapped out in front of him, with John's death, like it or not, the family mantle fell upon him.

The misfortune that befell Kitty Dillon was of a very different nature, and yet it was misfortune, in a way, that brought them together. Tim only lasted one year at Sandhurst, though it had been obvious to him from day one that, with the best will in the world, he was never cut out to be a soldier. It wasn't the physical demands of the training; he quite enjoyed that. At school, he had been that rarest of creatures – a star of the 1st XV, and the most talented musician in the Sixth Form. His constant worry was that he might damage his fingers in a mistimed tackle or at the bottom of a ruck, but it never stopped him. His father was utterly delighted when Tim announced that he had decided to go for Sandhurst instead of applying for a scholarship at the Royal College of Music. He had done it with a heavy heart, knowing it was really a mistake. Once there, it was the sheer mindlessness of so much of what they were supposed to do that Tim found hardest to take, and he had already been in trouble on numerous occasions during that first year, mostly for insubordination, so it was a disappointment rather than a shock when he told his parents that he had had enough. He would leave it a year then apply for university to read Music, and in the meantime, he got himself a job in a music shop in Portsmouth.

Kitty was at Portsmouth University reading Biology, but it was water sports that were her passion: sailing, surfing, water skiing; you name it, she did it, and did it exceptionally well. The car accident that she was involved in coming back from a party one Saturday evening was just one of those freak events, not really anybody's fault, but it resulted in her losing both her legs from the knee downwards. The day the doctors broke the news to her was the day she started thinking about what sports she could do without legs.

Portsmouth Sea Rowing Club consisted, at this time, of a dozen or so individuals of all shapes and sizes, all ages, both sexes and with pretty much nothing in common except a love of the sea and a delight in taking it on in little rowing boats. Tim joined because he needed something physically demanding, not to punish himself so much as to embrace a new challenge, and one that was sufficiently obscure so as to not attract any attention.

Kitty's rehab was long and painful, with endless hours of physiotherapy followed by weeks on end in the gym, which is where she established her relationship with the rowing machine, or to be more precise, her version of it, specially adapted to take account of her absent lower legs. By the time Kitty discovered the PSRC, Tim was already an established member of the club, and he was delighted when a new face, especially a young and very pretty one, appeared at a Tuesday evening training session. After a little initial awkwardness about Kitty's legs, they hit it off really well, being the same sort of age and relatively normal, by club standards.

The former sports fanatic had become extraordinarily proficient on her prosthetics, and they quickly worked out that they could manage the two-man boat between them. It amused them that the name on the side of the little wooden vessel was *My Way*. Probably not surprisingly, Kitty was a natural oarswoman, well able to hold her own against Tim, and they spent an increasing amount of time together, battling the tides and currents. For obvious reasons, you don't talk much when you're actually rowing, but either side of their times on the oars, they talked the hind legs off each other, discussing everything from global geopolitics to deeply personal matters, and just like their approach to most things, their exchanges were of the "no-holes-barred" variety.

The sun room of Admiral's Cottage, with its wall of windows facing directly out to sea, was where Miss Schiller spent sixteen hours of most days. She sat in her high-backed wing armchair, surrounded by her eleven cats, and chain-smoked Benson and Hedges, lighting each new cigarette with the butt of its predecessor. It was a charming room, with chintz furnishings, dozens of exquisite cameo plaques and a bookcase full of European literature. She did not read any longer but listened instead to Radio 3, except when *Test Match Special* was on, when she listened to that instead. She had become inadvertently addicted to cricket when, at some point many years before, the Third Programme had switched to cricket when test matches were being played, and for some reason it had enthralled her ever since. When asked on one occasion to explain this strange phenomenon, she had compared cricket commentary with the slow movement of a Mahler symphony.

Apart from her bedroom and bathroom, Miss Schiller rarely visited any of the other rooms in her house, which were all tastefully decorated and kept in readiness for visitors who almost never came. Her family had arrived in England at the start of the Second World War, but now she was the only one left, apart from a dubious nephew who visited her once a year, probably to ensure his inheritance, Miss Schiller thought.

Admiral's Cottage had, as its name suggests, been a Navy property and originally part of a lookout chain, watching the waters along the south coast of the Isle of Wight. Miss Schiller had purchased it in the 1950s and completely remodelled it as a comfortable home, its principle virtue being its remote location, insofar as it was possible to be remote on the holiday island. Her reclusive existence was softened by the daily attendance of her cook/ housekeeper, the dour Mrs Brackon, who arrived on the stroke of ten o'clock each morning and left promptly at four, and Mr Netherton, a kindly man but somewhat past his sell-by date when it came to heavy lifting, whom she employed two days a week to do the garden and any odd jobs required. The cottage was situated overlooking a tiny inlet between Chale Chine and Brightstone Bay, with a beach that was only accessible from the sea or a steep path running directly from the bottom of the cottage's garden.

After rowing together three or four times a week for a couple of months, Tim and Kitty felt ready for a challenge. The PSRC wasn't a competitive sort of set-up; its members rowed for the fun of it, so even had there been competitions to enter, they probably wouldn't have bothered, so its two newest members would have to arrange their own excitement.

'How about round the island?' Kitty had suggested after one session, and Tim found himself agreeing to the idea without even really thinking about it.

'To make it worthwhile, we should go from the mainland, say, Lymington, round the Wight and back to Lymington.' She was clearly excited by the prospect. 'What d'you reckon?'

'How long do you think it would take us?' Tim asked, trying to sound casual.

'Say, twenty strokes a minute… if we can keep that up, so about three knots on average, I reckon we might do it in five hours.' Kitty was really buzzing now.

'And you think we could keep going for that long?' Tim was obviously doubtful.

'We'd need to train a bit more, obviously… but yes, I think so… don't you?'

He really didn't want to be the one to back out.

'I guess,' he said, without much conviction, but it was enough for Kitty. Round the island was on, but it was another two months of distance training before they felt ready to go.

Crossing the Solent proved no problem at all; light breeze, calm water, and they had rowed past Hurst Castle before they knew where they were, and aiming for the Needles. Anti-clockwise round the island seemed the best bet, taking the tides into account, and the plan was to give the Needles themselves a good wide berth, but the moment they were round the jutting rocks, the weather started to change. The skies darkened and a wind sprung up from nowhere.

They had been rowing for just over two hours and the first wave of fatigue was beginning to hit. They knew they could row through it, but it was bad timing. They decided to down oars for ten minutes just to settle themselves, but within that time the weather worsened dramatically, and suddenly they thought they might be in trouble. They had studied the detailed map of the southern coastline, and they knew that there was no immediate chance to put in on a beach; they would have to row on until they reached Freshwater Bay. By now, the sea was rising, and controlling their tiny boat was becoming increasingly difficult, and whilst neither of them was panicking yet, they were both privately anxious.

As Freshwater Bay came into view and they began to relax a bit, surging currents hit them and drove them away from the shore. However hard they pulled, they couldn't make land, and suddenly they were back 300 yards or more from the shoreline and drifting along the coast. With the wind whipping up ever more strongly, they now had sizeable waves to contend with, most of which they rode, but occasionally one broke right over their craft, and taking on water raised the possibility the boat might actually sink eventually.

An hour past the Needles and with no immediate landing place in prospect, both rowers were now nearing exhaustion, when a freak wave rose high in the air and broke directly on top of them, tossing the boat over and its two occupants into the water. Even with life jackets on, the danger of being swept ever further out to sea was terrifying, and Tim realised that Kitty, with two prosthetic legs, was in dire peril. He grabbed hold of her and together they kicked for the shore with all the strength left in them. His lungs were on fire, every muscle in his body was screaming, but he drove himself on and on, until eventually everything went black.

Poor old Mr Netherton didn't know which body to shake first. He wasn't sure whether they were alive or not, when Tim groaned, coughed and started to shake, which he took as a good sign, so the gardener turned his attention to the girl with the iron legs. He tried raising her head and shoulders, and by the time Tim had got himself onto all fours and crawled the few feet across the pebbles to reach them, Kitty was on her side choking up salt water.

It had been Miss Schiller who had spotted the bodies on the beach and dispatched her handyman to the scene, not knowing whether or not it would be corpses he would have to deal with. She raised the binoculars that she kept to hand on her window sill, though she seldom used them, to see the two invaders sitting up, gratefully alive, if clearly distressed and battered by their ordeal. She wondered fleetingly whether they were asylum seekers washed overboard some ghastly people smugglers' vessel laden with human cargo, but dismissed the thought, concerning herself instead with offering assistance to these forlorn-looking seafarers.

An hour later, Tim and Kitty were sitting in Miss,Schiller's sun room, in an interesting array of dry clothes, sipping tea from delicate china cups, and massively grateful just to be alive. They realised, of course, that friends in Portsmouth would be worried about them before long, so one or two phone calls were made to allay fears, and then the two intrepid rowers happily accepted Miss Schiller's invitation to rest at Admiral's Cottage for the time being, at least until they sorted out arrangements for their return to the mainland.

It took four days for the couple to finalise plans for their trip back to Portsmouth, though it wasn't clear why it took so long. They thoroughly enjoyed Miss Schiller's company, as she did theirs, and it turned out to be a friendship that brightened the old lady's latter years.

The salty baptism of their adventure had secured an enduring partnership, and Tim and Kitty announced their engagement during his final year studying Music at Portsmouth whilst Kitty was completing her post-graduate PGCE at the same university, and training as a water sports coach for the British Para Olympic squad. Each summer, they would return to Admiral's Cottage to spend a week with Miss Schiller, for whom it was the highlight of the year.

At ninety-seven, the old lady contracted pneumonia and a few days later died peacefully in her sleep. A letter arrived for Mr and Mrs Barrington from Brownlows Solicitors, dealing with Miss Schiller's estate; she had left Admiral's Cottage to them with her love and gratitude for their friendship. When Tim's father heard of the bequest, his comment was typical: well, if he couldn't manage a military connection, at least he had made a naval one.

THE UNDERSTUDY

…when, after ten years in the wilderness, she is suddenly offered a wonderful "swansong" role, is the price she may have to pay too high?

Maria Torres (not her real name) had coal-black eyes, raven-black hair and an irredeemably black soul. She was forty-three years old but in the right light could pass for ten years younger. Twenty years ago, she had seduced Jean-François Bisset, the then darling director of the French *film noir* movement, and had become pregnant. Announcing her condition and its source, she declared that she was determined to keep the baby and bring it up *alone*. She then sat back and revelled in the prolonged publicity this provoked. When the baby was eighteen months old and all the fuss had well and truly died down, and the extreme inconvenience of motherhood had kicked in, she put Antoinette, as she had named the infant, up for adoption. This was her Faustian pact, not to achieve immortality but, more modestly, worldly fame as a movie star. And thus was her soul forever blackened.

Now, with her greatest years tragically behind her, she mused on the price she had paid, and the unknown future that lay before her. It was seven or eight years since she had had any sort of role in a film, and even then they had been well down the credits, so whilst she had made enough money in her heyday to live comfortably, she still craved the thrill of a new script, a new character to explore, a new audience to conquer.

Her phone rang. Ted Walters had been Maria's agent since he spotted her, twenty-two years before, at her final LAMDA Showcase performance; the loud, lanky but undeniably talented student, Mary Turner. Ted had seen Maria through triumphs and disasters; through movies and stagework and TV, through three husbands and three divorces; through alcoholism and rehab; through premature retirement and unwise revivals, and through it all he had adored her, secretly, and without the slightest possibility of his feelings ever being reciprocated.

'Peter Thorn is planning a provincial tour of *Hedda Gabler* in the autumn,' he said excitedly. 'The money's not great, but he needs a name for Hedda.' There was a pause. 'What do you think? You've always talked about wanting to do Ibsen.' Silence. 'Hedda would be perfect for you, sweetheart.'

'You're sure he doesn't want me for Aunt Juliana?' Maria quipped, expecting the swift rebuttal.

'Hardly, sweetheart; he needs a genuine leading lady, someone audiences around the country will recognise.'

'Ten years ago, maybe, Ted,' Maria sighed. 'Ten years ago maybe... but now... at forty... something.'

'You'd be sensational, sweetheart. Hedda's made for you, you know she is.'

'I don't know, Ted, I'm not sure...'

'Think about it, sweetheart. It's just what you need right now.'

'Okay, I'll think about it. When did you say the run was?'

'September to mid-November, then London, maybe, if it goes well.'

'Who's he got so far?'

'Reese Naylor for Tesman... umm... Tim Cornwell as Brack.'

'Naylor's good. Not done much recently, I don't think.'

'Hence the provinces, sweetheart.'

'And who's this Cornwell?'

'*EastEnders*?'

'Right! And Mrs Elusted?'

'Still looking for her, and Lövborg,' Ted added, sensing Maria's resistance beginning to crumble.

'Okay, Ted, I'll think about it... I won't have to audition, will I?' she added, with just a hint of nervousness in her voice.

'Maria, sweetheart, he'd die to have you,' he said, and then almost added that he had just taken on an amazing new girl; early twenties, good-looker, but more importantly, real class. Then he decided it probably wasn't the right moment.

In more than twenty years' association with the London Academy of Music and Dramatic Arts, Stefan Khroll had been thought only to have used the term "gifted" about a student on half a dozen occasions, in fact, so infrequently that nobody could even remember the last recipient of the honour. When Anette Rollands was interviewed for a place on the acting course, she looked like an extremely unlikely candidate; her academic history was one of unparalleled failure, her appearance seemed designed to offend, and her general demeanour was uncooperative and ill-mannered. So why was her application even being considered?

Lindsey Hazel ran a youth theatre project in the East End that was known to be a honey pot for lost causes (of which Anette was almost certainly the most lost), and she and

Khroll went back a very long way. Lindsey was well aware of the sort of students that LAMDA routinely accepted, and she almost never recommended her students to her old friend. However, on this occasion, she made an exception. In a note to Khroll she had written:

I do realise exactly how Anette appears, so reject her if you must. In her life so far she has grown well used to that, but take a look at her first, please. I think she will astonish you.

And she did. Against all Lindsey's advice, not for the first time, she chose to do Lady Macbeth's "Unsex me" speech, and she delivered it with such passion, such rage, such uninhibited emotional vulnerability, that she quite simply paralysed the interviewing panel.

She finished her piece, stood rigid with her back to her assessors, and there was utter silence in the room for what seemed like an eternity, but in reality was probably half a minute. No discussion of her application followed. Stefan Khroll simply glanced at his three colleagues, raised his eyebrows for an instant and said, 'So, who do we have next?'

Anette's passage through the disciplines of her course was not a smooth one – it was never going to be – but in the end, her raw talent always came to her rescue. Somehow, she always got away with it, because, at the end of the day, she simply was exceptional.

At the end of her first turbulent year, she decided to drop the Anette; she would be called Nan. And then a few months later, the "Rollands" was replaced with "Tuckett". The combination amused her. Whilst – now – Nan struggled with the more formal and academic elements of her training, her direct personal experience of the lamentable childcare system in this country, of physical as well as substance abuse, and of the iniquities of the legal system, gave her a pool of knowledge and empathy on which to draw in practical work that emphasised social realism, that set her apart from and beyond her fellow students. Khroll took this damaged and volatile girl and nurtured her towards the social norms that would allow her to function in the world outside LAMDA's cloistered protection.

Read-through was in a grimy church hall in Paddington on the Saturday afternoon of the August bank holiday. It was stiflingly hot, over 80 degrees outside, and the hall still stank of the previous night's disco; stale beer, sweat and overactive adolescent libido, with just a hint of vomit in the ladies' loos. Peter Thorn was going to be late; he *graciously* sent a message of welcome and suggested that they make a start without him. Tony Davidson, the SM for the tour, would deputise. Maria was, in a word, outraged. This was absolutely no way to treat professionals, and she was all for abandoning the read-through until the director had the courtesy to grace them with his presence. Ted had turned up unexpectedly, with some young girl in tow, and he prevailed on Maria to give Peter half an hour before storming off. The rest of the cast agreed and they all sat around in sweaty silence with their noses in their scripts. Thorn breezed in just as they had decided that fifty minutes really was long enough, full of apologies and *bonhomie*, which didn't go down particularly well.

Surprisingly, considering the prologue, the read went pretty well. They were, in fact, quite a classy ensemble, largely because straight acting opportunities, according to Maria, were few and far between these days, what with all the bloody musicals. But one thing you could never accuse her of was lack of preparation; she had read the script four or five times, and with the blessing of an astonishing memory she was halfway to being off-script already. This, however, had the disadvantage of allowing her to repeatedly prompt the other cast members if they missed a cue, or even hesitated, which provoked considerable irritation.

'Oh, do keep up, darling,' she interjected, in her best "theatrical dame" voice.

Rather as the alignment of the stars can sometimes portend some tumultuous astrological event, so three disparate elements in the life of Maria Torres appeared to be on a collision course that could only result in catastrophe: the appearance of Nan "somebody or other", Ted's latest ingénue, had upset her far more than it should have; the actual plot of play in which she was engaged; and a totally unexpected echo from her distant past that threatened to upset her, already rather precarious, apple cart.

Two months prior to the Paddington read-through, Nan sat in her bedroom in the shared flat in Earl's Court and reread the letter for the tenth time. Throughout her chaotic, dysfunctional childhood and even during her relatively stable period at LAMDA, Nan had made no attempt to discover who her birth mother was. It was not so much a matter of lack of interest, but rather more of a resentment that festered within her, and would, if she ever released it, consume her completely.

She didn't need any psychologist to tell her she was angry, she knew that already, and acting was her way of managing a condition that she felt would always be with her. In the end, there were no cures for what was broken in her. So she really couldn't explain, even to herself, what at this point in her life drove her to enquire.

She stared at the words – *Mother's name: Mary Turner*, which meant nothing to her. She could have happily accepted an anonymous Mary Turner; it was what appeared in the brackets that followed that name. Her stomach twisted, her eyes filled with hot tears and her mind tilted slightly; there would be consequences.

The following Wednesday, Nan was in Ted's office asking about any possible auditions when she saw on the board behind Ted's desk, where he pinned up forthcoming events, the Hedda tour, and who was involved. She shivered, and tried to think what this might mean. In the end, she persuaded Ted to suggest her for tour DSM, understudying for Hedda. Strictly speaking, there were no parts for someone of her age, but a bit of experience in stage management would be really useful on her CV. Thorn agreed to take her, on Ted's recommendation, as long as she was cheap enough.

Guns play a very important role in *Hedda Gabler*. They represent danger, threat, power, revenge, escape and fantasy, amongst other things. The duelling pistols that Hedda plays with in the first act and with which she kills herself at the climax of the play are, as working props, the responsibility of the DSM, the Deputy Stage Manager.

It had taken some time and effort for Nan to obtain live ammunition for the pistols. She made sure she kept it safely away from the blanks that came with the pistols from Mammary, the munitions hiring company that they used in rehearsals. The mechanics of her plan were simple enough. As a matter of professional routine, Maria always checked her props immediately prior to curtain-up, so Nan planned to switch the pistol on stage from a blank one to loaded between Act II and Act III. The final scene, as rehearsed, involved Hedda, viewed by the audience through a transformation gauze, taking the pistol from its case, pointing it at her forehead and firing on cue, instantly followed by a snap blackout. Nan would watch events from her position in the wings and afterwards she would go down to Maria's dressing room, taking the second pistol, reload that and shoot herself. She wasn't planning to escape so preferred that option to any other one.

Hedda Gabler opened in Leeds on Tuesday, 3rd September, having dress rehearsed on the Monday. Ticket sales had been encouraging; a near capacity crowd for an opening night was a bonus. The inevitable few lines dropped, but nothing that couldn't be covered up smoothly, and as the action moved into Act III, Maria felt good. She was Hedda – powerful, independent, stylish, and, yes, with a blackness in her soul she couldn't deny. The audience lapped it up, loving her, and loving to hate her.

As the act draws towards its climax, Hedda withdraws up stage to an alcove masked by the transformation gauze and backlit by a red floodlight to throw the character's silhouette out to the stalls. Hedda is playing a piano with ever-increasing mania when she suddenly stops. She raises the gun to her head, there is a pause which lasts fractionally too long, and then the gunshot and blackout. Tesman and Brack in distress and shock bring the play to its melodramatic end. The curtains close and then open again, the cast gather in a line and walk forward to take their bow. Maria Torres is not amongst them. And then they separate in the middle and the star of the production appears in a spotlight upstage centre, bows deeply, savours the moment, then slowly glides forward to meet the cast line, where they dip twice more in unison before the lights go down for the final time.

Maria grabbed Tony Davidson in the wings. 'What the bloody hell happened then?' she hissed at him through gritted teeth.

'The pistol must have jammed, love. It happens with these antique weapons sometimes.' 'Jammed?' she said.

'I'd cued up Trevor with a sound effect just in case, never thought we'd have to use it, but he was ready, thank God. I think we got away with it, don't you?'

Maria, still in a state of shock, wandered back onto the set, now illuminated only by blue working light. She picked up the pistol and examined it. A small voice came from the wings.

'I'd be careful with that if I were you.'

Maria turned and peered into the gloom. 'Careful?' she asked. 'Why ?'

'Because it's loaded, properly loaded,' the voice replied.

'Don't be ridiculous,' Maria sneered. Nan walked slowly out onto the stage.

'I wanted to kill you, actually kill you... The gun is properly loaded. It just failed to go off, that's all.'

Maria dropped the pistol as if it had burnt her hand. 'Why?' she said. 'Why would you want to kill me?'

Nan was calm by now. The terror and exhilaration of the past fifteen minutes had passed. The mental anguish of the past two weeks had drained away. The suffering and sadness of the past twenty years felt exposed. Suddenly she saw the utter madness of what she had been trying to do, and she resigned herself to whatever fate destiny had in store for her.

'I found out that you were my mother,' she said, 'and I couldn't bear it, I just couldn't, so I thought I'd kill you, and then kill myself, and the pain would stop. Are you going to tell the police?'

The run was a spectacular success with audiences. After Leeds came Manchester, Liverpool, Norwich and all stops to Exeter, Southampton and finally the Theatre Royal Brighton. A London venue hadn't been finalised but certainly wasn't out of the question in the New Year. At Maria's insistence, Nan remained with the tour as DSM, and as she and her mother inched towards a new understanding of one another, she began to feel, for the first time in her troubled life, some solid ground under her feet. And whilst the critics were lukewarm about Peter Thorn's production in general – *rather conventional... unambitious... not edgy enough* – they were, by contrast, unstinting in their praise of Maria's Hedda – *stunning... breathtaking... a star reborn.*

And yet, despite everything she knew about herself, Maria found that all the praise heaped upon her paled into insignificance against the filling of the hole that had existed in her life for the past two decades. Perhaps that black soul of hers was not totally irredeemable after all.

HELMET

…Helmet enjoyed Mr Dawson reading the newspaper to him each morning; he took a great interest in what was going on in the world, but unfortunately he was unable to express his appreciation because…

Although they had lived together for almost forty years now, it still didn't really seem as though they had much of a relationship. For instance, Mr Dawson had always enjoyed reading the newspaper out loud, and after Mrs Dawson (with whom he certainly did have a relationship) had expressed her determined lack of interest in hearing it, he had transferred his attentions to Helmet, who did enjoy being read to, and took a great interest in what was going on in the world. Unfortunately, Helmet was unable to convey this enthusiasm to Mr Dawson; it was one of the many drawbacks with being a tortoise.

Helmet had already lived in the garden shed for many years; he wasn't sure exactly how many, prior to the Dawsons taking possession of their first, and only, home. Mr Dawson had considered returning the creature to Mr and Mrs Doolan, the former owners of the property, but had then remembered that they had been planning to emigrate to Australia, for the princely sum of ten pounds, he believed, and he felt it would be inhumane to inflict transportation on a guiltless, if inconvenient, tortoise.

Mrs Dawson had tolerated it on the strict understanding that she would have nothing whatsoever to do with it; so it was left to Mr Dawson to feed it, which was, apparently, all that was required. Once their daughter, Amy, was old enough, at the relatively tender age of six, she took over even these modest duties. Mrs Dawson had heard that tortoises lived to be a great age and she wondered how one went about estimating that sort of thing; looking at its teeth perhaps, or the pattern on its shell? She was also highly suspicious of the choice of name, which had been painted in white gloss paint on its shell at some point long ago, but was still just decipherable.

'Sounds a bit German to me,' she had said, with a face that looked as though she had bitten into a chocolate expecting to find a nutty centre but discovered a very disappointing orange cream.

'You will be thinking of the former German Chancellor, Herr Kohl,' suggested Mr Dawson, in a political allusion that merely served to confuse his wife still further.

The newspaper was generally delivered between 8 and 8.30 each morning, except if there had been snow, when it was either late or didn't arrive at all. Mrs Dawson habitually woke up at 8.15 and took her breakfast, in bed, around 8.30. Mrs Dawson took all her meals in bed. Breakfast consisted of four slices of toast, made with thick-cut white sliced – two spread with Marmite and two with Robinson's Golden Shred marmalade – and a large mug of tea. In between Marmite and marmalade, Mrs Dawson switched on her television set, which lived on the chest of drawers at the end of her bed. If she wasn't interested in whatever Richard or Judy were offering at that moment, she would mute the sound and switch to Five Live radio. This was her alternating routine throughout the day; TV, radio, TV, radio.

What she particularly loved was a phone-in, even tuning into Talk Sport on occasions. Much to Mr Dawson's irritation, she frequently referred to the presenters on the radio and television as her family and friends. He refused to point out the obvious, that she actually had family, even if she no longer had many friends.

Amy Dawson was now twenty-seven, very unmarried, worked in a rather grubby local insurance office and visited her parents twice a week, on Tuesdays and Sundays usually. She spent half an hour sitting awkwardly beside her bedridden mother, desperately, and often unsuccessfully, trying to think what to talk about, then a couple more hours with Mr Dawson discussing the state of the world, before returning to the sickroom for a final ten-minute stint. These two hours were the highlight of Mr Dawson's week.

It was, in fact, Amy that suggested the idea of a dog. The Dawsons had never had a dog; they weren't really dog people. Anyway, they already had Helmet, and two pets somehow seemed rather excessive. Looking after Mrs Dawson, or "waiting on Her Ladyship, hand, foot and finger" as he referred to it (strictly to himself), took up much of Mr Dawson's time.

After breakfast came lunch, or dinner as Mrs Dawson insisted on calling it, which alternated between a Sainsbury's Meal for One and a Heinz Big Soup with a small buttered baguette, followed by tinned fruit of some description with custard or ice cream, whilst Mr Dawson usually had a pork pie, or a pasty, or something of that nature, with a large bag of cheese and onion crisps and a bottle of light ale. Tea, or supper as Mr Dawson preferred to say, was always something on toast – beans, scrambled egg, sardines, or if there had been a problem with the shopping, sometimes just Marmite again. This was taken at five o'clock.

Mr Dawson's final trip up to his wife's bedroom was with her ten o'clock milky hot chocolate and a Kit Kat, the four-finger version. Except for these visits, the couple did not see each other unless there were emergencies, which usually happened about three or four times a week, and were never really emergencies anyway.

'A dog would be a bit of company for you, Dad,' Amy had said as she pulled on her anorak to leave. Mr Dawson agreed to think about it, even though he really had no intention of doing so. However, the following morning, after reading the paper to Helmet, and somewhat against his better judgement, he decided to discuss the "dog" suggestion with his tortoise, but despite Helmet having extremely strong views on the matter, Mr Dawson's mind was no clearer afterwards.

When Amy arrived on the Sunday, she presented her father with the address of the local dog rescue service, insisting that a companion would be "just the ticket" for him. It has to be said that Helmet was distinctly unhappy when, two days later, Mr Dawson explained to him why the reading of the newspaper would have to be postponed until that afternoon, as he was visiting the "Dogs' Home" as he called it. Helmet didn't know whether to be alarmed or angry; neither was a natural emotion for a tortoise.

On his initial visit, Mr Dawson was only allowed to look at the dogs, to see if there were any that took his fancy, and to discuss the responsibilities of dog ownership, and that sort of thing. Most of them were far too big; he could see that straight away. He certainly didn't want a big dog, not an Alsation or a Setter or anything like that. He thought something like a Jack Russell might suit him, that sort of size anyway. The girl at the "Dogs' Home" was polite but really rather intimidating; he wondered if she might be one of those lady rugby players that you see in the newspaper occasionally. You certainly wouldn't want to argue with her. Mr Dawson had imagined he would be able to just go down to the compound, pick a dog out and take it home; but it wasn't like that at all. There were countless questions to answer and forms to fill in; you'd have thought he was adopting a child of the aristocracy. In his favour, he stressed, he didn't mind taking an old dog, which seemed to go down well with the girl, and he certainly wasn't worried if it was a mongrel; he'd heard they were less problematic in general.

On his second visit, he spotted a little ginger dog that quite appealed to him; the girl thought it was probably about seven or eight and seemed to have a quiet nature, which pleased Mr Dawson. So after all the necessary paperwork had been completed, he popped the little chap into the back of his car and headed home. When he took up Mrs Dawson's Sainsbury's lunch, Mr Dawson mentioned the dog for the first time; he hadn't wanted to get into an argument about it, so was delighted when his wife didn't seem bothered one way or another.

'Just so long as it doesn't come up here,' she said. 'So what's it called?'

'I thought I'd call him Ginger,' Mr Dawson said.

273

It was, of course, too much to hope that Ginger and Helmet would be friends; they didn't really have much in common, except Mr Dawson, of course. Whilst Ginger thought of Helmet as ancient, which he certainly was, and stupid, which he most certainly was not, Helmet considered Ginger to be intrusive, manipulative and quite possibly flea-ridden. However, they kept their views to themselves and a sort of uneasy truce was established, with the garden shed the undisputed territory of the tortoise, and the rug in front of the sitting room fire the dog's domain.

Flushed with the excitement of trying new things, Mr Dawson decided he would take up smoking a pipe. It was clearly a very unfashionable thing to do, which only added to its appeal, and the whole ritual of loading and lighting, and then constantly having to relight, and then the delight of cleaning out and preparing the bowl for the next pipeful, was simply a joy to him. Not so to Mrs Dawson for whom the upward-drifting smoke presented a cause for the utmost concern.

'If you must engage in these filthy habits,' she declared, 'you will do so in the garden shed. Do I make myself clear, Mr Dawson?'

Mr Dawson wilted, and conceded. Ginger had displayed a disappointing lack of interest in listening to the newspaper being read to him, so Mr Dawson continued to recite the news to his tortoise, with the additional delight, from Helmet's point of view, of the atmosphere in the shed now sweetly scented with rich tobacco.

And so things remained in the Dawson household much as they had been before, but with the novel canine addition.

Mrs Dawson neither improved nor deteriorated, and showed no signs of dissatisfaction with the domestic arrangements. The doctor visited her on a monthly basis, prescribed the same remedies and suggested, rather unhelpfully, that "time would tell", with which it was impossible to argue.

On the afternoon of the third Wednesday of each month, Joyce, from the "Heads Up" hairdresser's on the estate, would come to do Mrs Dawson's hair, and leave with only the faintest blue tinge to show for her efforts. Mr Dawson always felt obliged to offer her a cup of tea, and the enthusiasm with which she invariably replied, 'Oh go on then, if you insist,' suggested to him that the hairdresser had a bit of a soft spot for him. He was careful never to offer her a second cup, lest she misinterpret his motives.

Ginger settled in seamlessly, and despite the "tentative" relationship between dog and tortoise, all remained calm for a number of years, until one evening something took place to shatter that happy state, and threw Mr Dawson into a mental turmoil from which he thought he might never recover.

Supper dispensed, sardines on toast, Mr Dawson sat down in front of his own, slightly superior, television set to watch a football match, with Ginger happily curled up in front of the unlit fire. As the game kicked off, Ginger sat up and repositioned himself with his back against the settee in order to watch the match. This was something that Mr Dawson had noticed on several previous occasions, especially, it seemed, when Tottenham Hotspur were playing. Tonight, the Spurs were pitted against Mr Dawson's own team Crystal Palace in a cup quarter-final. It had been a tense encounter, with neither side ever really gaining the upper hand, and with just five minutes to play, the Palace centre-forward was brought down in the Spurs box.

The home crowd erupted in a chorus of 'Penalty Ref' at which point, to poor Mr Dawson's utter astonishment, Ginger leapt at the screen and shouted, 'No way, Ref – he dived.' Of course, Ginger knew at once what he had done. It was a disaster, a catastrophe, a breaking of the most solemn of all the animal vows – he had spoken "human". Mr Dawson sat in his seat, rigid with fear, whilst Ginger slunk onto his mat, his tail so far between his legs that it disappeared altogether, and his front paw placed on top of his head in a firm act of contrition. And there they remained. The penalty was missed, and the game drifted into extra time without man or dog even noticing. When he eventually returned to his senses, Mr Dawson tried to persuade himself that he had misheard, but, in truth, he knew he had not, and now the genie was out of the bottle, and nothing would ever be the same again.

Time went on; Mrs Dawson went on; Joyce's cups of tea went on. Helmet added a few more years to his grand total, and Ginger…? Well, Ginger tried to pretend nothing had happened, but of course there was no escaping what he'd done. Word got out somehow; it might have been an insect or a moth that had been in the room at the time that started it off, but soon it was common knowledge locally, and once the birds had got hold of the story, there was no stopping it.

Poor Ginger faced the situation stoically, knowing that he would be shunned wherever he went. Even Mr Dawson could hardly bring himself to look at the dog for fear of reviving that terrible moment. It was only Helmet who showed the poor beast any charity. Helmet, who had once been so antagonistic in his attitude towards Ginger, now became his only friend. But despite Helmet's best efforts, Ginger went into a slow decline; his fur turned grey, his limbs stiffened and his heart faltered.

It was a silly habit of Mr Dawson's, he knew, but it was one that he still kept up; he always left a ginger biscuit on the dog's bed before he retired for the night and, unsurprisingly, it would always be gone in the morning. So when, on a sunny April morning, Mr Dawson came down the stairs to see the dog curled up in his basket, with the ginger biscuit still untouched, he knew it was over.

Later that morning when he went out to the shed to read Helmet the newspaper, he gave the tortoise the sad news, and when he had pondered it for a while, the ancient creature, in a soft, husky voice that he trusted Mr Dawson wouldn't hear, whispered, 'Cheerio, Ginger.'

THE RAISING
OF LAZARUS

Nobody believes in miracles these days,
not until they happen to you, that is

'We'll be closing in about five minutes, sir.' The tall gallery attendant loomed over him as he sat on the battered leather bench in front of the painting. He really wasn't sure how long he'd been sitting there, in a sort of daydream, with Monteverdi's *Vespers* floating through his brain and this extraordinary unsigned painting of *The Raising of Lazarus* transporting him onto some... some higher plain. If he thought about it in those terms, it would all sound rather pretentious, but he couldn't deny how he felt; indeed, he didn't want to. He gathered up his bits and pieces – his notebook and pencil, a chocolate bar wrapper and the exhibition catalogue – stood up, gave a nodding 'thank you' to the attendant, though he wasn't quite sure what for, and made his way towards the entrance. He resolved to return, tomorrow if possible, as he had unfinished business with this work of art.

Franco Alberti had opened his little gallery in Milan some ten years earlier. It was a project to keep him out of mischief since he had retired, and it was his wife Sophia's idea, so it had to be a good one. Franco, now silver-maned but still dapper, had made his money, and a great deal of it, in cars; not new cars, of course, the competition was far too great on that forecourt, but in vintage cars – Ferraris, Lamborghinis, even the occasional Aston Martin. They always cost him a small fortune to buy, but then if you could double their price to resell to the right buyer at the right moment, that was the trick. He had caught a cold on one or two occasions, usually because he had been over-sentimental about a particular model, but as a rule it had worked out well, and although he wasn't a man who wore his bank balance on his sleeve, everyone knew he had made millions of Euros over the years.

He had spent his money on living well, on spoiling Sophia and on paintings – hundreds of paintings. He still remembered the moment his particular passion for collecting began, standing in the Galleria Massimo De Carlo in Milan, in front of two paintings of the Madonna and Child, enthralled by the richness of the paint and the tenderness of the subject treatment. Both paintings seemed to him a wonderful expression of man's achievement through art. A small, round man in a pinstriped suit and very shiny shoes turned to him, without invitation, and asked, 'What do you think the difference is between these two paintings?'

Franco had no idea how to answer the question; he thought them both exquisite.

'I'll tell you,' said the man. 'Two million Euros.'

'Really?' Franco was astonished. 'But why?'

The little man pointed to the bottom right-hand corner of one of the paintings.

'That's why,' he said.

And so began Franco's incredible collection of unattributed paintings. The little man's name was Giacomo Marconi, the assistant curator of the Galleria Massimo, and what he didn't know about Italian religious painting really wasn't worth knowing. He became first a friend of Franco, then his purchasing agent and finally the first director of the Alberti Gallery, a small but beautiful space, dedicated to some of the finest unattributed Italian paintings in Italy, and each and every one of them belonging to Franco Alberti. There was no entrance charge to visit his gallery, but always a charity box at the exit, collecting for some arts organisation or another. Franco didn't need any income to support his hobby, and he was convinced that people were always more generous if they chose to donate freely.

It was only a short walk from the Alberti Gallery to the Instituto Sacerdotale Maria Immacolata, where Pius XI, Pope from 1922 until 1939, had trained as a priest, but Sergio Orlandi was in no great rush to get there. His poor brain was in turmoil; an ecstasy of delight and an agony doubt at the same time. Sergio had decided that he was going to become a priest when he was fourteen years old, and he had been in a state of perpetual doubt ever since. Fr Alessandro, the novice Master at the seminary, had told him the year he arrived at the college that doubt was a gift, and that doubters invariably made the finest priests; it had seemed glib to him even then, but now it felt more like cruelty.

It was not as though Sergio had lost his desire to serve God and his fellow man, rather that he had lost the conviction that Holy Orders was the best way for him to do this, so he constantly looked for some sort of sign from God, not really believing that one would ever come. It was only in art, and in religious paintings in particular, that he did

283

discover some answers, a kind of truth within himself. It was possible, somehow, for him to immerse himself in the spirit of a painting far more easily than in a theological text or even, though he barely dared say it, in the Scriptures themselves. Had he been an artist himself... but he had not.

The Raising of Lazarus , probably by a contemporary of Giotto, in the Alberti, had had a particularly profound effect on him; the bewilderment of the man brought back to life, the unspeakable joy of his mother, and the extraordinary reticence of the figure of Christ himself, standing to one side, almost like a spectator at the miracle. For Sergio, faith was a practical matter, not an abstract one, and whether or not you believed in the historical truth of events, such as miraculous cures, or walking on water, didn't ultimately matter; it was how people's lives were actually affected that concerned him.

It was two more days before Sergio was able to return to the gallery, but when he got there... the painting was gone.

It had been another one of Sophia's ideas; she was always having them. She knew how much her husband loved his paintings, perhaps even more than he had loved his old cars, but he wasn't good at ideas. That was her speciality. Franco had accumulated some 300 paintings over the years, but the gallery could only ever display thirty-five to forty at one time.

'Why not lend some out?' she had suggested in a moment of inspiration. 'To places where they never get to see such wonderful works of art.' She was very pleased with this idea, and her little sapphire blue eyes glinted in her pink marshmallow face.

'Could we do such a thing?' Franco asked his director.

'It's possible, I suppose,' Giacomo had replied hesitantly. 'It would need to be very carefully planned.'

'Tiny churches in remote rural villages,' Sophia suggested excitedly, 'or run-down churches in city slums.'

The idea was growing on Franco. A whole new audience for his beloved collection. If the practicalities could be arranged, and the paintings properly protected, then he liked his wife's suggestion very much indeed; in fact, he thought it was brilliant.

The scheme had started off slowly, just a couple of paintings lent to local churches, but it got the ball rolling. Within one year, Franco had specially employed a young man, fresh from completing a degree in Fine Arts at the city's university, to arrange a programme of loans to forty-five modest venues, mostly churches, all within one hundred kilometres of Milan. Typically, a loan consisted of three or four paintings, on a related theme ideally, and for a period of a month at a time. Venues were not allowed to charge people to see the paintings, but a voluntary contribution to a charity was permitted. *The Raising of Lazarus* with two other miracle paintings, had been loaned to the church of the Sacra Famiglia, in the Vaiano Valle, one of the most deprived slum areas in Milan.

It had taken considerable persuasion, and certain liberties with the truth, before Sergio Orlandi was granted special permission to visit Vaiano Valle, ostensibly to gain more experience working with marginalised groups, Romany families in this case, because that was the area of mission that especially interested him. He failed to mention the painting to Fr Alessandro, feeling it might compromise their relationship. Even the tall attendant at the Alberti Gallery who had informed Sergio of the whereabouts of the painting was unaware that the inquisitive seminarian would be following the artwork to its insalubrious new location.

Without seeing it for yourself, it is difficult to imagine the wretchedness in which the inhabitants of the Vaiano Valle existed. Most of the housing lacked even basic sanitation or heating; in fact, if a property was weatherproof at all, it was a miracle. Men without jobs or hope or self-respect lounged around in makeshift bars, playing cards and watching football whenever it was on the stolen television. The scrawny women attempted to keep a semblance of normal life going; preparing pauper meals, washing ragged clothes and simply surviving in their barely habitable homes. The barefoot children roamed the streets, semi-feral, uneducated, unwashed, but not unloved. It was like a scene from Dante, and it shook Sergio to his core; a fifteen-minute drive in his old Fiat and he could be in the centre of fashionable, sophisticated, affluent Milan. How in God's name was such iniquity possible?

The Sacra Famiglia had been a fine building in its day, but that was more than a century ago now, and its Rococo facade had never been repaired after the damage inflicted on it by Allied bombers during a raid in 1943. Its cracked bell still rang out discordantly at 8.20 each Sunday morning, summoning the few dozen middle-aged and elderly women who now constituted the church's congregation, to the one mass celebrated each week by Fr Paulo Capaldi, Papa Paulo as he was universally called.

Instead of religious services, the church offered food to the hungry, shelter to the destitute, care for the sick and dying, and a refuge for the battered, abused and suicidal. It was not a small job description for Papa Paulo, now in his eighty-second year, having first arrived in the parish as a newly ordained and innocent curate at the age of twenty-eight. In the intervening half-century or so, he had hardly left the place, except to attend the funerals of his close relatives. He worked all the hours God sent him, from Sunday morning to Saturday night, and whilst he still had the heart of a lion, his old bones increasingly objected to carrying him around his extensive domain. The completely unexpected arrival of Sergio Orlando was, quite literally, the answer to his prayers.

The three paintings were placed, on their custom-made easels, in what had once been the Lady Chapel, to the south of the main aisle. The Lazarus painting in the centre was flanked by the *Marriage Feast at Cana* and the *Woman with Palsy*. The small altar area where they stood was roped off, but visitors could still get to within two metres of the works, and despite initial concerns about the safety of the treasures, the exhibition had been treated with the utmost reverence and respect. At first, the arrival of such beautiful objects in this unlikeliest of settings had caused little, if any, interest amongst the local inhabitants. A few of the regular mass-goers were joined by an assortment of curious agnostics and some children hoping, forlornly, for a bit of excitement. But once Papa Paulo announced that a little pilgrimage might be rewarded with some refreshments – a bowl of pasta perhaps or a small glass of beer – then numbers picked up dramatically. A dribble turned into a trickle and then a stream, albeit a spasmodic one. Old men stood in front of the paintings with tears in their eyes; old women, with rosary beads wrapped tightly around their gnarled knuckles, descended painfully to their knees, reaching out to touch even the frame of a painting and then crossing themselves repeatedly; children asked endless questions about the stories depicted, whilst young mothers, with babies in arms, took the opportunity to sit quietly in a pew and rest. And whilst all this was taking place in the ancient church, Sergio, now renamed Baba Paulo, despite his protestations, was accompanying the old priest around his wider congregation, on a strictly secular, perpetual mission of mercy. He witnessed deadly drunken fights and tender reconciliations; painful deaths and unwelcome births; unimaginable suffering and inspiring courage; and above all else, he witnessed humanity in the raw, people with nothing, clinging to life as if they really understood its divine value. If he stopped to think about it, Sergio could not imagine how he was going to return to the seminary and his life before Vaiano Valle.

It was three days before he was due to leave that Sergio fell ill. Unbeknown to him at the time, Papa Paulo had also contracted what the locals called "slum fever", and both men were confined to their beds with an illness that claimed the lives of as many as it spared. Once, there had been a doctor who served this blighted community, but not for many years now, so some of the older women, Gypsies often, assumed the task of comforting the afflicted as best they could, with herbs and poultices and distinctly unchristian incantations.

Maria Fellini seemed as ancient as the church itself, but as a girl she had served the young Paulo Capaldi when he first arrived in the parish, and she sat now, beside his bed, pressing cool clothes on his beloved forehead as his temperature raged and his remaining strength slowly ebbed away. In the next room lay Sergio, and it was as though the fires of hell were consuming him as he thrashed around, crying out deliriously, his eyes rolling and his mouth foaming. In brief moments, from time to time, his mind would clear, like breaks in the clouds on a stormy day, and then he noticed beside him the figure of a child, with wild, matted black hair, and huge melancholy brown eyes, but a body so emaciated that the sick man couldn't tell if it was a boy or girl, and the child was offering him a mug of water to quench his flames. And at the end of his bed he saw that they had placed the painting of Lazarus, as though to watch over him.

For three days and nights, his fever raged unabated, and each time his mind cleared momentarily, he would notice the painting watching him. And then on the fourth morning, the fever left him. When he opened his eyes, he saw the child of his ordeal, laid across his bed, asleep, so he closed his eyes and slept again. When he woke for the second time, the child was sat up beside him, smiling, and it was then that Sergio noticed that the painting had been removed.

'Did Papa Paulo take the painting back to the church?' he asked.

'Papa Paulo has been called to God,' the child replied.

'Called to God?' There was both fear and horror in Sergio's voice.

'Two days ago, Baba Paulo,' said the child. 'So now you will be... the new Papa Paulo.'

Sergio's mind was struggling to understand.

'So you mean... Papa Paulo has died?'

'God called him,' said the child, 'so he had to go.'

'But then who moved the painting?' Sergio asked again.

'The men from the gallery came,' said the child, 'and they took the pictures from the church.'

'Not from this room?' Sergio asked.

'From the church,' the child repeated.

'But when... when did they take my painting?'

'They took it four days ago, Papa.'

ATISHOO! ATISHOO!

...romance for starters, then cloak and dagger with a side serving of chess were all on the menu at the Lyons Corner House, Tottenham Court Road

T he threateningly elegant wood-panelled room smelt of polish and fear. The large hand on the elaborate Art Nouveau clock jumped on another minute. The unsmiling secretary, perched at her desk in the far corner of the room next to the enormous double doors, dressed in her navy blue suit, with starched white blouse and a handsome oval broach at its collar, peered over her spectacles at the four remaining applicants almost as if to say, *Haven't you girls got homes to go to?* Dorothy Foster, "Dot" to her family, "Dolly" to her friends, was beginning to regret ever seeing the advertisement, let alone answering it, but her mother had been adamant.

'It'd be perfect for you, our Dot; just the ticket.'

'I'm not sure, Mum,' Dolly had pleaded.

'Nonsense, my girl, they'll be lucky to have you. Isn't that right, Father?'

'Waiting on tables? And for a lot of snobs, I dare say.' Charlie, having looked up briefly, reburied his face in the *Daily Herald*.

'Well, I think it's a wonderful opportunity for her. And you know what they say, Father, at least half the Nippys end up marrying one of their customers.'

Dolly relived the moment when she had opened the letter offering her the interview; she could hardly believe it at the time, but now… the large hand clicked on again, and suddenly the great doors opened, and a young woman, who had, barely fifteen minutes earlier, entered the fray with such apparent confidence, now emerged battle-scarred and utterly defeated, or so it seemed to Dolly.

'Gillian Protheroe?' barked the gorgon, and the slim, mousey girl beside Dolly rose nervously to her feet, smoothed down her gabardine skirt, and with a deep breath and a brave smile set off for her "chance of a lifetime" as the advert had described it. Dolly was next; there was still time to back out; make a run for it; tell her mum that she had done her best but they had said… she was a bit too tall. She was seriously contemplating this course of action when the doors suddenly burst open again. "Mousey" had only been in there five minutes, but the merest shrug of her shoulders and a sad smile on her way out said it all.

Sod 'em, thought Dolly. *They won't do that to me,* and she lifted her chin, pulled back her shoulders and was halfway to the great doors before the fearsome secretary had even had time to call her name.

Twenty-five minutes later, Dorothy Foster strode back through those mighty doors, feeling six inches taller and ready to take on the world. She was now employed by the largest restaurant in the world. She was a Nippy at Lyons Corner House in Tottenham Court Road.

The tour had not been a success. It was the combination of an unusually early rainy season in the Punjab, rendering open-air performances almost impossible (and it was these performances, attracting huge crowds, happy to part with their Rupees in exchange for a slice of British culture, that paid the bills), together with an almost permanent list of company members down with one "exotic" ailment or another, and the increasingly hysterical rumours of imminent war in Europe, that had, finally, decided Barty (aka Sir Bartholomew Bancroft) to curtail what would be his final tour of India and take ship for Southampton. There would then just be time for one more short tour, to South Africa and Rhodesia, before Hitler would put an end to the theatrical globetrotting of the Imperial Theatre Company and its sadly predictable offerings of "*The Greatest Plays Ever Written*" or "Shakespeare for the great unwashed", as one rather acerbic Delhi critic had once described it.

The last performance was of *Measure for Measure*. A problem play at the best of times, but with all three of his leading ladies "indisposed", Barty had been forced to turn to Florence, his wife, to assume the role of Isabella, an undertaking clearly beyond her capabilities. Florence had been exceptionally pretty when young, and this had been sufficient to get her minor roles, typically in light comedies; she had even been in one or two things by a fledging Noel Coward. Her high cheekbones, startling blue eyes and captivating smile had also been enough to bewitch the young Barty, who had made it his mission to transform her into an acclaimed leading lady, the "jewel" in the Imperial Theatre Company's crown. Alas, it was not to be, and Florence, after an embarrassingly high number of woeful performances – her Cleopatra was especially cringeworthy – abandoned the footlights to occupy a happier role as Company Stage Manager, only standing in for absent actresses on the rarest of occasions, and even then under extreme duress.

Sebastian, the youngest of the Bancrofts' three sons, had recently finished at Cambridge, where he had gained his expected First, though in History not Classics as his father would have preferred, sat and sailed through the Civil Service exams and was waiting to take up a position in the Ministry of Labour. At a loose end for a couple of months, Sebastian had agreed to join the company bound for the subcontinent as a jobbing actor/technician/general dogsbody. His acting experience, for what it was worth, was limited to school and university roles, but suddenly his father was asking him to take on the part of Angelo, playing opposite his mother – "scraping the barrel" almost flattered him. It was to provide an ignominious conclusion to a less-than-triumphant tour.

You only ever see these scenes played out on the silver screen, not in real life, but when Sebastian Bancroft, recently returned to London, walked into Lyons Corner House on the Tottenham Court Road on Dolly's first full day, it was... well... you know what.

The novice Nippy had spent the previous three days preparing for her launch. She had had her uniform fitted – starched white cap worn to just above the eyebrows, with a large red "L" embroidered in the centre of her forehead; tailored black dress to just below the knee, with two neat rows of pearl buttons down the front, sewn on with red thread; a pristine white apron tied at dropped waist height; detachable white cuffs and collar; black stockings and sensible black shoes. She had been instructed in how to address customers, especially difficult ones; how to carry, load and unload a tray with grace and efficiency; how to add up a customer's bill in her head (this had been an area where Dolly had shone at her interview, mental arithmetic being a particular hobby of hers) and, most importantly of all, how to commit to memory the entire menu, together with any additional information that might be useful when engaging with a customer.

She had received instruction in personal hygiene, tidiness, hairstyling (bobs were the company's preferred choice) and, crucially and not forgetting, hand and nail care. Make-up was not permitted. She was prepared for anything... well, almost anything. Despite his ever-growing ardour, it had taken Sebastian four trips to Tottenham Court Road, on consecutive days, before he managed to pluck up the courage to ask Dolly for anything other than a pot of tea and a Swiss bun, even though the love-struck Nippy had ruthlessly contrived to be his waitress on each occasion.

'I don't suppose...' the poor lad stuttered nervously '...you'd fancy going to the pictures sometime... with me, I mean?'

There was a brief pause.

'Sounds lovely,' replied Dolly, almost as tongue-tied as her suitor.

'Really?' Sebastian was trembling with excitement.

'I loves goin' to the flicks.' Dolly looked around furtively to check no one was watching. Fraternising with customers was strictly forbidden.

'Do you?' was all Sebastian managed to stutter out.

A pregnant pause.

'Gosh... right then... how about tomorrow evening?'

'Sounds lovely,' repeated Dolly. 'I finish at five thirty.'

'I'll pick you up at five thirty then,' said Sebastian.

Another pause.

'So… what's on?' asked Dolly, casually.

'Umm… not sure.' Sebastian hadn't really expected her to agree to his request, and suddenly he felt hopelessly unprepared.

'That's fine,' said Dolly. 'I'm not fussy.'

'How wonderful,' said Sebastian. 'Pick you up at five thirty then.'

'Five thirty,' confirmed Dolly.

'Right,' said Sebastian as he stood up to leave, knocking his chair over backwards in the process.

He was halfway to the door when he suddenly turned, hurrying back to his table, which Dolly was still in the process of clearing.

'Sorry,' he said, 'I… don't know your name.'

'Dorothy,' she said. 'No, Dot… Dolly… everyone calls me Dolly.'

'Wonderful. See you tomorrow then… Dolly,' and he turned again.

'What about you?'

'Me?'

'Your name?'

'Oh, yes, of course. I'm Sebastian. Everyone calls me… well… Sebastian.'

From the smile on the young man's face, you'd have thought he'd come up on the horses.

As for Dolly… well, it had simply been the most thrilling day of her life… so far.

Six months, twenty-three feature films, numerous dances – Dolly loved the Roy Fox band, and Jack Hilton, and Joe Loss for a bit of the old Latin American; all of them, in fact

– dozens of walks around Hyde Park and God knows how many cups of tea and Swiss buns (what was it with Sebastian and Swiss buns?) later, and the Nippy and her beau were still going strong. But they came from such utterly different worlds, and they knew it. Neither of their families, and probably none of their friends, would approve, so they kept a low profile and revelled in the conspiratorial nature of their relationship.

Dolly soon found her feet at the Corner House; charming with the customers and even better with the figures, whether it was cashing up at the end of the day, or estimating orders, or assessing discounts for party rates, it just came so easily to her, and her talent did not go unnoticed. Sebastian's position at the Ministry appeared to be pretty straightforward, but what he couldn't tell anyone, not Dolly, not even his parents, was that his role as a civil servant was just a cover, and his real job, for which he had been recruited even before leaving university, was far more interesting and about to become infinitely more important. One day, the couple may have to brave the glare of public disapproval, but not just yet.

It had been one of those strange quirks of fate that Sir Joseph Lyon had happened to sit in on Dolly's initial interview as a Nippy. He did that sort of thing from time to time, just to keep in touch with the "factory floor" as he called it, and he remembered Dolly. She had been quick and positive and a bit feisty, and he liked that, so he had made a mental note of the name – Dorothy Foster. Once war broke out, as a leading industrialist, Sir Joseph, or Uncle Joe as the Lyons people called him (not to be confused with the Stalin version), was approached by the Government to see what contribution he might make to the war effort.

By this time, Lyons was the largest food manufacturer in Europe, employing tens of thousands of workers in numerous areas of the economy, not just the hospitality sector.

Over the months that followed, Lyons began to redirect their production into providing rations for the troops on an enormous scale, as well as reassigning a good deal of their factory capacity into producing armaments of various sorts. This vital involvement brought Sir Joe into close contact with several senior government figures, and he got to know Sir Stewart Menzies pretty well; they were both members of the Athenaeum. Menzies had just been appointed head of SIS, later known as MI6, a post he held right up to 1952, and the two knights would often chat matters over long into the early hours, slumped in the well-worn leather Chesterfields of the club, with a brandy goblet in one hand and a fine Havana in the other.

It was during one such late-night conversation that Sir Joe mentioned a rather interesting girl, working for him in Tottenham Court Road, that he had been keeping a close eye on because she clearly had an exceptional gift for numbers and he knew that "the Service" was always on the lookout for suitable candidates. Nothing more was said about it, but Sir Stewart noted the name and did have someone run the usual background checks on the girl, just in case she might prove useful.

When the Blitz started, in September 1940, Barty and Florence moved out of their Richmond house, heading down to what seemed to be the relative safety of Devon. They had frequently holidayed in Torquay so knew the area well, and as they were both highly sociable creatures, they quickly became assimilated into the local community. Indeed, it wasn't long before the old thespian was arranging entertainment for the returning wounded soldiers, sailors and airmen being treated at the military hospital in Exeter, whilst Florence threw herself into fundraising for the Red Cross.

The Richmond house was handed over to the Army for the billeting of officers who needed to be in London for one reason or another. This meant, of course, that Sebastian had to move out, so he rented a rather nice, if small, flat overlooking Regent's Park. Dolly and he spent as much time there together as they could, though she never stayed the night. It was tastefully furnished in the Art Deco style, with fun prints of the great silent movie stars – Pickford, Bow, Fairbanks, and so on – decorating the sitting-room walls. But the thing that Dolly liked most was Sebastian's stunning modern chess set, which took pride of place on the sleek walnut sideboard.

'It's an original Bauhaus 1922 set,' Sebastian told her.

'But does anybody ever play with it?' she asked once, at which Sebastian dramatically feigned hurt.

'I'll have you know I was Haberdasher's school champion two years in a row, *and* I was captain of my college chess team,' he boasted. 'This was the set I learnt on.'

'Could you teach me to play?' Dolly had no idea what she was asking.

'I suppose I could show you how the various pieces move,' he offered, rather patronisingly. 'But it takes years to learn to play seriously.'

Well, it took Dolly about two months to get up to Sebastian's standard, after which he really struggled to give her a decent game. He should have minded, but he really didn't.

As the war dragged on, the couple fell into a sort of irregular routine. Sebastian was frequently away from London; sometimes for a few days, other times for weeks on end. He never said where he was going, or why, and on his return he would always take a few days to get himself together before contacting Dolly. After eighteen months at the Corner House, Dolly was unexpectedly asked to attend an interview at an obscure office in Whitehall. She started work at Bletchley Park exactly a week later, so now, though they never said it, they at least had the Official Secrets Act in common.

Then one Saturday evening in late April 1941, completely out of the blue, Sebastian suggested they go down to Devon the following weekend, to meet his parents.

'But they don't even know I exist, do they?' Dolly was completely taken aback.

They were sitting on the small sofa together, and Sebastian took Dolly's hand. 'It's about time they did, isn't it?' he said, and in a tone which suggested the question was actually rhetorical.

'But are you going to warn them, Sebastian? What if they don't like me? What if...' she tailed off, confused, bewildered and if she actually thought about it... distinctly scared.

'It'll be fine, Dolly, they'll love you... honestly.'

Dolly wished she could be so sure.

His parents were at Exeter train station to greet their favourite son, and this mystery girlfriend of his. Sebastian had phoned them up on the Friday to warn them that he was coming... and that he would be bringing the girl he hoped would, one day, be another Mrs Bancroft. Barty had always been a sucker for a pretty face, so as soon as he laid eyes on Dolly he was smitten. As she walked through the turnstile, the old man enfolded her in an embrace as if she were his own long-lost daughter. Florence was equally warm in her welcome, if rather less demonstrative, and the four of them had a marvellous weekend of sitting around talking and laughing and walking along the promenade with Monty, the newly acquired spaniel, to say nothing of eating their way through about a month's worth of rations – Florence was an unexpectedly good cook.

By Sunday afternoon, Dolly really felt as though she was a proper member of the Bancroft family. Did this mean that she now had to introduce Sebastian to her own parents? She turned cold at the mere thought of it.

'Told you,' said Sebastian as they pulled out of the station. 'They absolutely loved you.'

He couldn't work out why they hadn't done it ages ago.

Henri le Clerc shone his torch on the rickety old ladder that led to the hay loft.

'You will be fine up there,' he said, and Sebastian nodded. 'And there is a hatch at the far end if you did need it... but you won't, I'm sure.' He waited until the Englishman had reached the platform. 'Good night. I'll see you in the morning.'

Sebastian had been in France for five days already, and he really needed to make contact with the Resistance group west of Paris in order to report back to London on the situation. He only had two more days before the rendezvous with his rescue boat outside Calais.

It was Friday and Dolly hadn't heard from Sebastian, so she assumed she wouldn't be seeing him at the weekend. She had already decided to grasp the nettle and tell her parents about the public school boy and Cambridge graduate with the dodgy job whom she was going out with. She didn't have to guess at her father's reaction, but she hoped that her mum at least might be a bit more understanding. They had been funny about her new job when she had left Lyons, especially since she was now living away during the week; this new revelation might just be a bit too much for them.

'But you were so happy as a Nippy,' her mum had said, and it was true. How could she hope to explain her new situation to them?

A squadron of German bombers were approaching the Kent coast; their target, as usual was London.

It was the shouting that woke Sebastian. He crawled to the edge of the platform and peered over, but it was too dark to see anything. Suddenly, amid all the German voices, he heard Henri… demanding to know what they wanted… pleading his ignorance… he was shouting at the top of his voice, clearly desperate to warn Sebastian. Scrambling back to the far end of the platform, he found the hatch, but it was jammed solid; it can't have been opened for years. He clawed at the edge, but it wouldn't budge as orders, shouted in German, seemed to surround the barn. He felt around in the gloom, and almost miraculously his hand discovered something hard, metal, the broken-off end of a scythe or something like it. He managed to work it into the slit between the trap and the frame and using all his strength, he was finally able to move the lid fractionally, then a bit more, till eventually the lid sprung up and he could swing the trap open. There was a drop of about fifteen feet into total darkness, but Sebastian didn't stop to think. As he landed on the soft ground with a painful thud, a brilliant light dazzled him momentarily, and an order was shouted.

Hansi Muller was nineteen, and this was his first bombing mission. He had joined the Luftwaffe on his birthday, and he was both proud and excited to be serving the Führer. He was piloting a Heinkel He 177 Greif, in a squadron of twenty-six planes, and this being his maiden raid, he was flying on the outer edge of the formation, which was generally considered to be a safer position; however, it did have the occasional disadvantage of dislocation from the main body of the flight during bad weather.

As they approached their target area, the German planes ran into dense low cloud, any pilot's nightmare, and almost without warning, Hansi found he had lost contact with the squadron. Panic suddenly overwhelmed the young man. He banked his aircraft steeply to see if he could regain visual contact, at which precise moment his plane was fatally hit by a stream of anti-aircraft fire from the ground. His last act was to release his entire payload of deadly Minol bombs; what else could he do?

With her mum and dad and two elderly neighbours from next door, Dolly was last into the flimsy air raid shelter that Charlie had built almost two years before. It was a cloudy night, so the Ack Ack gunners were simply firing blind into the sky in the hope that they might hit something, though it would be more by luck than judgement. Before she closed the shelter door, Dolly looked up briefly to see the firework display of tracers disappearing into the sky. After a while, the sound of aircraft engines started to fade, and the little group gave a collective sigh of relief. They were just waiting for the "all-clear" when the small rear garden of the Fosters' humble terraced house in Clapham took a massive direct hit.

All fall down.

THE HERO

…what had young Charlie been up to in the old abandoned rectory, and what had it to do with the disappearance of Tilly Laidlaw?

The dried tears left streaks down the small boy's dirty face. His head was bowed as he examined the toes of his birthday trainers, one resting awkwardly on top of the other. The elbows of his sweatshirt and the knees of his jeans were stained with mud. He was a forlorn little figure. The large hand that had a firm grip on his left shoulder, as he stood reluctantly on his own front doorstep, belonged to PC Wilkinson, and the lady standing in front of them was the boy's distressed mother, Marilyn Burrows.

'Been up to mischief again, I'm afraid, Marilyn.' P C Wilkinson called her Marilyn because she was his sister.

'A stern talking-to, that's what the lad needs,' was the policeman's advice. 'And maybe a bit more than just words,' he added for good measure.

'Thanks, George,' said Marilyn. 'His father will deal with him when he gets home.'

Fat lot of good that'll do, thought George to himself.

'Just make sure he does, will you,' said the constable, cuffing the boy round the ears, sending him stumbling unexpectedly into the hall.

After a prolonged description of what had gone on, PC Wilkinson drained his mug of tea, and his sister accompanied him back to the front door.

'He might not get off so lightly next time,' was his departing threat as he trudged back down the garden path.

'What were you up to, Charlie?' asked the boy's mother, once they were back in the kitchen.

'Nothing,' said Charlie. 'Just messing about.'

'Just messing about? What were you doing messing about in the Old Rectory? You know you shouldn't be in there.'

'I was just exploring,' Charlie said, 'and no one lives there, do they?'

'That's not the point, Charlie. You shouldn't have been there, should you? How did you get in anyway?'

'There was a window open at the back, Mum, honest, so I just climbed in, for fun.'

'And then you lit a fire inside, just for fun, did you, Charlie?'

'Only a little one,' Charlie said sheepishly. 'In the grate. It wasn't dangerous or anything.'

'And then why did you run off like that,' his mother asked, 'when your Uncle George saw you through the window? He said when he shouted to you, you charged out the back and through the churchyard like a madman.'

'No, I didn't,' said Charlie.

'And it took him best part of ten minutes to catch up with you. So what was that all about, Charlie?'

'Nothing,' said Charlie. 'I… must've panicked, I think.'

It wasn't a very convincing answer.

Tilly Laidlaw was a strange little girl; everybody knew that. Mr and Mrs Laidlaw weren't exactly pillars of the community, that was true, but people felt they had their hands full with Tilly, whose behaviour was… well… erratic, to say the least. And now she had disappeared… or run away again, most likely; that's what people were saying. She had gone off before, of course, stayed out all night once and was picked up five miles away at a coach station with a ticket for Glasgow in her coat pocket. The thing was, Tilly wasn't stupid, not by a long way.

At school, Brentfield Primary, she was very nearly top of her class, but that didn't stop her being the naughtiest girl in the school, and Miss Stockwell, the Headmistress, was at a loss to know what to do next with her wayward pupil. Despite numerous warnings, Tilly was always getting into fights, sometimes with other girls, but mostly with the boys, who teased her a lot, and, it has to be said, frequently regretted it afterwards. She was always a mass of bruises.

Mr Laidlaw was a lorry driver; a burly chap who you wouldn't want to argue with, and it was generally thought that he had done his best to discipline his daughter – perhaps even to the point of being over-strict. Miss Stockwell had thought so on occasions.

Tilly's mother worked at the local supermarket, often doing evening shifts, so if her husband was away on one of his – slightly suspicious – long distance jobs, Tilly was regularly left at home on her own until quite late at night. When Miss Stockwell discovered this, she confronted the parents, who promised to rectify the situation but, unsurprisingly, never did.

When the Headmistress asked Tilly herself about it, she was astonished by the girl's response…

'It's not a problem, Miss, honest,' she had said. 'I prefer it, actually, Miss.'

And now Tilly had done a runner again, and she had been gone for over twenty-four hours.

The Burrows had two sheds at the end of their large garden, which backed onto farm land. A rather smart large new shed which they had only acquired a year ago, and the original, rather dilapidated, one that came with the house when they bought it. They had moved all the garden equipment and anything useful into the new one, and Mr Burrows had promised his wife that he would dismantle the old one and burn it, with the rubbish it still contained, as soon as he had a free moment. That was about five or six months ago now.

Charlie was pleased that the old shed was still there because he used it as his secret den; he knew his mum was never going to go in there, because she thought it had rats in it, and his dad… well, it would probably be years before he ever got round to knocking it down.

When his dad got home, the evening of the Old Rectory incident, his mum explained to him what Charlie had been up to, and said he should "have words" with his son. This wasn't something that came naturally to Mr Burrows; he generally left dealing with Charlie to his wife, but he made an attempt at being the stern father, with Marilyn standing behind him giving him a poke now and then. Charlie looked appropriately contrite and promised not to do it again. After supper, he went out to his den; he had things to deal with.

Mr Baxter's shop simply wasn't big enough for all the things he wanted to sell, not since his wife had requisitioned the back room of the shop to become their new kitchen. It was all part of her grand design to "remodel" their living quarters since the arrival of the new baby. It was a general store, so he needed to offer a bit of everything, which now entailed spilling out of the shop proper onto the pavement. It had been necessary to obtain council permission to do this and, if he was honest about it, Mr Baxter was not all that happy about his merchandise being out of his sight, so when he started to suspect that some things were disappearing from his pavement display, his anxiety seemed justified. It was mostly his fruit and veg on display outside, but he had also located his fresh bread racks in the doorway, in an attempt to lure in customers with the delicious smells. It was the disappearance of a bunch of bananas and a French stick that Mr Baxter noticed first, and he reported the matter to PC Wilkinson on the day that the constable was making door-to-door enquiries about a missing girl.

It took all of Charlie's courage to stand outside Miss Stockwell's office after school, with his speech prepared and his fingers firmly crossed. He had had to go to the toilet three times.

'It's about Tilly, Miss Stockwell,' he managed to blurt out, before terror silenced him.

'Tilly, Charlie? What about Tilly?' asked the Headmistress, in a firm but friendly voice.

'It's just... it's just...' He had completely forgotten his speech.

'Do you know where Tilly is, Charlie?' asked Miss Stockwell.

'Noooo,' said Charlie. He obviously didn't realise that he was the world's worst liar.

'You must tell me the truth, Charlie,' she said, sounding very serious.

'Honest, Miss Stockwell,' he said. He wished now he had never come to see her.

'Well, what did you want to tell me about Tilly then, Charlie?' asked Miss Stockwell, more sympathetically this time.

'I don't know... I've forgotten, Miss,' whimpered Charlie, almost under his breath.

'Charlie,' she questioned, 'is that the truth?'

At which point, blind panic took over and Charlie darted for the door and, after a fleeting glance back over his shoulder, to see if the Headmistress was going to follow him, he fled from her office.

'You'll be safe in here,' Charlie said, and Tilly nodded, unconvinced. It had been a close shave in the Old Rectory. He hadn't realised that Tilly was in there at first, but when he discovered her curled up in the corner of the hall, and she had obviously been crying, he realised that it was a serious situation, and maybe he had to do something about it.

'I'm not going back,' Tilly kept saying. 'They can't make me.'

Charlie really didn't know what to say, so he just sat down beside her and listened.

'I won't go home, I won't,' she said. 'Whatever they try to do, I won't go.'

It took Tilly a while to explain it all to Charlie. They didn't really even know each other very well, so it seemed a bit strange for her to be talking to him like this, but he was happy to listen anyway. By the time Tilly had run out of things to say, Charlie was completely amazed. He had no idea that adults would behave so badly, or that parents could be so unkind to their children. Poor old Tilly, he kept thinking; he began to see his dad's "having words" in a very different light. If he were Tilly, he'd definitely run away.

It was then he decided to light a bit of a fire, to keep Tilly warm; it's what he'd seen them do in films. He found plenty of dry stuff in the outhouse, and he always had a box of matches on him, though his mum certainly didn't know about that. It was beginning to get dark outside and the fire gave a nice warm glow to the room. The fire, however, turned out to be a big mistake. They heard Charlie's uncle, who had spotted smoke coming from the chimney of an empty house, shouting as he approached. Charlie's own house was only five minutes away, so he explained as quickly as he could how to get to his back garden through the farmer's field, and about the old shed.

Tilly dashed out through the open window at the back and Charlie waited until his uncle had seen him through the front window, then he made his dash for it, knowing that he would be followed. He headed for the woods that were in the opposite direction from his home, and he just kept running as fast as he could. In the end, he was exhausted and collapsed onto the muddy ground just as his uncle reached him. PC Wilkinson was not a happy policeman.

On the evening of the second day after Tilly had gone missing, Uncle George was talking to Charlie's mum in their kitchen, whilst Charlie was doing his history homework in the dining room next door, and their conversation was considerably more interesting than drawing a map of Daneland .

'Drawn a total blank so far, Mari,' said the constable. He called her Mari sometimes.

'And no one's seen her at all?' asked his sister.

He shrugged his broad shoulders as he slurped his mug of tea.

'So what d'you do next then, George?'

'Start searching outbuildings round the village,' he said. 'She might just be holed up somewhere.'

Charlie swallowed hard.

'Probably start up the top end by the church, then work our way down.'

'Well, I can check our sheds for you, George,' his mum offered helpfully.

'Thanks anyway, but we have to do them all… just for the record, you know.'

So the next morning, from her look-out position on the far side of the field, Tilly could watch as the policemen steadily made their way across the gardens, looking in every shed, garage, caravan and even coal bunkers. Charlie had told her that he would give her the "all-clear" when it was safe to come back, but as she watched, it became clear that something was going on in Charlie's garden. The police seemed to have found something.

'Well, Mari,' said George, 'it looks as though she *has* been here.' And he produced three banana skins.

Charlie was loitering about, trying to find out what the police were going to do next.

'Great heavens!' said his mum. 'She must have been here, and we had no idea.'

'Well, at least that gives us a bit of a lead,' said George. 'Something to go on—'

'No,' interrupted Charlie, acting on impulse. 'The bananas were me.'

'You, Charlie? What do you mean?'

'I was eating them yesterday, out in my den.'

His mum looked at her son, and a worried expression appeared on her face.

'So where did you get bananas from then, Charlie?' she asked, though she had a pretty good idea.

Charlie just hung his head as the two adults looked at him, and then at each other, and then at him again.

'Well, Charlie... I'm waiting for an answer,' said his mum.

He didn't have much alternative if he was going to help Tilly.

'Mr Baxter's,' he whispered, with his eyes still on the floor.

'You mean you stole those bananas, Charlie?' asked his uncle, very slowly and seriously.

Charlie nodded. He knew it would mean big trouble.

School wasn't much fun the next day. Charlie didn't eat his packed lunch; he was saving it to give to Tilly later. His mum picked him up at 3.30 and marched him straight round to the general store, where he had to apologise to Mr Baxter for stealing the bananas. It was so embarrassing, but Mr Baxter was okay about it in the end.

When they got home, Charlie had to go to his room and stay there till dinner time; he was still in disgrace. It was almost seven o'clock by the time the boy managed to sneak out to his den, and he wondered if Tilly would still be there, and if she wasn't, where she would have gone to.

'Are you in there, Tilly?' he whispered as he peered into the gloomy shed.

'No, I'm in Glasgow, stupid,' she replied.

'I've brought you some grub,' he said, 'and a carton of orange.'

'Thanks, Charlie,' she said, emerging from behind a stack of old boxes. 'I'm starving.'

As Tilly tucked into his mum's cheese and pickle sandwiches, Charlie wondered if the girl had a plan of any sort.

'I've got to get to Glasgow, Charlie. I've got an aunty there,' she said whilst she munched away.

Charlie's mum always said, 'Don't talk with your mouth full,' but these were exceptional circumstances, he decided.

'So I need to get hold of some money,' she added, swallowing.

'I've got about two pounds in my savings tin,' Charlie offered, 'but that's not enough, is it?'

'I need to get to my mum's purse,' Tilly whispered, as if someone might overhear them. 'It'll be in her handbag on top of the fridge, in our kitchen.'

It took Charlie a while to fully grasp the implications of this plan.

'You mean, go back to your house?' he said.

'Got to,' she said. 'Will you come with me?'

He nodded his consent. 'Okay,' he said, but his brain was screaming that it was crazy. What if they were caught?

It was half past ten, and his mum and dad had gone up to bed, when Charlie crept downstairs, praying that he wouldn't make a sound as he let himself out of the back door and made his way up the garden to the old shed. Tilly was waiting for him outside, shivering in the cold air and clearly annoyed she had had to hang about so long.

'I had to wait till they had gone to bed,' Charlie offered by way of apology.

'Come on then, let's go,' Tilly said, already setting off across the field.

It only took them about fifteen minutes to reach Tilly's house, which was in darkness except for one bedroom window at the front.

'Should we wait till they turn their light out?' asked Charlie nervously.

'That could be ages,' said Tilly. 'It'll be all right if we're quiet. The kitchen's at the back in the extension.'

The spare back door key was under the third flowerpot along on the top shelf inside the greenhouse.

'You wait out here,' Tilly instructed Charlie, 'ready to make a quick getaway if we need to.'

That was fine by Charlie.

It was really dark in the kitchen as Tilly felt her way across the room and around the table to the fridge. The handbag was there, as she expected. She clicked it open and took out her mum's purse, trying to decide if she should actually take the purse or just some of the money in it. Then, just as she stuffed the purse into her pocket, the door flew open and the light flashed on.

'Got you, you little madam... caught red-handed,' and Mr Laidlaw lunged at his daughter, grabbing hold of both her arms. Tilly screamed and struggled and tried to kick, but it was useless; her father was far too strong even for a fighter like her.

'I'll teach you a lesson once and for all, young lady,' Mr Laidlaw growled, and he let go with one hand, swung the yelling girl round to face him and started slapping her around her head with his other hand. Charlie had been watching all this transfixed with fear, but now a courage that he didn't know he had swelled up in him, and he burst into the room.

'Let her go, you... you big bully,' Charlie shouted at the top of his voice.

Mr Laidlaw, still with his grip on Tilly, turned to look directly at the boy, then he laughed, a loud, menacing laugh.

'Well,' he said, 'what have we here? The cavalry has arrived,' and then he laughed even harder.

'Let go of her NOW,' shouted Charlie, 'or I'm calling the police.'

'Run away home, little boy,' threatened Mr Laidlaw, 'before I start on you.'

By now, Charlie was beside himself. He took a huge breath and then snarled back at Mr Laidlaw, 'You're... you're... you're a FAT BASTARD,' straight into Mr Laidlaw's face.

Mr Laidlaw's face changed. Gone was the mean smile; now his eyes were popping out of his head and they were filled with rage. He dropped his daughter onto the floor and rushed at Charlie, who had no time to avoid him. He picked the boy up like a rag doll and hurled him against the kitchen wall, his head crashing against the white tiles before he sank to the floor, motionless.

Mrs Laidlaw suddenly appeared at the door and screamed at the horror that greeted her. 'My God, what have you done…? Have you gone mad, Duncan?' she gasped as she went to pick up their daughter.

'Let me deal with this, woman,' Mr Laidlaw shouted as he pushed her away and she fell awkwardly onto one of the chairs. Now he grabbed the delirious Tilly and started shaking her violently again as the poor girl screamed for help. Then suddenly, out of the blue, came the sound of a huge gong being struck, and then, silence… Mr Laidlaw was sinking, in slow motion, to the floor.

When PC Wilkinson, who had been summoned by a desperate phone call from Tilly, arrived about ten minutes later, he was greeted by a scene that took even his breath away. Mr Laidlaw, who three months later would be given a long prison sentence for a string of offences that later came to light, lay in an ugly heap on the floor; Mrs Laidlaw sat at the table, trembling, staring blankly into space, and with a large iron wok still in her hand; and Tilly was kneeling beside Charlie begging him to wake up.

'You gave us quite a fright, Charlie,' said the boy's mum, when he did eventually regain consciousness.

He was lying in an unfamiliar bed, with white walls and strange bits of equipment around him. It took him a while to gather exactly where he was, and then his first question was, 'Is Tilly all right?'

'I'm fine,' said a voice from the foot of the bed, 'thanks to you, Charlie.'

THE MCALBY FOLLY

...the demise of Margo Burns, otherwise known as Margo McAlby, precipitated an astonishing and quite unexpected sequence of events, which would resonate far beyond their Highland roots

It was not until she belatedly, and rather ignominiously, "shuffled off this mortal coil" that it transpired the late Mrs Margo McAlby, wife of the even later Hector McAlby, was, in reality, no such person. The truth of the matter was that for over twenty years Margo *Burns* had enjoyed, if that's the correct term, a duplicitous existence, ostensibly the respectable wife of the Laird of Lochnafoyle, whilst in reality, as well as in law, she remained the wife and accomplice of a notorious Edinburgh confidence trickster.

According to her death certificate, the lady succumbed to alcohol poisoning, her co-conspirator, and legal husband, predeceasing her by only a matter of months, and with little mourning involved. Her demise precipitated an astonishing and quite unexpected sequence of events, which would resonate far beyond their Highland roots.

The first, indeed the only legitimate, Mrs McAlby had, before her death at a relatively young age, dutifully provided her husband with the requisite male descendants; "an heir and a spare" as the saying goes, Alistair and Gordon, to secure the family line. It was, alas, a line more notable for its profligacy and ineptitude than anything else, having, over the course of three consecutive generations, squandered an enormous

Highland estate to the point where little of its original grandeur remained, other than a rather fine, if now somewhat shabby, townhouse in Edinburgh and a modest hunting lodge-cum-folly, on the banks of Lochnafoyle, together with a few acres of forest and lakeside. It was to Foyle Folly that Hector McAlby had retreated in his latter years, as much to escape the tortures of his domestic discomfort as to enjoy the pleasures of Highland solitude, and so it was to here that Gordon "the spare" would regularly come to visit his ailing father.

His elder brother, Alistair, was, to his father's eternal regret and sadness, a lost soul. Meanwhile, the avaricious and misanthropic Margo remained immovably ensconced at Connaught House in Princes Street, the Edinburgh residence, from where she initially transferred what little remained in the family coffers into an account of her own, and then went on systematically to sell any family items of value that the city auctioneers would take off her hands.

By the time of her death, after two score years of plundering, there was very little remaining in Connaught House worth selling, and yet, quite extraordinarily, there appeared to be nothing whatsoever upon which the pecuniary rewards of this labour had been spent. Margo's inexplicable control over the hapless Hector for so many years would remain a mystery, even beyond the Laird's death.

And so it was to Foyle Folly, not Connaught House, that Gordon McAlby now came to look into what might remain of his father's estate. Ironically, Hector had slipped peacefully away at almost the same time as the unscrupulous Mr Burns.

Indeed, if to lose two husbands *looked like carelessness* on Margo's part, to then die so abruptly herself of the drink seems positively obtuse. Gordon was, of course, very familiar with much of the property, having spent many a happy summer holiday on the loch, but now he explored it more thoroughly for the first time.

Describing it as a folly perhaps gives a false impression of the size of the place. It still had six guest bedrooms, a handsome dining hall and spacious reception rooms, as well as adequate accommodation for a small staff. Hector had lived there more or less contentedly for his final decade with just a butler and cook, and very little about the interior had altered over the years; none of it was cleaned very often.

Hector's study, only a small room but comfortable, was of particular interest to Gordon, because it was here that his father had spent much of his time, reading, smoking cigars and poring over ancient maps of his beloved Highlands. It was in this room that the son imagined he would discover his father's papers, uncovering anything pertinent they might contain, a task centred around the enormous oak desk that stood in the stone bay window which had been its home for the last hundred years. The three deep drawers on either side were stuffed to overflowing with a miscellany of bills, letters, invoices and notices, as well as advertisements and pamphlets for a vast variety of causes. In the bottom right-hand drawer was a stained manila folder with the word *Certificates* scribbled on the front. As well as numerous official documents relating to the running of the estate, when there had still been an estate to run, there were also various birth, death and marriage certificates, dating back over the years, with the most glaring and significant absence being a second marriage certificate, that for Hector and Margo.

It certainly appeared that the estate of Hector McAlby, 22nd Laird of Lochnafoyle, would be a very straightforward affair. In Alistair's absence, Gordon was named in his father's will as his principal heir, with a number of small bequests left to close friends, and somewhat larger ones to Angus McCloud, his butler at the Folly for more than thirty years, and Mary Carr, his loyal cook and housekeeper.

At one point, soon after Hector's death and before Margo's, a young man, barely twenty years of age, calling himself Robert McAlby, made himself know to Campbell and Partners, the McAlby estate solicitors, claiming to be an unrecognised son of the Laird. The matter, which unsurprisingly turned out to be another of Margo's schemes, was soon dismissed by the lawyers as without foundation, and the boy unceremoniously sent packing.

Gordon's wife, Teresa, was herself a solicitor, albeit an English one, and so took a particular interest in the business of her husband's inheritance. With the departure of Margo from Connaught House, the property could be put on the market and the proceeds set against the not insubstantial death duties on the estate. Clearing out the old house proved a simple enough task, with so many of the rooms denuded of much of their furniture or ornament, and with no sentimental attachment to the little that did remain, the majority of the house was soon cleared, with the exception of the enormous outdated kitchen in which Mr and Mrs Burns would appear to have spent their days, and the two separate second-floor bedrooms, where they presumably spent their solitary nights. Numerous items of kitchen equipment were old enough to prove of interest to the Edinburgh City Museum, to which they were duly donated, but it was to be the swindler's sleeping quarters that would provide the most astonishing revelations. Teresa appointed Gordon to clear Mr Burns' room whilst she attacked Margo's, armed with rubber gloves and bin liners, and it was she who made the first discovery.

Having stripped the bed of its unsavoury clothing, she knelt down to check underneath the iron frame and innocently withdrew a heavy, old-fashioned leather suitcase. It was, perhaps surprisingly for its location, locked, and no amount of wrenching on her part would allow Teresa access to the portmanteau. Just as frustration was beginning to get the better of her, Gordon appeared in the doorway, hauling by his side an object identical to her own discovery. They set the two cases side by side, and clearly to ensure that no mistake was ever made, the lid of each bore initials, boldly painted in cream gloss; MB on the one, presumably for Margo, and KB on the other, for whatever Mr Burns was called, Kenneth probably. Gordon produced an uncompromising–looking screwdriver and, with little effort this time, the locks succumbed. They took hold of a lid each.

'After three,' said Teresa. 'One, two, three.' Nothing could possibly have prepared them for the sight that greeted their eyes.

With Edinburgh's leading estate agents duly instructed, and a remarkably high estimated valuation on the old house, Gordon and Teresa returned to Lochnafoyle to continue the job of putting the Folly in order. Mr McCloud and Mrs Carr were still in residence, and happy to remain so as long as required, which meant until they died, as far as they were concerned. Teresa set about making systematic lists, room by room, of necessary repairs, improvements and additions that would be essential if the old place was to be turned into a habitable modern home. The exterior was, of course, wonderful as it was, with its mock battlements, its two towers – Great Tower and Wee Tower – and its entirely superfluous moat and permanently lowered drawbridge, but the interior had been due, indeed long overdue, a major facelift, and Teresa felt that she was the woman for the task. Gordon resumed his investigations in Hector's study, which for some unknown family reason had always been referred to as the Book Room. As he lowered himself into the desk chair, Gordon could picture his father sat there, crouched over his desk, often scribbling away in his ever-present black diary, and now he thought about it, the very same image came to him of his grandfather, all those years earlier, doing the very same thing, in his own diary.

The moment passed, and the new Laird glanced around at everything in the room that seemed so familiar, and yet at the same time strange. As a boy, he had stood in that room so many times, not infrequently in trouble, and even, in later years, sat in it, discussing matters with his ageing parent, but he had never really known the room, and now it was his. His eye travelled to the oak bookcase with its ancient sets of books. Nothing published in the last half-century, Gordon thought to himself. Then one set of volumes caught his notice; it was at head height, all plain black leather spines, each apparently emblazoned with a year date in gold tooling, and on closer inspection, the strangest thing was that the dates did not stop at the current year but instead progressed on, at one per year, until 2029.

Fascinated by this, Gordon removed a couple of the post-dated books only to find, to his enormous disappointment, that they were entirely blank, as were the rest of these post-dated books. They were clearly destined for some future purpose. Gordon now turned his attention to the remaining books on the same shelf, the editions running the full width of the bookcase, and now, he noticed, spilling onto the shelf below. Every book, identical in its binding, bore dates stretching back to 1929. He looked across at the desk, and there in the very same livery sat his father's diary. Gordon shivered, as one does when sensing something is about to happen. There were exactly one hundred of these books, and it now occurred to Gordon – had it not been obvious? – that they must be diaries. Was that possible? Almost a hundred years of McAlby history?

Gordon hardly dare look. He called to Teresa, who was clearly in some far-flung corner of the Folly and out of earshot. He went out into the passageway and called again, and this time the urgency in his voice reached his wife's hearing, and when she arrived, and his speculation was explained, they ventured into the Book Room together and stood in front of the bookcase.

With something akin to religious reverence, Gordon ran his finger gently across the spines of the books until he reached 1929. His fingers tingled with anticipation as he carefully withdrew the volume and opened it. *Mullach* was the single word inscribed, almost carelessly, on the inside cover, and it meant nothing to him. The husband and wife looked at each other and shrugged. On the following pages it became clear that what they had discovered was indeed a diary; the diary of Hamish McAlby, 18th Laird of Lochnafoyle, and whilst it was by no means an exhaustive daily account of the life of the Laird, it was nonetheless a personal record of the comings and goings of Lochnafoyle during the year in question. As the couple methodically took down further copies, the significance of their discovery began to dawn on them; if this really turned out to be a continuous personal record of life of the McAlby estate over almost a hundred years, surely it would be an amazing find. Housekeeping records of great estates, dating back centuries, were not uncommon, but a continuous personal diary over such a time span, such a thing might well be unique. Added to the contents of the Connaught suitcases, this was turning out to be a revelation on an epic scale.

Despite the security of his inheritance, perhaps even because of it, Gordon felt resolved, if not obliged, to make further attempts at contacting his lost brother, last thought to be living somewhere in the West Indies. Through various connections in the international media, and rather more tenuous ones in the Foreign Office, Gordon made valiant efforts to reach his brother, or at the very least, let him know somehow that their father had died, but without success. It was some eighteen months after the events that immediately followed Margo Burn's death that a letter arrived at

Lochnafoyle Folly, having originated in St Lucia. Apparently, it had been misaddressed and thereby delayed. It read quite simply –

> *My Dear Gordon,*
>
> *Just found out on the grapevine about the old boy's departure – sad and all that, etc. Best of luck with Lochnafoyle – rather you than me – all's well at this end – do feel free to visit.*

And it was signed –

> *The prodigal son – Alistair*

No address was included.

It had clearly been necessary, at Teresa's insistence, it has to be said, to inform the police when the contents of the suitcases had been revealed, but despite the Edinburgh Constabulary's best efforts to the contrary, there appeared to be no legitimate reason why the McAlby family could not keep their newly discovered treasure trove. And what a trove it was; Teresa's best guess, when she first saw the money, was about ten thousand pounds in each case, but if you have never seen such a vast quantity of cash, it's really very tricky to estimate. The actual amount was three hundred and eighty– five thousand, four hundred and fifteen pounds... in each suitcase, in hundreds, twenties, tens and five-pound notes. The amount was identical in each hoard, down to the fifteen pounds, but what seemed so utterly inexplicable was the pleasure that Margo and… Kenneth, if that was his name, what strange pleasure they must have derived simply from knowing that all that cash was resting directly beneath them. It was quite beyond Gordon and Teresa, but of course it was double-edged in that this new figure had now to be added to the estate when estimating the death duties.

'I knew we should have kept quiet about it,' Gordon had moaned to his wife, who simply rolled her eyes and said nothing.

Whilst there was an inordinate amount of Hector's unattended business to deal with, matters that had been building up over many years, it was the diaries that Gordon found himself returning to repeatedly, and in particular his own father's incomplete, and occasionally incoherent, writings and that first edition of 1929. In a strange way, his father's concerns were frequently for the future; what would become of the Folly, of the redoubtable staff, of what was left of the McAlby inheritance and of Gordon and his family. Hamish, the 18th Laird, appeared more vexed about the past, constantly referring back to earlier better days. He frequently mentioned the views and actions of his predecessors, both recent and from further back in time, and he did so with such clarity, it was almost as though he had been party to these events in person.

In 1929, Hamish had succeeded his father as Laird, Lochnafoyle Castle had reluctantly been sold and the family had moved into the Folly with whatever possessions could be squeezed into, what felt to the family like, a tiny space. Every inch of the Folly was crammed with precious family treasures, and yet still, to the distress of the new Laird, much had to be disposed of. Gordon could feel the tragedy scrawled across the diary pages, but there was also a vague feeling that somehow he was missing something. The other thing that nagged away at him was that word printed so hastily on the inside of the first volume – *MULLACH*. It must mean something, he supposed, and perhaps characteristically it was the house itself that eventually provided the answer, at least the house in the guise of Mr McCloud.

'Mullach, aye, it means roof, plain enough,' said the old butler, 'and we've plenty of those to choose from,' he added helpfully.

The Folly had indeed numerous roofs and roof voids, eleven in total, from the huge space suspended above the massive beamed ceiling of the dining hall to the tiny conical that topped out Wee Tower, but it was in the loft above the Laird's bedroom that the chests, which nobody knew they were actually looking for, were eventually found. It was no small task to remove the six solid oak coffers from their dusty resting place, but when eventually they were arrayed across the floor of the gallery, it was with an air of almost unbearable excitement that Gordon, his wife, Angus McCloud and Mary Carr stood over them, speculating on their possible contents.

This time, Gordon was gentler in prising apart the latches and it was not until the final lid was up that anyone of them could quite believe what lay in front of them. In each box were various bundles of books, neatly tied together with ribbon, and on the identical spines of each set, sometimes clearly visible, other times needing closer scrutiny, were dates, consecutive year dates. They were, it seemed, sets of diaries, and whilst the binding had changed from time to time, and some were clearly in far better condition than others, they appeared to date back to 1610 in an unbroken line.

The rest of the story is part, and a very major part, of Scottish literary history. The diaries were authenticated by Professor John Stride from the Department of Antiquities at Edinburgh University, and heralded as one of the greatest literary discoveries in the English-speaking world. In terms of their age, the Lochnafoyle Folly Diaries could not match the 10th-century "Pillow Book" Diaries of the Japanese court ladies, but they did outdate Mr Pepys' celebrated journals, and whilst his spanned a mere ten years, the McAlby literary line endured for almost 400 years, so far, that is. Their monetary value was inestimable, but that was immaterial since the family donated the bulk of the dairies to the National Museum of Scotland, with the understanding that one diary would always be on public display, a handsome cabinet being specially commissioned to house the treasure, and with a different page open each day for visitors to read.

The most recent diaries, from 1929 onwards, remained at Lochnafoyle Folly, where they are still treasured by the current Laird and his family to this day. An interesting footnote to the story: the Lochnafoyle Folly Diaries became so famous that in time the name became shortened, for convenience, to the *Folly Diaries,* and so the term folly became synonymous with the literary form, to the extent that whilst south of Berwick, a collection of diaries is correctly known as a "Dork", north of the border, it is frequently described as a "Folly".

ACKNOWDEDGEMENTS

M y warmest and most sincere thanks to Kevin O'Sullivan whithout whose encouragement and support this book would never have been published.

My thanks also to everyone at Troubador for their kindness and professionalism. You really did make the whole mysterious publishing process thoroughly enjoyable.

R ory O'Sullivan is a former teacher and director of youth theatre. He worked extensively in this country and abroad on touring productions, to Japan, Canada and Singapore amongst other places, and organised large scale school Arts Festivals, involving all the principal national performance companies. He has written numerous plays, which have been produced at the Edinburgh Festival and various prestigious venues including The Fortune Theatre in London's West End. He lives in Gloucestershire with his wife, Jackie, and Paddy the chocolate Labrador.